What the critics are saying…

"Full of action and lots of sex, it keeps you on the edge of your seat and rooting for the characters the whole way." ~ *Romance Junkies*

"This is an imaginative fantasy with very hot sex." ~ *Romantic Times BookClub*

"…it's romantic, funny, sexy as hell, the plot is creative and surprising, the hero and heroine make you sympathize and easily capture your heart…it's also sizzling hot…Romantica-fantasy at its best." ~ *Mon-boudoir Reviews*

Tielle St. Clare

Dragon's Rise

ELLORA'S CAVE
ROMANTICA PUBLISHING

An Ellora's Cave Romantica Publication

www.ellorascave.com

Dragon's Rise

ISBN # 1419952668
ALL RIGHTS RESERVED.
Dragon's Rise Copyright© 2004 Tielle St. Clare
Edited by: Briana St. James
Cover art by: Syneca

Electronic book Publication: October, 2004
Trade paperback Publication: October, 2005

Excerpt from *Dragon's Kiss* Copyright © Tielle St. Clare, 2003

Warning:

The following material contains graphic sexual content meant for mature readers. *Dragon's Rise* has been rated *E-rotic* by a minimum of three independent reviewers.

Ellora's Cave Publishing offers three levels of Romantica™ reading entertainment: S (S-ensuous), E (E-rotic), and X (X-treme).

S-ensuous love scenes are explicit and leave nothing to the imagination.

E-rotic love scenes are explicit, leave nothing to the imagination, and are high in volume per the overall word count. In addition, some E-rated titles might contain fantasy material that some readers find objectionable, such as bondage, submission, same sex encounters, forced seductions, etc. E-rated titles are the most graphic titles we carry; it is common, for instance, for an author to use words such as "fucking", "cock", "pussy", etc., within their work of literature.

X-treme titles differ from E-rated titles only in plot premise and storyline execution. Unlike E-rated titles, stories designated with the letter X tend to contain controversial subject matter not for the faint of heart.

Also by Tielle St. Clare:

Dragon's Rise
Shadow of the Dragon

Prologue

Kei stepped cautiously toward the dragon's lair, his sword bared and held loose in his right hand. He hated to enter a dragon's home with a sword drawn but with this particular one, he needed to be prepared. The dragon had kidnapped four women in the past two weeks, snatching them from fields and farms, even the center of town. The creature had become the terror that legends warned. And Kei needed to stop him.

He had to see if he could talk to it first. He didn't want to destroy the dragon but there might not be another choice. He stopped at the entrance to the cave, marveling again that he himself might have ended up in a place like this, if Lorran hadn't saved him. Accepted him. Seduced him, really. He smiled at the memory and Nekane rumbled pleasurably inside his head. In the ten years since Kei had been bitten by a dragon and the animal had become a part of him, he'd learned to adapt to the creature who shared his soul. They'd adapted to each other.

Kei tilted his head to the side and listened, hoping for some sign that the dragon was sleeping or pacing. Any sound that the dragon was in his lair.

Instead, there was a rustle of leaves behind him.

Kei whipped around, crouched, sword ready.

Wide green eyes met his and both froze. Kei was the first to recover.

"By the Hells, Bren, what are you doing here?" he demanded of his oldest son. The boy, serious even at this young age, pulled his shoulders back and faced his father directly.

"I wanted to meet another dragon. A real one."

Nekane growled softly at the unintentional slight.

"Nekane is a real dragon and so is Tynan." Kei reprimanded gently, referring not only to the dragon who shared his mind but to the one who had been born a part of Bren.

Bren's cheeks hinted red and the boy nodded. "A wild dragon then. Whenever a dragon is causing problems, the villagers call you to handle it. I want to see what you do when you meet with them."

Kei nodded then paused. "How did you get here?"

"Tynan."

Meaning he'd turned into a dragon and flown across the land.

"You could have been seen." Dragons were so feared that if a villager saw one, it was considered brave and wise to fire arrows at the passing creature.

"I stayed in Nekane's shadow."

Kei had no answer for that. He'd turned into his dragon to fly to the location as well; he couldn't very well fault his son for it. Of course, Lorran was going to be royally pissed when she discovered what he'd done. "Fine, you can stay. But *you* get to explain this to your mother when we return."

The ten-year-old blanched. Lorran was definitely the fierce one in the household when it came to her children.

But she'll still blame me, Kei thought. Nekane quietly agreed.

"Come on. Let's go see what this dragon has to say."

With his son beside him, Kei knew he couldn't kill the dragon, so he returned his sword to its scabbard. Bren, like Kei, was dressed only in a loincloth. More for propriety's sake than modesty. If they should happen along a villager, a naked man walking through the woods would arouse comment.

They walked to the very entrance of the cave, where the light was swallowed by the dark. Kei placed his hand on Bren's shoulder and knelt down to look into his son's eyes.

"I don't know what we'll find in there. His fire can't hurt us but his teeth can. This is an angry, possibly wounded dragon. I want you to stay back."

Bren nodded. Kei stood and led his son into the dragon's lair. Though dark, he knew both he and Bren could see equally well. The dragon senses they shared allowed them clear night vision. Kei listened as he moved. There was no sound of rustling of scales. No low growls of warning to the invaders. And the scent of blood was strong.

They entered the wide cavern. Like many dragons, this one had collected bits of metal and jewelry — treasures — and stored them in his lair. Kei was pleased that Bren observed the jewels and gold cups but showed little interest in them. He wasn't a greedy child. He took his rank and position in life very seriously.

The dragon lay in the corner, huddled against the far wall. Blood poured from wounds across its hide and a spear stuck out of its back. The creature wasn't breathing.

Kei walked over to the beast, placing a hand on its cold carcass. The villagers had bragged that they'd managed to wound the dragon. No, they'd killed it.

"We're too late," Kei announced. He turned. Bren was no longer behind him. "Son?" Nekane quickly searched and sensed the boy not far away. Though Nekane didn't indicate that Bren was in danger, Kei didn't like that he was out of his sight. He followed Nekane's guidance down a short tunnel and found his son.

Staring at the naked, broken body of a woman.

Bruises and blood marred her flesh and fear was etched into her pale face and open eyes.

"What happened to her?" Bren asked, suddenly sounding very young. "Did the dragon do this?"

Kei dropped to one knee and tried to answer. "Yes, he did. You remember how we talked about the dragon seeking a mate—looking for the right woman to accept him?" Bren nodded but didn't look away from the woman's body.

"He hurt her."

Kei nodded.

"A new dragon's understanding is limited and if the woman he considers his mate rejects him, he becomes angry. He probably didn't even know what he was doing." Kei stared at the woman as well. "She could have been his mate who rejected him or another woman he'd taken and the instincts of the animal just consumed him."

Finally, Bren turned and looked at his father. The boy's lips were set in a tight line and his eyes were filled with determination. It seemed as if Bren had made a decision.

Chapter One

Prince Bren of Xicanth sat back in his chair and listened to his assistant recount the latest developments with the dragon proposal while he mentally calculated the hours until dinner. Not with anticipation. With dread. He had a long night ahead of him. As the host, King Ashure's idea of an evening of entertainment involved an elaborate banquet where wine flowed freely, causing normally rational people to behave in embarrassing and outrageous ways—followed by a night spent in a brothel. Definitely something Bren would have avoided...but he didn't dare refuse. Ashure saw his brothels as his kingdom's finest natural resource. And Bren couldn't afford to offend Ashure right now. He needed his support.

A rare gathering of the King's Council would occur in four days' time. Bren's father, Kei, would be arriving along with the other rulers of the seven kingdoms. The purpose of the Council was primarily to eliminate wars between the nations but every ten years the group gathered to discuss changes in their charter. The work done this week by delegates and diplomats from each kingdom would be finalized when the kings arrived. Though *they* officially made the decisions, almost everything would be decided before they arrived.

And Bren was intent on making sure that the ban on dragon hunting was included in the list of approved proposals. With all the work that needed to be done, he didn't have time to spend three hours watching other people drink themselves stupid.

Bren sighed, mentally resigning himself to a long night with a woman he didn't know and couldn't fuck. Maybe I could bring some documents to read, he thought. *It would give me something to do if the courtesan Jaqis selects isn't interesting.* That was highly unlikely. Madam Jaqis' pleasure workers were trained to serve princes and kings. They could converse about many subjects, dance, play instruments and were willing to perform most, if not all, of the known sex acts.

Not that the last item on the list impacted Bren in the least. Still he hoped she assigned him a woman who was well versed enough in the political climate that they could have a decent conversation. One who might have some insight that would help him on his quest.

"I really don't think we're going to get King Evelant's support. He's stalwart in his dislike of dragons." Wrea's comment interrupted Bren's musings.

"Yes, he's had a fear of dragons ever since my uncle accused my father of becoming one." Bren tapped this fingertip against his lower lip as he thought. "Still, I'm not quite ready to give up." He sat forward in his chair. "He has a son Kayla's age. It's really too bad I can't offer him my sister in exchange for his support."

Wrea laughed softly and Bren looked at him. Wrea's lips bent up in a hesitant smile. "That was a joke, wasn't it, Your Highness?"

"No," Bren replied in all seriousness. If only Kayla had been willing to ignore the dictates of her dragon, she could have been married by now—and most advantageously to their family. Princes and kings from across the lands had come to meet her but none had pleased her dragon. So none had pleased her. She was waiting for the damned creature to select her mate. "But it doesn't signify. She's not available. I'll have to find something else to sway Evelant."

"Yes, Your Highness."

Closing the thick parchment book he used for his notes, Bren stood. "I'm going take a walk. I probably won't be back before the banquet so just finish these notes and I'll see you in the morning."

"Enjoy yourself tonight, Your Highness," Wrea said, his eyes twinkling with the light of males bonding over the thought of pleasures of the night.

Bren didn't respond. Wrea wouldn't understand. No one could understand, except perhaps his brother and sister...and Rainek was so happy fucking his mate he'd have no sympathy for Bren's situation.

The thought of Rainek almost made Bren reach for the amulet he wore around his neck. Created by dragon blood and wizard's magic, the amulets connected the three siblings across long distances. Bren could contact Rainek or Kayla merely by holding it and concentrating on whichever sibling he needed to reach. If he called on Rainek now, he would no doubt interrupt a lovemaking session between his brother and Tiana, his brother's new wife. Though it might be entertaining—a minor payback for years of being tortured by his younger brother—Bren knew he wouldn't do it. The amulet wasn't used for games or playing tricks. It was designed to help when they were in danger.

Instead, Bren walked toward the south entrance of the castle. A forest lay just beyond the castle grounds and there was a secluded spot where he could release Tynan. Though he continually battled with the dragon who shared his existence, Bren understood the creature's need for space—for time in his true form.

Ashure's castle was a maze of long, seemingly random hallways. It was a little harder to track the sun's movements from inside the castle walls but Bren extended Tynan's senses and determined which way was east. That would lead him to the nearest garden exit. He turned the corner and collided with a servant coming from the other direction. Their chests slammed into each other and their foreheads cracked together.

"Owww," the other man whimpered, touching his fingers lightly to the spot where they'd hit. Bren silently echoed the sound. "I'm so sorry, Your Highness. I wasn't watching where I was going."

Bren blinked and looked at the servant. Except for the rough clothes, he didn't look much like the serving class. He wore his hair too long and there was a spark of arrogance in his eyes that didn't seem to match a servant's position. He was tall and broad-shouldered, appearing more like a warrior than a house worker. Bren silently asked Tynan for an opinion. The dragon mentally shrugged, indicating he sensed no danger from the man.

"Don't worry."

"Thank you, Your Highness." He grabbed Bren's hand in both of his and bowed over it, touching his forehead to Bren's skin. "Thank you," he said again. He straightened and was gone. Bren turned and watched him. The servant took long strides away, with the strength of someone who knew he wouldn't be stopped to serve.

I think I'll keep watch for that one, he said to Tynan. The dragon agreed with little interest but he did prod Bren to get them outside.

He turned and continued on his way. He'd almost reached the garden door when a tiny feminine figure entered the far end of the hall. He slowed. Tynan growled his displeasure. Bren ignored him, focused on the woman.

Nerra. He hadn't seen her in almost five years—when she'd left to marry another. He should have known she would be here. Her lord was one of the delegates. Naturally she traveled with him.

She took three dainty steps along the hall before raising her gaze. She gasped as she skidded to a stop. Bren's throat tightened. She was as beautiful as ever. Delicate and ethereal with blond curls bouncing against her pink cheeks, eyes wide and innocent.

"Bren." Her voice was still soft and breathy. It left an ache in his chest but did nothing for his flesh farther down.

Bren growled his frustration. Tynan stubbornly refused to show any interest in this woman—the one Bren had chosen.

Why couldn't the damned dragon see she would have made the perfect wife for him? She understood politics. She knew how to organize parties and banquets. She was sweet and gentle. The perfect helpmate. If only the dragon would have permitted it. But Bren knew he couldn't marry a woman knowing he could never give her children. Or even consummate the marriage.

He'd seen the passion between his parents and knew it was possible for a dragon to find its true mate—he'd also seen the results when the woman refused. Most women weren't as accepting as his mother. Nerra, despite her willingness to support Bren, would have fainted at the thought of a dragon loving her.

No, even if Tynan chose a mate, Bren had no intention of accepting her as a wife. He would never risk his dragon harming a woman simply because she feared the creature.

None of this mattered now. Nerra was wed to another.

"Nerra," Bren said, stepping forward and automatically reaching for her hands. She responded in kind, her slim fingers curling lightly over his. Her hands were cool and trembled slightly as she touched him.

"It's been so long."

He squeezed her fingers and stepped back, looking at her once again. She was perfect. Tiny, beautiful beyond words, with wide blue eyes. Even after five years of marriage, she carried herself with her an air of purity.

"It's good to see you," he said, dropping into a courtly bow. "How are you?"

She hesitated then smiled. "I'm well. My husband is here as the king's advisor."

"Of course." Bren had yet to meet Lord Herenson but he knew the man by reputation. He was second hand to King Evelant and that meant they would be involved in many discussions over the next four days.

Bren looked around the empty hallway. He didn't know what to say. Before she'd married he would have spoken of her beauty or shared some confidence. But now, he could think of nothing to say that wasn't out of the bounds of propriety.

So he finally asked the one question he needed an answer to. "Are you happy?"

Tears welled in her mystic blue eyes. "I am content." She placed her hand on his chest and leaned closer. "Nothing could ever match the love that we shared. I cling to those memories when I am lonely."

Regret lanced Bren's heart. Content seemed like such a weak word. But would her life with him have been any different? At least with her husband she had the opportunity to have the children she'd always longed for.

"Nerra?"

As a new masculine voice rang down the hall, she snatched her hand away. She lifted her chin and flashed Bren what could only be called a brave smile before she turned. A well-dressed courtier strode purposefully toward them.

"My lord," she greeted with a shallow curtsy. It seemed like a formal way to greet one's husband—she didn't even use the more familiar address of "milord"—but Nerra had always been conscious of proper etiquette.

"I had thought you were walking in the gardens." The note of censure made Bren's back straighten but he held back. It wasn't his place to come between a wife and husband.

"I was heading that direction when I ran into an old friend. My lord, this is—"

"Prince Bren of Xicanth. Of course. I recognize you from the many descriptions I've received."

The hint of jealousy made Bren relax. That would account for the irritation in the man's voice. Finding one's wife in conversation with a previous love had to be unsettling. He hoped it wouldn't influence the discussions during the week. He would have to assure Lord Herenson that there was no chance of him and his wife resuming their former association. Nerra sidled up to her husband. Close but not touching. Reserved but supportive.

"Lord Herenson, it's an honor to meet you. My father has spoken often of your clear advice to King Evelant." He hadn't, but Bren hoped the political lie would smooth their future relations. After all, King Evelant was a judicious king. Surely, he'd surrounded himself with wise advisors. "I'm anxious to get started tomorrow on details."

Some of the tension eased from Herenson's shoulders. "I agree. I hope for some major corrections to the agreements stretching across the kingdoms."

Corrections? thought Bren. *As if we've been doing it wrong all this time?*

"I hope to see some changes as well," he responded diplomatically.

"Well, Nerra wanted to rest herself in the gardens before the festivities begin tonight. Shall I escort you, my dear?"

Nerra's eyes grew wide and she looked from Bren to her husband and back again before agreeing. "Thank you, my lord. Prince Bren, it was a pleasure to see you again."

Maintaining the formality that she did, he bowed slightly. "The pleasure was all mine, Lady Nerra. Lord Herenson, I'm sure we'll have some interesting discussions over the next few days."

Herenson nodded but didn't smile. "I'm sure. Come along, my dear."

Bren continued down the hall, not turning and watching the two of them walk the opposite direction. He didn't want to appear the lovesick swain and cause Nerra any more difficulties. It was strange that, after five years of marriage, Herenson would find cause to be jealous of an old love. Surely he realized that Nerra would never break her vows. She was nothing if not proper.

Dull.

Bren rolled his eyes at the muttered comment inside his head. Tynan was always there but stayed silent most of the time. Unless the topic turned to women and mates. And it was a topic Bren refused to discuss with his dragon.

But he felt compelled to defend Nerra. "She's a perfect lady."

Dull. And I don't like the male.

Tynan had to be referring to Herenson. "He doesn't much like me either," Bren murmured as he stepped outside. "Hopefully, that won't make him difficult to deal with." Pushing thoughts of Nerra and her husband aside, he drew in a long breath. The smell of the castle with its bodies and machines clashed with the faint hint of clean crisp air. Bren followed that scent.

When he'd arrived two days before, he'd done a quick search of the forest. There was a secluded pond, easily defensible and difficult for prying eyes to view. It was the perfect place to hide a dragon. As he entered the heavy tree line, he began to run, allowing the dragon's strength to flow through his body and give him speed beyond a human's ability.

Tynan's excitement grew as they neared the water. It had been several days since the dragon had been freed. Bren ran down the path, easily bounding over tree roots and stumps until he came to a clearing. The pond, fed by a river, rippled softly with the afternoon breeze. The trees were tall and dense, making it almost impossible to walk through the underbrush. The only access to the site was down the path Bren had walked.

He scanned the clearing—listening to the forest sounds, making sure he was alone.

Bren had more control over his dragon than many who made the transition. His father had been bitten by a dragon more than thirty years ago. At the time, it was believed that once the human turned into the dragon form, they could never return. Bren's mother had discovered the secret to reversing the dragon's transition.

Bren and his brother and sister had been born with dragons as part of their souls. They'd learned from an early age to control the creatures inside them. But the dragon was a powerful beast and needed its freedom.

It would be nice not to think about the conference for a few minutes, Bren justified. To let the dragon's senses command and enjoy the sheer power of the creature. Though they were at odds about the search for a mate, Tynan was a part of him. Bren took a deep breath and relaxed, letting the dragon take him.

* * * * *

"What are we waiting for?" Keene asked as she kicked her boots up onto the table and leaned back in her chair, balancing on the rear two legs. Risa glowered at Keene's feet but said nothing. Keene ignored the glare. Risa might be team leader on this mission but she wasn't the arbitrator of etiquette.

"Triant. He's checking on the prince right now," Risa answered.

Keene nodded and settled in to wait. It would be a while before Triant returned. The prince's chambers were located on the opposite side of the castle from the small two-chamber suite Keene had managed to secure for the team. With kings, princes and delegates arriving from all seven kingdoms, there wasn't an open room in the castle. They were lucky they had two rooms to split between the four of them. To get the small suite, Keene had cozied up to the castle steward and dropped hints that the prince would need her "close, but not too close". She smiled. Somehow the steward had gotten the impression that she was the prince's mistress.

She glanced at Marvis, the final member of their team. He sat beside her, his elbows resting on his knees, his eyes focused on a blank spot on the far wall. Keene hadn't worked with him before but knew by reputation that he was the strong, silent type. His dark hair was cut short, which did nothing to soften the hard edges of his face. *It's almost too bad he prefers men,* she thought.

Not that she would get involved with a team member. The Guild frowned on its members forming attachments to anyone— in or out of the Guild.

Risa paced slowly across the length of the room growing more tense with each step.

Finally, the door snapped open and Triant strode inside, his long blond hair tied at the base of his neck. Keene turned her head to watch him, keeping her body precariously balanced in the chair. The coarse material of his clothing said he'd chosen to move through the castle dressed as a servant.

"Is he here?" Risa demanded.

Triant nodded. "Been here for two days already."

"Why? The conference doesn't start until tonight," Keene pointed out.

"What can I say? The man likes to be prompt."

Keene chuckled softly.

"So—" Risa said, stepping between them. "Anything?"

Triant shook his head. "Just like in Xicanth, I made contact but couldn't get anything from him."

"So, we do it the hard way," Risa announced.

Keene felt her stomach roll over and was silently glad she was just here in a support role for this mission. Triant was up this time and she would let him lead. From what she'd read of Risa's plan, Risa and Marvis had one target; Keene and Triant were assigned to Prince Bren. Keene's main task was to provide distraction for the prince. To get him out of the way when they needed it.

Jumping back into the conversation, she looked up at Risa. "What's the schedule?"

"All seven kings of the Council will arrive at the end of the week. We have to get to Prince Bren before then." Risa pulled out a sketch of the prince and placed it on the table. Marvis leaned forward to inspect it and gave a low whistle before sliding it across the table to Keene.

She accepted the parchment with a nod.

An instinctive gasp threatened but she brutally crushed it before it had a chance to escape. Taking a shallow breath, she willed herself to stare at the parchment with the same reserve the others had shown. The drawing couldn't be accurate. The image was too lovely for this world. His face came alive from the paper, his eyes staring wild and dangerous out of the piece of parchment. The strong jaw line and etched cheekbones—no doubt enhanced by the artist—indicated a powerful, tightly contained man resided inside the body. Even his hair was trimmed short, almost to his scalp, as if he would let nothing out of his control.

"He's going to be surrounded by people all the time. How do we get to him?" Marvis asked.

"Thankfully, King Ashure is the host," Risa answered, unaware of Keene's fascination with the sketch. "Which means that, every night, all of the unwed men of a certain rank will be taken to the king's favorite brothel and given the use of a woman for the night. Keene—"

Keene snapped her head up, suddenly realizing she was still staring that drawing.

"You'll go in as a courtesan. We'll get you assigned to Prince Bren."

"Whoo-hoo." Marvis slapped her shoulder. "Lucky you."

Keene wiggled her eyebrows up and down while she ignored the hints of arousal starting between her legs. "Looks like I get to have all the fun on this assignment."

Even Risa smiled. Then she shook her head. "Probably not."

"Why?" Keene winked. "Just because I have to knock him out doesn't mean I can't make use of him first." She glanced at the sketch and wondered what those dangerous eyes would look like as he held himself above her, driving deep into her wet sex. A flutter of desire moved through her pussy, as if it too was anticipating just such an event. It would certainly make the mission more interesting.

"From the information I've gathered, Prince Bren doesn't indulge."

Keene slowly straightened in her chair. Marvis leaned forward as well. "What do you mean?"

"I've spoken with a number of King Ashure's courtesans and while Bren accepts the king's gift—it would the height of rudeness for him to refuse the ladies' services—he doesn't touch them."

The room fell into a confused, rather stunned silence. Being that it would be *her* in the chamber with the prince all night, Keene finally asked the question she knew Marvis and Triant were thinking as well.

"So, if he doesn't have sex them, what do they do all night?" she asked.

Risa looked at her notes. "Talk, drink, eat. Play chess. One or two of the women have reported that he brought them to orgasm with his mouth or hands but never takes any for himself."

"Maybe we should be sending Marvis. He might prefer men." *And what a loss that would be to women across the land.*

Risa shook his head. "No, they tried that as well. He simply doesn't seem interested. So you'll go in, put the potion into his drink and when he wakes up the next morning he won't remember a thing. Simple. Easy."

Even you can't screw it up, was the silent message. Keene ignored it. Risa didn't like her. She didn't know why but it didn't matter. The Guild actually preferred that members didn't become attached to their teammates. It interfered with the success of a mission. The Guild was to be protected and served—even if it meant losing a team member. And Keene knew that Risa would love a reason to sacrifice her.

Knowing it would annoy Risa, Keene sighed dramatically. "Too bad. I was hoping to have some fun."

Triant laughed softly. "Highly unlikely. From what I can tell, Prince Bren doesn't understand the meaning of the word."

Keene smiled. She'd worked with Triant on several other missions and found him not only a good partner but a fun companion as well. When she'd come of age, he'd been one of the men chosen by the Guild to introduce her to sex. The connection had stayed with her though they were both careful not to let it move beyond a casual friendship.

Risa tapped her fingernails on the table and looked at Triant. "Any idea what type of woman the prince might be interested in? Blonde? Brunette? Redhead?"

The drawing of Bren lay on the table. Keene gnawed on the inside of her lip and stared at the sketch. A man like that—strong, powerful, controlled—what kind of woman would he want?

"When I was in Xicanth, I heard that several years ago Prince Bren was in love with a woman in his kingdom." Triant shook his head. "The match wasn't approved. Everyone I spoke with was very vague as to why but, from what I could gather, she was a tiny little thing." He looked at Keene. "Delicate, petite. A true gentlewoman. Maybe that's a way to go."

"Hair color?" Risa asked.

"Blonde."

"There you go, Keene," Risa said with a smug smile.

Keene just smiled back. It shouldn't be hard to convince a prince with such obviously conventional tastes in women to have a drink with her.

"Fine. One blonde, dainty female courtesan coming up."

It didn't take her long to find a courtesan to match the description. King Ashure's brothel had women of every shape, style and coloring. But convincing Cissa to take the night off was more difficult than she'd expected. The courtesan was cautious and obviously loved her work. Keene tilted her head and waited for an answer on her proposal.

"I'm not sure it's a good idea," Cissa said. Keene marveled at the shrewd look in the courtesan's eyes. Her clothes and body gave the impression of innocence but her eyes showed intelligence and caution.

"It will be fine," Keene assured her.

"You won't hurt him? I'll be fired and probably executed if anything happens to him."

"Nothing will happen. All I want to do is take your place and you have the night off." Before Cissa could speak, Keene continued. "You'll receive double your evening's pay and any tip that Prince Bren might provide." Keene knew from Risa's information Bren always left large tips even though he didn't use the services offered.

Cissa tapped her perfectly manicured fingertips on the countertop as she considered the idea.

"What if someone finds out?"

"They won't. Only you and I will know. You've never serviced Prince Bren before, have you?" Cissa shook her head. "Then he'll never know. He'll just assume I'm you. I just want to meet him. I've heard stories but I can never get close enough to him." Keene tried to sound eager without being too scary. "This way, I'll pose as you and I'll get to spend the night talking with the prince. It couldn't be more perfect."

"But what if he wants to fuck? I mean, I know he never has before but Madam keeps offering him different women hoping that one of us will please him. What if you actually end up having to service him?"

The center of Keene's stomach dropped away. It was a possibility—a slight possibility—that she had to deal with. Despite her teasing with her teammates, the intensity of the man's stare—even from the sketch—made her shiver with a strange fear. This would be a difficult man to manage. But she was a professional and if the job required it, she would follow through.

Keene shrugged, showing a casualness she didn't feel. "Then I'll fuck him."

Cissa thought for a moment longer then nodded. "All right. I'll let you take my place but I won't have my reputation damaged."

Before Keene could even begin to think what that meant, Cissa grabbed her hand and dragged her across the room, seating them both on a couch. Cissa leaned away, rummaging through a drawer in a small table at the end of the couch. When she sat back up, she held the largest phallus Keene had ever seen. It was made of sleek, smooth wood, lovingly carved into perfect shape.

"What are you going to do with that?" Keene asked, her heart now pounding in her throat and moving upward. Surely the courtesan wasn't expecting Keene to show her —

"My specialty is oral attention. I mean, all of the women do it, of course, but I'm particularly known for my talents." She held the phallus casually in one hand, tipping the point toward Keene. "Have you ever sucked cock before?"

Nervous as a virgin, Keene shook her head.

"Well, we don't have time for you to learn everything but if you're going to take my place you need to know a few tricks that will please almost any man."

Keene shook her head again — but with little conviction. "But, Prince Bren doesn't use the courtesans. You said so yourself."

"And if tonight he changes his mind, I don't want him reporting to the world that Cissa's cocksucking talents were vastly overstated." The pert tone of the courtesan's voice made Keene wince. She could see the woman's point. She just wasn't sure she was ready for lessons. "Now," Cissa started, placing the phallus in Keene's hands but not releasing it. "The main skill of sucking cock — like any other aspect of fucking — is you have to want to do it, you have to love it." Cissa licked her lips. Her eyes drooped to half-mast. "I love feeling a cock slide in and out of my mouth, feeling all that strength, that power." Her voice grew breathless. Her chest rose and fell and the tight points of her nipples pressed against her thin top. "Rubbing my tongue against that firm flesh, knowing it's so fragile underneath that strength. Knowing that I hold the power of his pleasure between my lips."

Cissa groaned and the sound seemed to shake her from her thoughts. She sat up straight and giggled.

"Sorry. I get a little carried away."

Keene swallowed and nodded, not wanting to admit that her nipples were hard underneath her leather vest or that hot liquid was forming between her thighs.

"Now, let's go over some of the basics." She lifted the phallus to Keene's lips. "Open wide, dear."

For the next hour, Keene learned Cissa's secrets, practicing until the courtesan felt she wouldn't be embarrassed. She taught Keene to lick the shaft and ease her lips around it. Flick her tongue against the head and swallow it deep, pointing out sensitive places to make a man groan.

"That's it." Cissa lifted the phallus as Keene kissed her way down it. "Take time to suck on his balls."

Keene opened her mouth wide to accept the wooden bollocks. "Always start out gently and then increase pressure. Having him scream ruins all the delicious tension you've created. That's it." The phallus moved again, slipping the wooden balls from between her lips. "Now, imagine it's the prince and you've been pleasuring him for hours. He's screaming with the need to come. The need to fuck someone."

The image of Prince Bren, naked on his back, his hands tied to the bedposts so he couldn't reach for her, totally at her mercy, exploded into her head. The light heat between her legs enflamed, sending liquid dripping down her pussy.

She swiped her tongue across the base of the phallus.

"That's it. Now, lick your way back up his shaft. He's desperate to come."

Keene's heart pounded as she wrapped her lips over the wooden head and repeated the motions Cissa had taught her, sliding back and forth, pressing the flat of her tongue against the shaft as it glided past, adding suction each time she pulled back. Keene closed her eyes. The wooden phallus became Prince Bren's cock, hard and hungry.

"Perfect," Cissa whispered, her breathlessness matching Keene's pounding heart. "You've got it. Suck him just a little harder, use your hands." Keene wrapped her fingers around the part of the shaft she couldn't take into her mouth. Cissa held the end of the phallus and gently pushed it in and out, keeping the thrusts deliberately shallow. "More, yes, take him. Feel him. Love what you are doing to him. Want it." Cissa's voice reached a fever pitch. "Make him beg, hear him pleading with you to let him come. He's yours to control. Take him. Swallow him." Keene's body hummed with hunger. She sucked, pumping her mouth to keep the rapid pace, craving this release.

"That's it. One more long pull and let him come."

The phallus thrust between her lips one final time and stopped.

Keene waited. There was more. There had to be more.

"Excellent lesson," Cissa announced, sliding the wooden cock out of Keene's mouth. She followed it with her eyes, feeling a little lost, a little empty. "Oh yes, you'll do fine. You sure you've never done this before?"

Keene shook her head. Something about the courtesan's sultry, teasing question made Keene look down.

At some point, she'd gone from sitting on the couch to kneeling—straining to reach the cock as Cissa had moved it just out of reach. Keene's leather vest was open and the blouse inside unbuttoned. Keene vaguely remembered Cissa's instructions to touch her breasts, to find the pleasure in her body as she sucked on the wooden shaft.

"Well, I'd say you have a natural talent for it." Cissa reached forward and stroked her finger down the center of

Keene's blouse. A faint glimmer of sweat shone between her breasts. "I think you'll *really* enjoy it once you try it on a real cock." Cissa's eyes twinkled with warm laughter. "After all that, it's almost too bad you'll be assigned to Prince Bren. You won't get to try it out."

That's probably a good thing, Keene thought, feeling her cheeks heat.

"I'll just have to…"

Cissa looked at her expectantly.

"Find someone else to try."

Cissa smiled and winked. "Good for you." With that, she turned away and began washing the cock, her hands lovingly stroking the wooden shaft. "You'll need to be here before nine. We don't mingle with the guests beforehand. One of the eunuchs will bring him back here and he's yours for the night."

"Thanks." Keene stood, finding her knees a little shaky. She'd been in control until Cissa had told her to imagine it was the prince's cock she was sucking. That's when the trouble began.

Cissa looked down at Keene's leather vest and pants outfit. "You might want to borrow something from my closet and do something about your hair."

Keene smiled, remembering the image they'd decided on to tempt the prince. "I'll do just that." She left the courtesan's chamber and wove through the castle hallways, back to the team chambers. As she reached for the doorknob, she made sure her countenance was calm. It wouldn't do for the team to realize how much she was looking forward to tonight.

Chapter Two

Bren wandered around the edges of the lounge, his glass of *burgenda* in his hand. The thick black liquid was bitter, making it almost impossible to drink more than a single glass. That was one of the many reasons Bren chose it as his liquor of preference. There was little chance of him getting drunk on *burgenda*. He finally settled himself along the side wall of the lounge watching the crowd of men mingle until Madam Jaqis would appear and distribute assignments for the evening. The laughter was bright and harsh as many grew deeper in their cups.

The banquet hadn't been a total loss of time as Bren had imagined. He'd been seated next to a nervous young aide who'd taken his lord's place when the man had fallen ill. So nervous was the young man that he'd barely touched is dinner or wine, leaving him clearheaded and at least able to carry on a conversation. With some subtle questioning, Bren had been able to induce the aide to report on his lord's plans for the conference. It was information Bren could use later.

Lost in thought, he observed the crowd of men. The noise level was growing. Bren sipped his drink, counted the hours until dawn and held back a sigh.

"Your Highness."

The vaguely familiar voice drew him out of his reverie. He turned, surprised to see Lord Herenson standing beside him. Though always invited, married men were exempted from having to attend the evenings at the brothel—particularly when their wives traveled with them.

"Lord Herenson." Bren bowed his head in greeting. It wasn't up to him to judge why Herenson was here instead of with his wife. "Good evening."

"Did you enjoy your *walk* today?"

Something about the sharpness of Herenson's tone made the hair on Bren's neck stand up. This seemed beyond just some minor jealousy. Was it possible he knew about Tynan? The truth about their dragons was an open secret within the kingdom. Servants and close friends knew but mostly it was rumors and fantastic tales, which Bren and his family ignored or flatly denied. The prejudice against dragons was too strong for them to be open about their situation.

"It was fine. Lord Herenson, is there something you wish to say to me?" Bren, a firm believer in diplomacy, also knew bluntness had its place.

Herenson opened his mouth to answer but never got the chance.

Silence built on the far side of the room and spread as the Madam Jaqis entered and walked through the crowd. Princes, lords and high-ranking officials stepped to the side to allow her to pass. She greeted each guest with a smile, designed to entice and enthrall and, from the reaction of the men in the room, it worked very well. Bren had to admire her. She ran an elegant brothel with well-trained courtesans. She'd even assigned herself to tend to Bren one night in the hopes that she could inspire him to use the brothel's services. Tynan had indicated no more interest in her than any other woman but Bren had used the night to have the madam instruct him on providing oral and manual stimulation. If the dragon didn't release its hold on Bren's body, that might be all he could ever give a woman.

She strolled through the crowd, finally stopping in front of Bren. As the highest-ranking person present—except for King Ashure—Bren would be the first led from the room.

"Your Highness." Madam Jaqis bowed her head in greeting then waved her hand toward the thick-muscled man waiting beside them. Bren was by no means a small man, standing over six feet tall, but Jaqis' eunuchs were chosen for their massive size. "Bardo will escort you to your room for the night. The young lady's name is Cissa and I think she will please you."

Though Jaqis accepted that Bren wouldn't use any of her women, she still provided choice and varied selections with the hope of finding one that inspired his cock to rise.

"Thank you, Madam. I'm sure she'll suit me well." He could say that in all honesty because Jaqis also knew enough to provide him a courtesan with some intelligence and conversation. The hours were long until morning and he'd have to fill the time somehow. As he followed Bardo out of the room, Bren considered the possibility of pleasuring the woman. Though he was unable to become aroused, the scent and touch of a woman's body was pleasing and, even if the woman wasn't the one chosen by the dragon, Bren knew Tynan found some comfort in the oral caresses.

It wasn't enough to satisfy either of them but the impasse between them had lasted since Bren was a child and showed no signs of abating.

The dragon was again silent as Bardo opened the next to the last door in the hall.

"These are Cissa's rooms," the eunuch announced. "May you find pleasure in this chamber."

Bren nodded and walked inside. The door snapped shut behind him sealing him in for the night. Though not specifically locked inside, it was considered rude to leave before dawn—an insult to the courtesan, Madam Jaqis and King Ashure. Bren needed Ashure's support on the dragon initiative. He wasn't going to offend the man by leaving before morning.

Taking a deep breath and mentally preparing to see who Jaqis had matched him with this evening, he stopped. There was something different. A scent. A feeling. Something in the air that had never been there before. Tynan rumbled softly in his head as if the dragon had also become alert. Clearing his own thoughts and silencing Tynan's curiosity, Bren looked around, searching for the woman assigned to him.

She stood in the center of the room, waiting. Bren felt his breath catch in his throat. There was something different about this one. Her long blonde hair was pulled up into two high ponytails near the top of her head, hanging down to brush her shoulders. She wore a pale pink top that stopped just above her belly button—inches away from where her low-slung skirt started. The skirt ended barely mid-way down her slim thighs. She was tiny, dainty, almost childlike. In fact, he might have mistaken her for a child if not for the full roundness of her breasts—visible and clearly unrestrained beneath her tiny blouse—and the sexual wisdom in her eyes. Still, she was young. Probably no more than twenty-one summers. An enticing blend of innocence and sensuality clearly cultivated for her guests' pleasure.

She waited patiently as he finished his perusal, then grabbed one thin strand of hair and drew it to her mouth, nibbling on the end in a coy flirtation.

"Good evening, milord." Her voice was soft and whispery, floating through the air like fine smoke, distracting him enough that he didn't correct her. He should be addressed as "Your Highness" and he found it odd that one of Jaqis' courtesans could have gotten it wrong. She twirled the strand of hair around her finger drawing his attention. "I hope you like what you see." Her eyes twinkled as if she was laughing at him.

The muscles at the back of his neck tightened at the thought of becoming a joke amongst the pleasure workers. He drew air into tense lungs and stopped. There it was again. That scent. Something compelling and intriguing. His cock twitched inside his hose.

Bren shook his head, knowing he was imagining things and instead focused on the diminutive courtesan before him.

"You are lovely, as I'm sure you know," he said stiffly.

Keene bit the inside of her cheek, trying to contain her smile. It beat trying to slow her pounding heart. Thankfully, while he'd been inspecting her, she'd had the chance to do the same to him. It gave her a moment to school her features. It wouldn't do for a supposedly skilled, experienced courtesan to let her tongue hang out of her mouth.

He was even more stunning than the sketch had indicated. And certainly bigger than she'd expected. She couldn't see much of his body—the formal court clothing masked his shape—but the danger and power that had leapt off the parchment was magnified in person. The artist hadn't been able to capture the innate command of his presence.

Like most of the other men visiting Ashure's court, he wore black woolen hose with a long heavy overshirt and jerkin that reached mid-thigh—longer than her own skirt. There was no way to see any muscle definition beneath the loose clothing. And if all their information was true, she would never get a chance to see what he looked like naked.

His eyes, glittering green, were brilliant, even from halfway across the room and Keene felt a warm reaction deep inside her sex. Like she'd been empty all her life and somehow her body knew this was the man to fill her. In all ways.

The thought quickly led her back to Cissa's lessons on cocksucking. The heat between her legs grew and turned liquid. Holding back a moan, she silently prayed to Goddesses long forgotten to speed this night.

"My name is Cissa, milord," she said, again deliberately lowering his rank. He hadn't corrected her the first time but she'd seen his jaw tighten as if he'd considered it. It helped remind her that he was a target, not a lover.

With a hopefully saucy sway of her hips, Keene stepped forward and waved her hand toward the couch. It was the same couch she'd sat on during her cocksucking lesson and would be the perfect place for their conversation. The potion was ready to go into his drink.

"Would you care to take a seat? We could talk for a moment." She lowered her arm and let her hand touch the bare skin of her thigh, just below the skirt. Then slowly, she dragged it upward, taking the material with her. More skin was revealed, not enough to bare her sex but teasing him with the hint of it. "Get to know each other."

His eyes followed her hand as she'd intended. Then, with a definitive jerk, he yanked his gaze away. Again, she indicated he should seat himself on the couch.

He hesitated, as if his body was fighting itself, before walking down the three steps into the sunken living room. Each step brought him closer. A shiver of fear raced down her spine. The intensity of his eyes blazed brighter than the torches lining the walls. He was watching her. Closely.

Could he suspect what she was up to? Was it possible that he knew he was a target? Not wanting to arouse his suspicions, she waited until he was seated then lowered herself onto the couch beside him, trying to remember the slow way Cissa had sunk down and the eager manner in which she sat, as if a child waiting for a surprise.

Think dainty, delicate, she told herself. And sensual. She had to remember that. She was supposed to a courtesan after all. It wasn't all that difficult. Something about this man inspired sexual thoughts.

Cissa didn't seem to own any undergarments so Keene was naked beneath the skirt. As she turned to face him, cool air brushed against her sex, alerting her to how wet she truly was.

She considered offering him a drink immediately—the sooner she drugged him, the sooner her mission was over and she could escape the strange draw of this man. But something about the way he watched her stalled her movements. Something had aroused his suspicions and suddenly slapping a glass in his hand might make it obvious.

"So, Lord Bren…" She pressed forward, allowing the top of her blouse to gape and reveal the inside curves of her breasts. "Tell me about yourself." As expected, his eyes dropped to her cleavage and lingered for a long moment. He shook his head. Like he was trying to erase an image. Without speaking, he leaned toward her and took a deep breath. He snapped back, as if he'd been thrown from a catapult, hitting the cushions of the couch with a heavy thump. His eyes never left her.

"By the Gods," he whispered, his hot gaze ran up and down her body, lingering on the apex of her thighs.

Keene stared back—unwilling to hide from the blatant inspection. She had nothing to fear. She looked good—Cissa's clothes had seen to that. And he was a man who didn't use the pleasure workers' services. Pushing aside his strange reaction, she focused on how a courtesan would think. Sex. Fucking. She had to at least appear to be heading that direction.

She lowered her gaze to his groin. The tails of his overshirt had flipped back when he'd thrown himself against the couch, baring his crotch. The heavy woolen hose were stretched tight, revealing a thick bulge. Air suddenly seemed in short supply in the room. She heard herself panting softly at the growing mound between his legs. All reports indicated that no matter what the courtesans had done, the prince simply never got hard. That didn't seem to be the situation here.

Oh my Goddesses, I might have to actually have sex with him. She licked her suddenly dry lips and tried to take a calming breath. She was a professional. She could do it. And it might be a lot of fun, her wicked inner voice whispered.

The prince continued his intense observation. Keene's first reaction was to pull away but duty demanded she continue the role she'd been assigned. She twisted, lifting herself until one foot was under her bottom and the other on the floor, separating her legs by mere inches. The scent of her own arousal floated up to her nose. She could only hope he didn't notice it.

His gaze dropped to that hot space between her thighs. Though still covered, she felt like he could see her pussy. Knew how wet and open she was.

The grim set of his mouth indicated that he wasn't pleased by what he found.

"Milord?" she prompted when he didn't move. "Are you all right? Perhaps I should get you a drink." She needed to get the potion inside him and get this over with before she ended up flat on her back with her legs in the air. Unfortunately, that image did nothing to diminish the warmth emanating from her sex. She stood up and turned. His hand snagged her wrist, jerking her to a halt.

"Mine."

The low, guttural word sent a shiver down Keene's spine and she slowly turned to face him.

"Or I could get you a drink later," she teased. He didn't smile.

His eyes locked onto hers and the spine shivers returned. What was it about this man that made her want to alternately escape and run to him? With his fingers still wrapped around her wrist, he drew her down until she sat beside him, her hip touching his knee. He made no other move to touch her.

Think like a courtesan. Think like a courtesan.

Of course. *She* should be touching *him*.

Taking a shallow breath, she placed her free hand on his knee. She waited for his response, any response. The only change was a brief tightening of his fingers around her wrist. The pressure immediately eased before he hurt her but he didn't release her. Keene took that as a sign she should continue. She slid her fingertips up, skimming softly across the inside of his thigh. Forcing a boldness she never would have felt under any other circumstance, she continued her path until she reached the hard press of his erection.

With the pad of her middle finger she stroked the length of his cock. His body tensed, every muscle tightening and pulling taut.

Remembering Cissa and the lesson from the afternoon—and her own feeling that there had to be more—Keene ignored the sensible voice in her head that screamed she should free herself. Instead, she placed her hand over the still-expanding bulge beneath the fine woolen hose.

"I would be pleased to…to take you in my mouth." Her words came out breathless and hesitant but a strange eagerness rumbled in her chest. She wanted to feel this man's cock moving between her lips, feel him slide inside her mouth—all the images Cissa had left in her head.

For a moment, she thought he would refuse. His hands curled into fists on the cushions next to his thighs as if he were fighting the urge to reach for her—or push her away. The tight clench of his jaw made her teeth ache in sympathy. Poor baby, she thought. He was battling some internal demon she didn't understand. Just when she was about to give up hope, he nodded. Once. Sharply.

She almost moaned as relief sparkled through her chest. She didn't want to lose her chance now.

With his silent permission, she reached up under the tails of his overshirt and grasped the waistband of his hose, pulling them down. The thick, full cock sprang free as she tugged the material clear.

"Oh my Goddesses," she whispered, unable to stop herself. She knew it was a very uncourtesan-like comment but his cock was bigger than she'd expected. Bigger than the phallus she'd practiced on. Definitely thicker.

Unable to bring herself to look up at him, she focused on the erect shaft presented to her. *You can do this. Don't embarrass Cissa.*

Then she remembered Cissa's first rule of cocksucking—*you have to want to do it.*

Keene licked her lips. She definitely wanted this.

Relying on her one meager lesson, she leaned forward and placed a light, delicate kiss on the head, greeting it, getting a hint of the heady masculine flavor.

He was so different from the wooden phallus Cissa had trained her on. This was alive and hot and hard. A flash through her brain told her that this wasn't right. That Prince Bren didn't get hard or allow the pleasure workers to suck his cock but none of the warnings settled into her head. She inhaled, breathing in the hot male scent.

Cissa's instructions returned, silently guiding Keene's mouth. Flicking her tongue out, she learned the warmth, the flavor of his skin, slowly moving down the shaft, interspersing licks with soft kisses. He was fire beneath her lips and Keene felt the warmth radiate through her own sex. The tiny glimmer of moisture she'd felt before flowed freely now and began to trickle down the inside of her thigh.

She shifted on the couch to get a better angle. Flattening her tongue against the underside of his cock, she slowly stroked up, and up, until she reached the tip. Cissa's silent guidance matched Keene's desires and she opened her mouth wide to take the thick head inside. The prince's hips convulsed up, as if he was resisting the need to thrust.

One of her ponytails fell forward. She brushed her long blonde hair back and looked up, watching him watch her. Keeping her eyes on him, she swallowed him, allowing his cock to invade her mouth. His girth didn't allow her to take much but what she received, she loved. She rubbed her tongue across the bottom of his shaft, massaging the sensitive place just below the head.

Bren groaned. His eyes glittered as he stared at her and Keene knew they'd made a mistake in coming here tonight. Whatever information they'd received was wrong. The lust emanating from this man's eyes was not going to be satisfied by one cocksucking, or even a single fuck.

The power of his stare bore into her and Keene dropped her eyes. *Focus on his pleasure. Focus on sucking him off. Then get him a drink and get this done.*

The mental instructions helped for a moment. She continued her loving attention to his cock, pulling back and again tasting his entire length. When her hair fell forward, he reached down and pulled it out the way so he could watch her. The gentle massage of his fingertips on her scalp translated into pressure in her sex.

Thoughts of her mission faded. She groaned, losing herself in him, his taste, his hardness. The smooth silk of his cock against her fingers, her tongue. With Cissa's wisdom guiding her, she alternated between sucking and licking, kissing and stroking.

As she lapped at his bollocks she understood Cissa's fascination with this activity. He was so sensitive, so alive. Every touch inspired a reaction — subtle, as if he was fighting every sensation. But she knew he couldn't resist what she was doing — knew her touch was pure pleasure. Knew he wanted more and that only *she* could give it to him. She wanted to suck on the twin sacs but the waistband of his hose didn't permit her full access.

Leaving that treat for later, she skimmed her mouth up the line of his cock. The harsh sound of his breath filled the room and Keene gloried in it. She wanted to give this to him. Wanted to be the woman who made him come. The woman he couldn't resist.

She risked another glance at him. His stare hadn't wavered — but this time, she didn't back away from his lust.

For the first time since she'd started, she lifted her mouth completely away from his cock. "Shall I make you come, Your Highness?" She scraped her teeth ever so lightly across his skin. She thought his eyes had burned before but they exploded with hunger now. The temptation to drive him higher — push him beyond his limits — urged her on.

His pulled his hand away from her and buried his fingers into the arm of the couch as if he was holding himself still. Holding himself back. The action dared her to break that iron control. "Would you like to come in my mouth?" she whispered against his shaft, knowing he'd hear and feel the words. "Release all that delicious seed into me." She paused to lick him, loving the hot flavor. He groaned and punched his hips upward. "Come inside me until you're drained." She placed another reverent kiss on the very tip, dribbles of pre-cum leaking out. "Would you like that, Prince Bren?"

She didn't know what instinct was driving her on but she needed to hear him say it. Needed him to admit that she was the one who gave him pleasure.

Swirling her tongue around the thick head, she waited, aware that her own body was aching and drenched with desire.

"Suck me," he commanded. There was no pleading. No begging. It was an order he expected to be followed. One that Keene felt deep in her pussy.

Still, she didn't want to be too easy on him. She hesitated—just long enough to see his eyes glow with the threat of retribution.

Flashing him a taunting smile, she opened her mouth and accepted him back inside. This time, the restrained thrust of his hips went a little higher, pushing him a little deeper. Joy burst in her chest. She had him. He might appear to be in control but he wanted this. She tightened her lips around his cock and began to pump. Cissa's instructions faded as Keene reveled in the sheer pleasure of Bren's shaft sliding in and out of her mouth. She wrapped her hand around the base, stroking him in time with her suckling.

Beneath her other hand, his thigh was like stone—locked in impossible strength. She kneaded the hard surface, loving the power of his body. He was close—she could feel it—but still he fought against his release.

She flung her head back, letting his shaft slip from her lips. Her heavy breathing matched his. She stared into those wild green eyes.

"Let me have it. Please." Barely breaking her rhythm, she took him again, driving her mouth down his cock, sending him to the back of her throat, relaxing to take more. She lost herself again—thinking only of drawing him deeper, pushing him farther. His hips rolled upwards and Keene knew she had him. He was hers.

Her cunt fluttered as if it too wanted to be filled and Keene couldn't contain the moan that broke from her throat.

A constrained groan was her only warning before his seed burst into her mouth.

Yes! She swallowed quickly, catching each pulsing wave as it flowed down her throat. When it subsided, she lifted her head and stared at the prince.

Strange. Hadn't his eyes been green before?

* * * * *

Bren felt his control waver as his seed flowed into the pretty courtesan's mouth. Tynan was pushing him.

Mine! The dragon's cries had given Bren strength to resist, to fight the pleasure the woman offered. Damn it, he wouldn't give in to Tynan's demands. He wouldn't release control to the beast inside him.

But when she'd looked up and asked for his cum—he couldn't fight her.

Tynan clawed at his insides, screaming for his mate.

The courtesan—Cissa—continued to lick him, as if she wanted to capture every last bit of his cum. She'd wanted this, wanted his seed.

She wanted him.

He knew she was a whore—that she pleasured men as her work—but the liquid pooling between her legs was no faked response. Tynan had sensed it almost from the beginning, pleading for a taste.

Bren licked his lips. He, too, wanted to taste her. To feel her climax against his mouth. Around his cock. He closed his eyes against the image, fighting it. Digging deep inside himself, he pulled Tynan back. The dragon fought him with an incredible strength. The beast's mate was near and the animal wasn't going to let her walk away.

"Lord Bren," she whispered, her breath teasing his still-hard cock. He looked down. Her blonde hair was tangled and wild. Her lips red. "You're still hard. Did I not please you?" The edge of her mouth curled up in a secret smile. "I could suck you again." He could hear her heart beat faster, smell her arousal. She *wanted* to suck him again, wanted to feel his cock in her mouth.

Tynan's roar blended with Bren's own and the human found he couldn't fight both. The desire was too strong. He would have her. Tynan craved her and so did Bren.

We'll have her, he assured the dragon, using a strangely soothing tone. He'd fought, sometimes even hated, the dragon in his head but tonight the beast and he would work together.

Mine!

We'll have her, he repeated.

"Lay back," he said aloud.

She blinked as if startled by the command and he thought he saw a glint of disappointment as she stared at his cock. He wanted to reassure her that she'd have more opportunities to suck his shaft before the night was through but now he needed to soothe the dragon.

"Lay back," he said again, using the same tone as when he commanded his men. The little courtesan nodded. She was on her knees on the couch—giving her the perfect angle to consume his cock. A bit awkwardly, she pulled her legs out from under her and followed his orders, resting back on the short couch until her head was propped up against the far arm and her feet were planted on the cushions, knees bent. Her body was graceful but without the practiced sensuality he might have expected from a trained courtesan.

As she settled on the couch, her skirt tumbled to her waist. Her captivating scent flooded his head. He watched, hungry for the first sight of her sex.

"Open your legs." She hesitated then moved, slowly spreading her thighs. Impatient, he reached out and lifted her right leg, placing it on the back of the couch. Her other foot he placed on his knee, so she was completely open and bare before him. Staring down at that pretty pink cunt, Bren felt his cock harden further.

His father had warned him about this—that even after his mate had satisfied him, he would want more. And Bren did. He wanted to drive himself into her, claim her with every inch of his shaft until she knew only the feel of him.

But still the dragon pressed on him and Bren couldn't deny him any longer. He'd dreaded this moment for years—when Tynan would claim a woman—and wondered if he would have the strength to fight the dragon. Inhaling her warm luscious scent, he knew he couldn't deny Tynan's needs. Not now.

He leaned forward. Thin trails of moisture wove across the insides of her thighs. She'd grown wet while sucking his cock.

"You liked taking my cock into your mouth, didn't you?" he whispered as he swiped his tongue across her skin, capturing the liquid heat. The flavor warmed his mouth and he lapped again. Tynan shuddered with pleasure inside his mind. "You're dripping all this delicious juice from your cunt just from having me come in your mouth." He raised his eyes to watch her.

For an experienced courtesan, there was an odd hint of trepidation in her eyes. And faint blush on her cheeks. It might have concerned him if the heady perfume of her pussy hadn't grown stronger with his words. Her body was still preparing for his penetration. He would fill her with his cock. Soon. But first, he had to ease the dragon. The creature's desires were spiraling out of control.

Yes. Mine.

Bren let Tynan guide him. He spread her sex wide with his thumbs and plunged his tongue into her passage. She screamed and arched her back. From the corner of his eye, he saw her fingernails claw at the cushions. Tynan howled his triumph and seized control of the body he shared with Bren. Bren was distantly aware of thrusting his tongue in and out of her pussy, shallow intense movements. The dragon seemed to know precisely where to touch. He worked her entrance hard until she was panting and moving against his mouth with a frantic rhythm.

A red haze welled up inside Bren, blurring the lines of power, clouding his sight. The delicious taste of her cunt and Tynan's hunger consumed his senses. The dragon wanted more, wanted all of her.

Bren's tenuous grip on his awareness slipped. Tynan was too strong and his need too great.

She rolled her hips upward, opening herself—as if silently pleading for a deeper touch.

Mine! the dragon shouted and blackness covered Bren's mind.

Keene grabbed at the cushions beneath her, needing something stable in her world. Her heart pounded loud in her ears—silencing all sound except the prince's low satisfied growls. He pushed his tongue into her again, as if trying to reach deeper. Her body screamed for more. She was so close. She planted her foot and drove her hips up, smashing her pussy against his mouth, desperately seeking the release she knew he could give her. The shallow punches of his tongue were mere teases, little bits of temptation to torment her. The sharp climb to the edge of climax left her begging.

"Please," she sighed. He lifted his mouth away and fear plummeted into her heart. He couldn't leave her like this. Reacting instinctively, she slapped her hand to the back of his head and shoved him back down. His raspy chuckle tickled her skin. The arrogance of it all should have slowed her desire but the light brush of his tongue, flicking across her lower lips distracted her from any irritation. She had to find the release. Nothing in her life had prepared her for this—this wild, exotic pleasure.

The sweet tension continued to build, growing higher and tighter with each stroke. He sank his tongue into her passage and fluttered the tip. The light touch sent warm flickers through her pussy. She arched her back and cried out. It was too much—and still not enough.

As if he knew he'd pushed her to the limit, he drew back and circled her clit with his tongue — slow swirling strokes. Her pussy shimmered with new fires. He placed his lips over her clit and began to suck.

"Bren!" she shouted, her body illuminated by the intimate kiss. His dark head bobbed between her thighs as he consumed her. He kept on — sucking and licking, returning and tasting her with delicious strokes. The pressure around her clit built, flowing into her pussy until it felt like her whole sex was contracting, tightening, desperate for release.

"Mine. Come," he growled. The light brush of his words and gentle pull from his lips sent her over the edge. She gasped as her world spiraled down to one central point in her body then exploded. Tension skittered through her limbs followed by melting fire. She sagged back onto the couch, her strength evaporating.

Hot liquid flowed through her veins, making everything slow and languorous. The climax had a narcotic effect on her body and she floated for a while, unable and unwilling to worry about anything. As she drifted back to full awareness, her team came to mind. They would never believe what the prince could do with his mouth, she thought with a smile. The reminder of her mission collected her scattered thoughts and prompted her to lift her head and stare at the man still crouched between her thighs. *Was now a good time to offer him a drink?* It didn't seem so. After that incredible tongue-fuck, he was going to want to have her for real.

She blinked, still feeling the after-effects of her orgasm, and realized Prince Bren hadn't stopped. The touch was lighter, almost soothing but still he tasted her, swirling his tongue across her flesh, pushing the tip into her passage. The nerve endings came alive again.

"Uh, Prince Bren, I—" She felt the need to explain that she'd already climaxed.

His mouth left her pussy for one moment, to growl the word "more" then he fell back on her, burying his face between her legs. Surely, he wouldn't continue. She'd climaxed. She was done…and oh, he was sucking on her clit again, lighter now and with wispy flickers of his tongue.

Her body didn't seem to grasp that one climax was enough either. It wanted more. Lulled by the first climax and tempted by the oncoming one, her head dropped to the side. A torch across the room illuminated the bar. That's right. She was supposed to drug him. She had a task to complete.

"Uh, Prince Bren, perhaps you'd…" He swirled his tongue around her clit and Keene couldn't find the breath to speak. "Oh my. Uh, Prince Bren—" she tried again. "Perhaps you'd like a drink."

He lifted his head and drilled her with those changeable eyes. They were black as he stared at her. "Drink from you."

Before she could respond, he'd spread her pussy lips wide and again thrust his tongue inside, reaching deep. He swirled the tip, teasing her inner tissues. Her eyes rolled into the back of her head. It wasn't possible for one body to contain all this pleasure.

She couldn't exactly stop him, she justified as she sank back down. What courtesan would do that?

She had all night. It was hours before sunrise and surely he would tire soon. She let her head fall back against the cushions and listened to her body's pleasure.

Chapter Three

Bren came back to his senses, his hands clamped around Cissa's hips, holding her still as he repeatedly drove his tongue into her passage.

Her back arched and she cried out. "Bren, oh please, Goddesses, Bren!" She twisted as if she wanted to escape—but pumped her hips upward as if begging for more. "Please stop. You have to stop." Her whimpered plea tore through the remainder of the dragon's control and Bren felt his power return. He stared at her. She was practically naked—her blouse open and hanging from her shoulders, her skirt shredded in pieces beneath her hips. He had no memory of it.

Bren looked down. His hose were still shoved down and there were traces of semen on the ground. He'd obviously jacked himself off as he'd licked her.

Now she begged him to stop. What had he done to her?

He sat back, trying to remember. Had he hurt her?

Then he heard it. "Fuck me, please." Her whisper was so soft he almost missed it. The haze of the dragon had retreated and the deep pink of her cunt called to Bren, tempting him to have her as Tynan had. He had no strength to resist. Moving slowly, he slipped his middle finger into her wet passage. She was swollen and tight. Her silky flesh clung to him as he penetrated her cunt, reaching deep. He ground his back teeth together to contain the dragon's growl of pleasure. She was so tight she would grip his cock like a fist. "Yes, please, Bren, fuck me."

He pumped his finger in and out of her pussy several times before he spoke.

"Is that what you want? Do you want my cock inside you?" he asked, his voice low and raspy.

"Please."

"Do you not like the feel of my mouth? My tongue in your cunt?" He pushed, needing time to regain his control and needing to hear that the dragon had not harmed her. But there was no way he could deny himself another taste. He followed the question with a deliberate swipe of his tongue around her clit.

She moaned and arched her back up. "I need you." Her plea was soft but the hunger within the words swirled around his cock, demanding that he satisfy her desire. "Inside me."

Keene could barely keep her eyes open. Her body bordered on exhaustion but the craving lingered. The prince had been steadily working her with his tongue for what seemed like hours—it could have been days, it could have been minutes. Wild intense minutes. She didn't know. Only that she'd come, and come. And again, until she'd lost track and her voice grew hoarse from her pleas.

Only her cries weren't for him to stop—they were for more. His tongue—his cock. She wanted it all. The thick rod rising from his groin would stretch her inner tissues but she wanted it.

He bent forward, as if he was going to return to licking her. She leveraged herself up, grabbed his head, the short spiky ends of his hair tickling her fingers, and held him away from her.

"Fuck me, please, Bren." She didn't care how desperate she sounded. Her pride had disappeared about the time he'd ripped her skirt into pieces to have better access to her flesh. He tensed, his hands tightening for a moment on her hips and Keene thought he would move away. His eyes drilled into her sex. The heat from his gaze warming her again, liquefying the desire in her cunt. He was fighting the desire.

She remembered the phrase that had sent him to release before and whispered, "Come inside me."

She felt the words move into him.

He pushed up, moving over her, until his cock was positioned at the edge of her entrance. The heat was incredible—just the tip of his shaft was touching her and it felt like a sword newly pulled from the blacksmith's fire. She wanted to move, to rock her hips up and force him deeper but he held her still.

"Is this what you want?" he asked, locking his eyes to hers.

Suddenly, Keene couldn't find the answer. This seemed to be so much more than a casual fuck between a courtesan and her client. Except she wasn't a courtesan and he was her target. If she said no, he would move off of her. She knew that. He was fighting it so hard that she knew if she gave the least sign of withdrawing, he'd pull away. But she couldn't do it. The desire thrumming through her veins wouldn't let her pull back.

"Yes," she whispered.

He drove forward. Their matching gasps echoed through the room. He was big but fit inside her nicely, stretching long and wide. She groaned and rolled her hips upward, inching that last little bit inside her.

His eyes were dark as he stared down at her. Amazement seemed to wash over his face and for a moment Keene thought she'd done something wrong. Maybe she wasn't supposed to find this much pleasure in the act. Perhaps a courtesan would be more controlled but Keene couldn't hide her eagerness.

She'd fucked before—it had been part of her training when she'd first joined the teams—but this was different. He was different.

He felt so good inside her. She let her head fall back against the cushion and met his gaze, silently daring him to fuck her until she screamed.

Neither spoke but he seemed to recognize her desire. He pulled back, the movement so slow she felt every inch of him. When he was almost clear, he stopped. His hands left her hips and gripped the couch below them as he started to push back into her. Slow and controlled. The muscles in his arms were singing with tension—his body practically screamed with it. His tight chest barely expanded as he inhaled.

This was the prince they'd discussed. The one who controlled his world and everything in it. Even controlling—resisting—his own pleasure. Damn, she'd broken that control before, she wanted to do it again—wanted his memories to be of release and shattered satisfaction.

She gripped his upper arms, her nails biting gently into his skin. "Prince Bren, you feel so good inside me." She let her desire reverberate through her words. "So thick and hard." He slammed into her, filling her completely. She gasped, feeling him once again stretch her. "Oh yes, just like that." He slowly retreated, as if he was using the time to recover. Keene squeezed around him, tightening her muscles around his shaft. His lips pulled back, baring clenched teeth. "I need you, my prince." In the torch light, his eyes seemed to change from green to black. She stroked her hand up his shoulder to his cheek. "I need you."

He tossed his head back and growled. It was a tortured sound, ripped from the darkness inside him. His hips began to pump, hard and fast. No slow penetrations. He pounded into her. Keene curled her legs up, wrapping around his waist, pulling him deeper. She didn't understand but this felt right—it felt real.

"Yes, Bren. Deeper, harder." The muscles beneath her hands tightened as he drove himself into her. Her body, primed from the steady licking he'd given her, was ready for a hard fuck. She opened herself and let him ride her. Every stroke brushed against her clit and teased the inside of her sex, deep—where only Bren could reach. She'd already experienced climaxes from his mouth but this was a new sensation—touching a place inside herself that she'd thought lost.

She knew it was only passion, lust really, but she felt a connection to him that she hadn't since she'd left her family as a child.

She pushed wildly against him, wanting all of him, begging with each thrust for more. Then she lost the ability to speak, crying out as he pushed into her, shattering the tenuous control she had on her body. Powerful contractions started deep inside her sex then spread, growing in waves as they radiated through her body. In the distance, she heard a cry and knew it was her. She didn't care. Lost in the feeling, she let the wicked sensations slip from her body. As she came back to herself, she realized Bren was still moving inside her. Slowly, gently, as if he wanted to stop but couldn't resist. Her eyelids fluttered open and she stared up at him. He watched her — the fire in him burning his eyes to blackness.

She smoothed her hands up his shoulders, massaging the tight skin as she pumped her hips up against him. Her tiny movements seemed to tear at his control. She pushed harder, driving him deeper. He growled, pulling his lips back like an animal's snarl. If she hadn't been so sure he was fighting his own desires, she might have been frightened but she knew, she could feel him. He wanted to fuck her, to drive hard and lose himself in her body.

"That's it," she encouraged. "Fill me. Let me feel all of you." His hips slammed forward and once again his body seemed in charge. "Yes. That's it." She reached up and gripped his head turning his face until he looked directly at her. "Come inside me, my prince," she whispered.

A cry that sounded suspiciously like a howl filled the chamber as he pounded into her, once and then again. The hot flood of his seed poured into her womb. Bren collapsed on top of her, settling his heavy weight on her chest. The lack of air didn't bother her.

She smiled tiredly as she stared into the torch-lit room. This was almost as satisfying as her own climax. Almost. She let her mind wander, listening to Bren's heartbeat slow and his breathing return to normal. This was the memory she would carry with her — when Prince Bren lost himself inside her body.

A long time later, he pulled back, stood and lifted her in one fluid movement.

"Bathing chamber," he demanded.

Keene pointed over his left shoulder and he turned in that direction. She curled into his warmth as he carried her, nuzzling her nose against his neck, inhaling the delicious masculine scent. Her body was pliant and weak, still relaxed from her climaxes. Unable to resist his nearness, she flicked her tongue out and captured the salty flavor of his skin. He tipped his head as if giving her free rein to taste him. She opened her mouth on his throat, placing hot kisses along the tight muscles.

Through drooping eyelids, she caught a glimpse of the bar as he stalked past it. Her purpose snapped back into her head.

"Would you like a drink?" she mumbled, her lips as tired as the rest of her body. He didn't even pause. Just shook his head.

"Later. I need more of you."

Her entire body shuddered with joy. Even tired and well satiated from the climaxes he'd given and shared with her, she wanted more. There was time later for her to complete her task. She had all night.

He stepped inside the bathing chamber. Torches burned around the walls giving the room a golden glow. The bath was a large tub with a slow spinning river of perfectly warmed water. Without breaking stride, Bren reached over the high edge and placed her inside. By the time she'd straightened, he'd dropped his hose and pulled off his shirt and jerkin. He tossed them casually on the ground outside the door. A flash of silver caught her attention. A heavy chunk of metal hung around his neck on a thin silver chain. He wrapped his hand around the medallion and removed it, hanging it on post on the door frame. When he turned back to her, he was naked and all interest in the medallion disappeared. She had only a moment to admire the full power of his body—his broad chest was etched with strong powerful muscles that tapered down to a tight, rippled stomach. Keene licked her upper lip imagining what it would feel like to trace each line with her tongue.

The center of her body began to ache with renewed energy. What was it about this man that he inspired such hunger?

Making another effort to regain control of her body—and hopefully the situation—she turned away as he climbed over the edge of the tub. The movement placed her in the path of the water and the slow swirl quickly washed away the traces of his seed. A strange sense of loss crept into her chest as the remnants of his lovemaking disappeared.

Bren came up behind her—his cock pressing against her backside as his hands drifted over her hips, her waist, skimming up to cup her breasts. He held her firm mounds in his palms, squeezing gently as he pulsed his cock against her ass. She shivered. She'd never taken a man there. Would he want that? The idea skirted through her mind. His strong fingers pinched her nipples…and all thought but the present faded.

By the Goddesses, it would be wonderful to have this every night, to know this lover waited for her, to be able to rely on someone else's strength. The traitorous thoughts made her straighten.

"Shh, shh. I've got you," he whispered. "Let me ease you." Knowing she had to complete her role, she sighed and let her body relax against his.

He began to stroke her and wash her, the delicate perfume of the soap filling the chamber. A vague nagging voice in the back of her head tried to break through—something about her being the courtesan and that she should be bathing him, but it was too wonderful to have his hands on her, soothing and cleaning. It was so easy to lose track of time, to forget the world beyond them as he touched her.

The warm moist air in the room stopped her from being chilled but didn't stop her nipples from staying hard. He lifted a soapy sponge, dribbling suds across her shoulders, down her breasts.

He was silent, guiding her movements with his hands, turning her, shifting her as he washed every part of her body, dipping down into the warm flowing water to cleanse and heal the space between her legs. The sponge disappeared and his fingers slipped into that still-hot place. Keene groaned, fighting the urge to succumb to his caresses. She didn't want to miss this opportunity. This would be her one chance to explore his body.

With languid ease, she turned to face him.

"Let me serve you, my prince." She gently pushed him against the opposite side, encouraging him to sit on one of the benches placed below the waterline. When he was seated, she backed away and stood before him. His eyes dipped down to her chest. She smiled, pleased to have his attention, knowing her breasts were firm and full, probably her best feature. She picked up a sponge and slowly squeezed until bubbles poured from the depths. Suds dripped down her arms, pooling into the flowing water. She took one step closer and brushed the sponge across his chest, leaving a trail of foam. She followed behind with her palm coaxing the soap into a thick lather.

Bren put his hands on her hips and pulled her forward until she straddled his knees. Positioned over him, she guided her hands across his skin—the tight muscles of his chest, his shoulders, the sharp ripples of his stomach. He was warm beneath her touch and she let herself linger, enjoying the delicious sensations.

The urgency faded and she indulged her desires— alternately washing and caressing. She teased the flat copper nipples and scraped her fingernails across his skin. The fire from his eyes encouraged each stroke. Reaching below the surface, she traced the sponge up his thighs, circling his rising cock. Bren grabbed her hands. So lost in her own world, she blinked as she looked up.

"I want to touch you," she whispered, hearing the pleading tone to her voice.

He shook his head. "Too much. I need to be inside you."

The nagging voice shouted in her head but she couldn't stop herself. How could she say no to him?

She nodded and inched forward, lifting her hips until she was above his cock. Placing the thick head to her entrance, she slowly sank down.

All her worries faded. It was too lovely—the thick shaft sliding into her, the grip of his fingers nipping into her hips. Laughter bubbled up in her throat. She curled her arms around his neck and settled her head on his shoulder, whispering his name as she slowly rocked against him, teasing her clit with each stroke. His hands stroked up her back, learning each curve, gently rubbing the tight muscles.

Contentment bubbled up inside her and Keene buried her face in his neck. This was dangerous, far worse than any physical threat. The pretense of the courtesan was gone—she was making love to the prince as herself, without concern for the mission. Despite the irritating conscience, she couldn't make herself withdraw. Her other sexual encounters had all been during training and had had a purpose. This was different. There was no goal except pleasuring each other. They moved together, matching rhythms. It was slow and luxurious, with little drive toward climax. Keene knew it would come but for now she was content with having him inside her and having free access to stroke his body. She rubbed her breasts against his chest and enjoyed the tiny jolts erupting from her nipples.

Just once more, she promised herself. She would have him one more time and then she'd return to her task.

"Let's get out of here," he muttered, though he made no move to push her away. She raised her head and smiled. She brushed her fingertip along his lower lip, fascinated by the smooth surface.

"I'm comfortable right where I am." The teasing tone was no longer the imagined timbre of the courtesan's voice. Keene knew her own personality was revealing itself but couldn't find the strength to fight it. She wanted him. Not as part of the mission but because he was too delicious to resist.

"Baby, we're going to get wrinkled."

She shrugged.

"Things might begin to shrink."

Her lips formed into a silent "Oh".

"You probably wouldn't like that," Bren said, amazed to discover a foreign undercurrent in his words—laughter. He was flirting with a courtesan...and she was flirting back. He didn't understand what was happening. The deliberate seduction in her voice when he'd first entered her chambers was gone and something far more powerful was in its place. The intriguing way she curled around him, snuggled against him. These weren't the actions of a trained courtesan.

Was it possible she felt the same connection that he did? It was unlikely. His passion came from the dragon.

"I don't know," she said with a soft groan. "You're so big, I think you could shrink and I'd still feel you—thick and hard inside me." She pumped her hips up and down—an action that would ensure he stayed hard.

He smacked his hand onto her backside—a firm but gentle tap. She straightened, her eyes widening and her beautiful breasts pushing forward.

"Don't push me too far, sweet," he warned. "It's taken me too long to get to this point. I'm not willing to waste a moment."

His advice had the desired effect—and it didn't. She stood up, disconnecting their bodies, but there was a hint of power that shone in her eyes as if he'd given too much away. She now knew how desperately he wanted her.

"Then perhaps we should move on." She stepped away, elegantly climbing out of the tub. Bren watched—hungry for the barest glimpse of her pussy as she exited the water.

More, Tynan urged, driving Bren in the direction of the woman he'd chosen.

Cissa picked up a towel and stroked it slowly across her skin. She held the cloth across her breasts and turned to the side, so he only had an obscured profile of her form. She rubbed the soft material across her body, bending forward to dry her legs, pushing her curved ass out. Bren curled his hand around his cock and stroked, matching the rhythm of her hands. The lazy way she flicked the droplets from her body made his mouth water.

Tynan growled inside Bren's head and Bren mirrored the sound out loud. She lifted her head and smiled.

"Something you wanted, my prince?" She dropped the towel but, before he could see all of her, she spun away and walked from the room—her beautifully rounded ass tempting him as she left. Leaving him alone.

Bren stared down. He was still in the pool, his cock hard and in his own hand, and he was alone. *How in the Hells had that happened?*

Mine?

"I'm going," he muttered and dragged himself out of the bath. She'd left him. It was strange behavior for a courtesan. Or maybe it wasn't. This was the first time he'd ever become involved with one.

Not that he was actually becoming "involved" with her, he assured his still-vocal conscience. This was a one night thing. He'd found a woman the dragon could enjoy and he would indulge the beast but it wouldn't go beyond that.

Mine!

Tynan's scream shook Bren's skull. He gripped the doorframe of the bathing chamber waiting until his head cleared. When the sound had faded, he opened his eyes and looked into the room. Cissa was on the bed—one leg bent, the other spread to the side in delectable invitation. Her enticing scent reached him from across the room. All thoughts of the future disappeared. He had to have her now, had to feel her against his mouth, feel his cock plunge into her.

"Mine," he said echoing the dragon's desire.

Water dripped from his body as he stopped at the bedside. She stared at him—at his cock in particular—and slowly dragged her tongue across her upper lip. Damn, just when it seemed he couldn't get harder, his cock would prove him wrong.

"I'm ready, my prince."

Her husky words spiraled through his chest, grabbing his heart and dragging him forward.

While he watched, she slipped her hand down until her fingers brushed the top of her pussy. "I'm ready to have you inside me. To feel that long, lovely cock pumping into me."

Tynan wailed with his need and Bren had to fight the dragon's strength to keep from falling on her. He drew himself back, holding his spine stick straight.

Keene held her breath. It was happening again. She could see him physically drawing back. A feminine urge—one that had nothing to do with the reason she'd been sent here—begged her to seduce him again. Give him that momentary release inside her body.

Just once more. She'd promised herself one more time and this was it. Keene spread her thighs. She dipped her fingers into her sex, teasing the delicate flesh that Bren had licked and fucked. Her own hand was fine but she wanted his—wanted to feel the hunger in his touch.

"More." The word rumbled from his throat as if dragged there by another source.

"Yes," she replied as she pushed her index finger into her pussy. "I want more."

It was nothing less than the truth. But now, seeing him beside the huge bed—his cock hungry and his control pushed to the limits—Keene felt the strange desire to tease him a little.

"I love your thick hard cock inside me," she whispered, knowing it would drive him insane. She continued to finger-fuck herself, watching his eyes glow with desperate heat. She'd never felt a sensual power like this before. An irritating voice in her head pointed out that he didn't really want *her*—he wanted the courtesan Cissa—but she pushed the negative thought aside and concentrated on seducing the prince. "Would you like to come inside me? Feel my cunt wrapped around your cock. Hmmm, it will feel so good."

He didn't speak. For a moment, he didn't move. He seemed locked in position. Then as if suddenly freed, he reached out and wrapped his fingers around her ankle. A slow steady pull brought her to the edge of the bed. Cool air brushed her wet flesh. She was bared and open to him but there was no shame in it.

He stared down at her pussy and Keene thought she would scream with the power of it. Pure wicked lust flowed from his eyes. She could barely find her breath. The desire to feel his mouth on her welled from deep inside her cunt and overcame her silence.

"Lick me, my prince." She watched in awe as he knelt beside the bed and followed her instruction, gently, oh so slowly, tasting her. Even as the sensations fought to consume her, she realized that he was licking her in a new way—slower, more subtly. And with a fiercely frustrating outcome. He lavished attention on her clit, licking and sucking until she was twisting within his grasp, so close to her climax. He moved away. Her moan turned to a sigh as the tight point of his tongue pushed into her opening. Good. He wasn't done with her yet. He withdrew, licking across her inner lips. The slow delicate strokes were delicious and lovely but they weren't giving her what she needed.

"Bren, please...I need to..." He brushed his thumb across her clit reminding her how close she was to coming. "Bren!"

He lifted his head and stood. Keene watched in disbelief. He couldn't leave her like this. He couldn't.

"Bren?" Her voice quivered.

"Perhaps that will teach you to tease me." With no prelude, he plunged his hand between her legs and drove two fingers into her cunt. She arched her hips as her passage molded around him. Her body shimmered at the edge of release.

"Please, my prince, I beg you. I promise I won't tease you."

"You'll not touch your cunt without my permission?"

"No."

"Make it your vow." The hard commanding phrase was like a new caress inside her sex.

"I vow not to touch my cunt without your permission."

He pumped his fingers in and out of her pussy in an achingly slow rhythm. Keene dropped her head back and groaned.

"This is mine to command and enjoy."

"Yes, my prince," she sighed, willing to agree to anything as long as he would let her come.

"Shall I fuck you now? Shall I come inside this sweet cunt I possess?"

"Yes, my prince. Come inside me. Please."

His fingers slipped slowly from her passage and Keene cried out from the loss.

"Don't worry," he soothed. "You've given me the answers I wanted—I will reward you." Moments later the thick head of his cock was once again pressed to her opening. Keene braced herself against the bed tensing as he began the slow penetration. "Look at me," he commanded. She forced her eyes to meet his, fearing what he would see in the depths.

He pushed the first few inches of his cock into her. The urge to close her eyes, to hide, was strong but she knew he'd never allow it. He held her gaze, as if staring beyond her eyes into her soul—all while he slid into her pussy. The thick girth stretched her passage almost to the point of pain but it was so delicious she didn't want it to stop. She'd had him inside her before but this was different—he felt wider and longer. Maybe it was the intensity in his eyes, fading slowly from green to black and back again.

As he settled himself inside her, Keene sighed with pleasure. She was stuffed full. It was wonderful. As he began to fuck her, new fears sparked inside her. She would feel empty when he left her.

She had no time to dwell on the concern. The slow, heavy assault on her pussy continued. Keene let go of the future and past and focused on Bren and his delicious cock gliding inside. She grabbed his arms and braced herself, preparing for what she knew was to come. He stood beside the bed, gripping her hips, and pumped into her, riding her deep as if this would be his one and only chance inside her.

Stretched out as she was, Keene couldn't do anything—she couldn't hold him or draw him deeper. She could only lie before him and accept each heavy thrust. He pulled her legs up and around his back, curling her hips upward and sliding his shaft along her clit with each thrust.

"Bren, please," she begged, needing one touch to send her over.

He lifted his head, baring his teeth as he pumped deep into her sex.

"Mine," he growled.

She had no choice but to answer. "Yes."

* * * * *

He pulled out of her, wincing as he heard her tiny hiss of pain. He rolled to his side next to her, their bodies still touching.

"I'm sorry," he said, smoothing his hand along the soft hair protecting her cunt. Keene marveled at the gentle stroke. It had been hours since he hadn't been inside her in some way and, even now, he continued to touch her. The caress wasn't sexual or designed to arouse but simply felt like he couldn't resist. Like touching her was soothing some need deep inside him. The thought brought a sad smile to her lips. He was a target. Nothing more.

It was time to complete her part of the mission but she needed a moment to collect her thoughts.

Her body ached, inside and out, from the long hours of fucking but even as exhaustion pulled her to sleep, she knew she needed more. One more thing.

He stared at his hand against her skin for a moment then raised his eyes to her face. Using what little strength she had,

Keene pushed herself up and placed her mouth against his. It was a soft, gentle kiss. Of thank you and love. He tensed for a moment then responded, keeping with the tone she set, never overwhelming or conquering. It was a lover's kiss, binding them.

Keene fell back on the bed, the lure of sleep too strong to resist. With the taste of him on her lips, she drifted off into her dreams.

Bren listened as her breathing slowed to the steady pace of sleep. He waited until he was sure she was deep in slumber then he rolled out of bed. He had to get out. The temptation to stay was too strong. The desire for her was too strong. Even now, with his cock soft and Tynan rumbling with satisfaction through his head, Bren wanted her. He wanted to watch her, touch her, taste her lips and hold her. Hells, he even wanted to talk to her. This was bad.

He paced around the end of the bed, unable to pull his gaze away from her. His seed dripped from between her legs marking his possession. She'd wanted it. Begged him for it. And he'd needed to give it to her.

His logical mind warred with his instincts. She was a trained courtesan. Of course she knew how to arouse him — knew the precise words that made him unable to resist her. But damn it, her arousal had been real as well. He'd sensed it. Tynan had sensed it. She'd wanted him.

He stared at her face. The very edge of her mouth was curled up — a satisfied smile. Somehow, that comforted him more than the desperate cries for release. Those could be faked but the little smile as she slept — that was real.

As real as that kiss.

He still felt the impact in his gut.

Courtesans didn't kiss their clients. It was an unspoken agreement between the parties. But she'd leaned forward and placed her mouth against his.

He stalked to the bar, desperate for something to drink. A bottle of *burgenda* waited. But sipping the bitter liquid wouldn't satisfy his thirst. Or soothe the wild flurry of his thoughts. He reached below the counter and found a bottle of *amber penanc.* He poured a shot into a glass and tossed it back. The liquor burned as it moved down his throat.

Damn, it might not calm my thoughts but it certainly will corrode my insides.

He placed the tumbler quietly on the counter, not wanting to wake Cissa. She deserved her rest.

Listening to the silence and extending the dragon's senses outward, he felt the sunrise nearing. Probably an hour away.

He couldn't leave. Not yet.

Bren wandered back to the bedside and stared down at her. She hadn't moved.

Mine, Tynan whispered. Bren noticed a change in the dragon's tone. They'd been at odds for so many years it was strange to hear calm in the words. Tynan had found his mate.

A woman Bren knew he could never take as his wife. It wasn't her profession that made her unsuitable. Ashure's courtesans were prized as wives. But now, more than ever, Bren knew he could never accept this woman. The crystal cut memories of that cave years ago slammed into head—only this time it was Cissa's body broken and bleeding on the rocks. Bile rose in his throat.

He'd lost control of Tynan tonight. His memories of those moments were blurry but it didn't lessen the impact. Tynan had been desperate to have the woman he thought belonged to him. Only the Gods knew what would have happened if Cissa had rejected him. Bren couldn't, wouldn't risk it again. The heavy weight of a leaden heart dragged him down.

Mine?

Bren found himself taking the coward's way out. He knew he would have to tell Tynan about his decision but that was a battle for another time. Tonight the dragon was at ease and Bren found himself wanting to keep the peace between them. He crawled back onto the high bed, close to, but not quite touching, Cissa. Her hair, long freed from the ties that held it in ponytails, lay spread across the pillows, tangled by his hands and her frantic movements.

As if she sensed his presence, she rolled toward him, cuddling into his chest, her hand curling between her breasts, her legs winding around his until they were bound together. He checked to see if she was awake but her eyes were still closed and, after a sigh, her breathing returned to the slow steady pace from before. He brushed his hands across her back. The room had cooled and her skin was chilly. He wrapped his arms around her and pulled her closer, sharing his warmth.

It was the least he could do, he told himself.

Sleep pulled at him as well but he didn't let himself drop into more than a light doze. He had to leave immediately after sunrise. He tried to think about all the work he had waiting for him but the smells of their loving and the press of her body against his distracted him. His hands continued to caress her smooth flesh. Another hour and he could leave.

Another hour and I'll be insane, he thought. His cock was aching to return to her heat, his body already seeking the connection. The night had been a revelation in so many ways. It had been the first time he'd actually had sex, though he hadn't felt like a virgin when the night had begun. Still, the sensations had been nothing like he'd expected. They'd been stronger and more demanding. Once the desire had taken hold of him it had been difficult to resist.

And the woman. Her body had matched his in a way he couldn't have imagined before experiencing it—her curves matched his angles until they fit together.

He stared down at her form and felt another slap from his conscience. Even in the pale light he could see the bruises from his hands on her fine skin, probably on the insides of her thighs as well. He brushed his fingertips over her arm, skimming across the faint purple marks. His control had been pushed to its limit tonight and there was the damage to prove it. He wished he could blame it on Tynan seizing control but, with the exception of the first time he'd licked her pussy, the dragon had never overwhelmed him. He'd exerted his power and joined Bren but the human had remained in command.

He closed his eyes. The sweet perfume of her cunt was permanently fixed in his memory.

More, the dragon prodded and Bren was too exhausted to deny him.

With gentle fingers, he rolled Cissa to her back and began to stroke her between her legs. Almost instantly she grew wet. The warm moisture amazed him. Even in her sleep she responded to him. Her eyes fluttered open as he spread her thighs and pushed the very tip of his cock into her passage.

"Once more," he said.

Keene nodded and reached for him. She was sore and tired but her body still craved his. As if he understood, he sank into her gently, giving her time to adjust, holding himself above her with a strength that amazed her. A lazy smile curled her lips once he was fully seated inside.

As they stared at each other, neither moving, she knew it was different. Something had changed.

He leaned down and kissed her. It seemed natural and right and loving. He flicked his tongue along her upper lip and she opened for him. He didn't drive into her mouth but licked inside, giving her mouth the same delicate touch he'd given her pussy. She curled her tongue around his and savored the hot masculine flavor.

This was no desperate fuck between bodies. He was loving her.

As if he couldn't stop himself, he rocked slowly inside her. She gasped and he moved his mouth down her neck, kissing and licking in slow progression toward her breasts. Keene ran her hands up his back, across his chest, teasing the tight, flat nipples.

It was beautiful, the slow way they touched and kissed, caressing each other's bodies as he stroked inside her. The rise to pleasure was slow and long and when it came, they reached it together.

"Bren," she sighed as she floated down from the high, the warmth of his cum filling her. He settled down on top of her, still inside her, holding his weight off her. Nuzzling her neck, tasting her with light kisses and teasing nibbles of his teeth.

"Sleep," he whispered, pulling out of her and again settling beside her.

Bren stared again at the sleeping woman in his arms and waited until she was deep in slumber before he eased her away and crept from the bed. The sun was rising. He could feel it in his blood and knew it was time to go.

Tynan's confusion slowed him down but there was no way he could explain his actions to the dragon. Bren clamped down on the beast's less vocal complaints, dressed, and headed toward the door. The jingle of coins in his pocket drew him to a stop.

He should leave her something. King Ashure paid for the courtesans but Bren always left a tip—usually a large one. He reached into his pocket and pulled out the coins. It felt wrong. Something about paying Cissa to fuck him felt wrong.

Because she's ours, Tynan said.

Bren scoffed. It might feel wrong to him but Cissa would expect it. She'd been doing her job after all. She'd just been damned good at it.

He stared at the eight *sentons* in his hand. One was a reasonable tip, two quite generous. He slapped all eight on the table and walked away. Whatever the cost, he had to get away from the woman.

She was too dangerous to his peace of mind.

* * * * *

Keene pushed on the door and was glad when it swung open easily. She didn't have the strength to fight inanimate objects. She needed to save her remaining energy to explain her failure to her teammates. She trudged into the meeting room. Triant, Risa and Marvis looked expectantly at her as they all waited for the door swing shut. Assured that they were protected against anyone listening, she sighed.

"I didn't get it."

"What?" Risa stood up and pushed away from the table. "Why not?"

Keene took the opportunity of the open chair and sank down. It was all she could do not to drop her head on the table and fall asleep. Her body was exhausted. And sore.

"I didn't exactly have time."

"How is that possible? You were gone all night."

She grimaced up at the team leader. "It seems your information that Prince Bren doesn't use the services of courtesans was incorrect. *Very* incorrect."

"You mean he actually…?" Triant left the term hanging.

"Oh yes. That, amongst other things." Many other things.

She sagged forward, resting her elbow on the table and her chin in her hand. She wasn't going to be able to stay upright much longer. Her energy was drained — physically and mentally. The prince was exhausting. And as dangerous as she'd first expected. She shifted in her chair and the inside of her thighs protested. She would have wondered how long it had been since she'd spent that much time with her legs spread open but she knew the answer — never. The inner lining of her pussy fluttered and Keene couldn't hold back her groan. It was as if her body missed him — missed his penetration, the long heavy thrusts and the short shallow pulses of his hips as he massaged the far reaches of her cunt.

She inhaled, full and deep, trying to clear the memory from her body.

"Well, not to be too intrusive into your part of the mission," Risa said, sarcasm dripping from her words. "But couldn't you have fed him the potion after you finished?"

"What *finished*?" Keene asked with equal attitude.

Risa's lips pinched tighter. Sex was joked about and referred to but rarely was it discussed openly among team members. It was just a part of their lives that didn't exist within the team.

"After he finished—" Risa waved her hand vaguely in the air.

"Fucking me?" Keene supplied.

"Yes. After he finished *fucking you*, couldn't you have suggested a drink?"

"I would have—"she said, enunciating each word. "But he didn't. Finish."

"I say again—you were gone all night," Marvis added eagerly. The wonder in his voice was almost enough to make Keene smile but it took too much energy. It was clear Bren's stamina was as impressive to males as it was to females.

"Yes. All night. He came in, we started to talk and the next thing I know, I'm flat on my back with my skirt flipped up."

"And you stayed like that all night?" Risa asked. The mocking disbelief in her question made Keene squint her eyes and glare at her.

"No. Sometimes he turned me over and took me from behind. And there was the time in the bath and on the bed…want me to continue?"

"Yes!" Triant and Marvis shouted in unison. Risa grimaced, glared at the two men and shook her head.

"I'm sure that's not necessary."

"I'm sure that if Keene could have broken away for a moment and drugged him, she would have," Triant said, placing a supportive hand on her shoulder. "If nothing else than to get a little rest." He winked at her.

Keene did her best to smile back in agreement but she wasn't sure that was the truth. She *could* have stopped him. He hadn't tied her down or forced her. If she'd pulled away, she didn't doubt that he would have let her go, but his growling demands for more just sank right into her sex and she'd had no strength to refuse him.

"Then we try again tonight," Risa announced. She nodded toward Marvis. "We've completed our half of the mission. We just need to get to the prince. I still think the best place is the brothel. He's with a stranger and no one will check on him until morning." She looked at Keene. "We wanted to find the type of woman that appealed to the prince. And it appears we did so. Let's give him someone a little less appealing. Let's see what he does with someone not petite and blonde."

Keene nodded then forced her trembling legs to stand her up.

"Where are you going?"

"Bed." The word tumbled out of her mouth through exhausted lips. Bless the Goddesses her whole body was tired. She would need the full day to recover from Prince Bren's delicious assault on her body.

Chapter Four

"Surely you don't expect the Council to approve this proposal, Prince Bren?"

At the sound of his name, Bren felt his attention yanked back to the meeting room. He blinked and looked up. Herenson towered over the table. The man stood whenever he spoke — a habit Bren found vastly annoying. If one couldn't be sufficiently intimidating while sitting, standing wasn't going to help.

Bren remained in his chair. That seemed to annoy Herenson even more.

"I must be blunt, Your Highness," Herenson continued. Bren tried to keep his tired mind on the discussion but it was challenging. "Your proposal must fail. It would take away our means to protect ourselves."

Several other heads nodded in tentative agreement. Bren glanced around the table. The head nodding stopped. He knew half the other delegates were slightly afraid of him and were definitely not interested in getting on the wrong side of his father's kingdom. He had no intention of intimidating the others into agreeing but neither would he let ancient prejudice stop him from succeeding.

"Lord Herenson, this proposal does no such thing. It merely seeks to end the hunting of dragons *without cause* and to eliminate 'recreational' hunting." He addressed his comments to the whole table. "My mother's research in the past thirty years has shown that dragons can be controlled and there is no need to destroy them. In fact, there is some indication that dragons can be returned to their human state." A rumble of interest moved through the twenty men in the room. Bren knew for a fact that dragons could be returned to human form but the family had decided to keep that knowledge private for now. "If that is possible," he continued. "Is it truly humane to kill the dragon?"

"But they attack villages…steal cattle and *women*."

"And if you have a dragon that cannot be controlled and is attacking people, that is not precluded from this proposal. Lord Starn—" He raised his eyes to the pudgy man in the corner. "You contacted me about a dragon that was tormenting a village within your lands and we were able to subdue the creature and now, most don't even believe a dragon lives nearby."

Starn nodded. "Yes, yes, you did. I, for one, am recommending King Wehan support the proposal. Having met the dragon Prince Bren is discussing, I see too much humanity in them to consider them beasts any longer."

Bren bowed his head in thanks to the advisor and stood, drawing himself to his full height so he could stare Lord Herenson in the eye. "I believe we're done for the day, gentleman," Bren announced to the room. Parchments shuffled around him as the others gathered their work and began to slip from the chamber before Herenson could object.

Herenson stalked across the chamber until he was inches away from Bren. "What did you have to give the dragon to pacify it? How many women were sacrificed before the creature was satisfied?"

"Lord Herenson, surely you don't think we'd resort to something so archaic as sacrificing virgins to appease a dragon." They hadn't…exactly. They'd merely paraded row after row of women through the dragon's cave until he'd picked one as his mate. The woman chosen in the end had needed a little time to adjust to the idea but from all reports she was content. The dragon was still too unsure of her affections to allow the human to return on a permanent basis but the creature was no longer tearing the world apart.

"I know why you want this proposal to pass. I know the truth about your family."

Bren smiled arrogantly. "Ah, you believe the rumors then?"

"I've got proof and when King Evelant arrives I will make it known to the world what unnatural creatures you are."

Bren felt his eyes tighten at Herenson's threat. Was it possible someone had seen him when he'd let Tynan take his corporeal form? His family had withstood attacks of gossip many times before. They would do so again. They'd all developed the ability to lie, wide-eyed and innocently, about their dragons. Besides if the Kings' Council made any attempt to remove Kei from power, Bren knew the battle would be epic.

"You must do what you feel is right, Lord Herenson, but know this—this proposal will pass, with or without King Evelant's signature on the parchment."

Before Herenson could protest, Bren spun away and left the room. He didn't bother to gather his papers—Wrea would collect them. Bren headed straight for the first open door he could find and into the gardens. Several small groups were wandering slowly in the late afternoon sun but he didn't stop or acknowledge them. He kept his attention focused on the trees before him.

He stalked through the forest, away from Ashure's Castle. His day had been worthless. He hadn't been able to concentrate on anything that anyone had said. And now he'd practically dared Herenson to tell the world his family was dragon spawn. But was he worried about that or the success of the dragon hunting prohibition? No. Even now, his concern was on the petite blond woman he'd fucked all night long. It was all he could do not storm back to the brothel and find Cissa.

Mine! Tynan screamed inside his head. He'd been shouting since sun up, demanding that Bren return them to his mate.

Bren ignored him. The dragon was only part of his troubles. Bren had long ago learned to place Tynan in a corner of his mind while he worked on business for the kingdom. His distraction this morning hadn't been solely the dragon's fault.

It was the memories. Sometimes so clear his cock would harden and he could feel Cissa's lips wrapped around his shaft. Even now, walking alone, his cock was lengthening.

Yes.

Bren knew that Tynan was enhancing his memories, making them sharper and more potent. Anything to draw Bren back to the woman the dragon claimed was his.

But that could never happen. If nothing else, last night had reinforced Bren's conviction that he could never allow Tynan to choose his wife or release the dragon on any woman.

He tensed, expecting the dragon to rebel—scream or struggle against his hold.

Tynan's response was almost worse. The dragon filled Bren's mind with images, pictures, scents and tastes—the hunger in her eyes, the musky perfume of her arousal and the hot, seductive flavor of her cunt. His body froze in desire, unable to move, sure that he would explode—or worse, run to her. He could almost feel the sensation of her inner walls as he slipped his tongue inside her. Bren licked his lips wanting more. *More.* His cock stretched the fabric of his hose. He cupped his hand over his shaft, imagining it was her, stroking him, sucking him.

The fantasy didn't last long. Tynan was controlling them and he led them back to the couch, where Bren had knelt before her, loving her with his mouth. His memories of those moments were hazy. Tynan had been in charge. When Bren had finally returned to himself, Cissa had practically been in tears.

What had Tynan done to her? The question cleared his head, giving him enough strength to force the images from his mind.

Tynan released an amused sigh and answered Bren's question. *Loved her. Fucked her with your tongue. She enjoyed it. She would enjoy mine even more. I could reach deep inside her. Bring out more of that delicious juice from her cunt.*

"She was begging me to stop," Bren said aloud, resisting the urge to sink back into fantasy. He clung to the actual memory of last night. He'd stopped licking her...just long enough to fuck her.

And that's what troubled him the most. He'd had no more control than Tynan. He'd fucked her on the couch, in the bath and then dragged her to the bed where he'd mounted her for the rest of the night. She'd been willing but damn it, she was a courtesan; she was supposed to be willing. That didn't excuse his behavior. Or the marks he'd left on her pale skin from taking her so hard.

Ever since he was a child and had seen the destruction a dragon could cause, he'd known he could never lose control of the beast inside him. And last night he had. But Tynan hadn't been the only "beast" to appear. He scraped his fingers through his short hair and walked toward the sound of running water.

The forest hummed around him—animals wary and on the verge of flight. It was as if they sensed the dragon's presence but couldn't find the creature. Didn't know in which direction to flee.

Bren sighed. He sometimes envied his brother's relationship with his dragon. Rainek and Denith were companions. Bren felt like he'd spent his life fighting with his dragon. And he had. Tynan had seen what he'd seen in that cave twenty-four years ago but the dragon, with the confidence of all dragons, didn't believe he would ever harm his mate.

Bren slowed his steps as he walked into a clearing by the water. On a normal day, he would have allowed Tynan to appear, given the dragon a few moments to stretch its wings out and feel the sun. Maybe even fly if there was a safe, hidden place to take to the air. But Bren knew that he couldn't give Tynan that freedom today. The dragon would snatch control and head to the brothel. He could just imagine the screams as Tynan ripped through walls to get to his mate.

In the natural silence of the forest, Tynan said, *she's mine.*

"I know," Bren agreed. "She's yours but she can never be mine."

The finality of the statement sent a wave of pain into Bren's chest. Most of the emotion belonged to Tynan but some came from Bren. No, damn it, he mentally corrected himself. There had been no emotion involved. He'd had *sex* with the woman. It wasn't, couldn't be, anything more than that. His father and brother had spoken of the emotions attached to finding a mate — that somehow the dragon's choice was someone that the human not only desired but loved. He knew his parents' affection and respect for each other went beyond the lust of the dragon. And he'd even seen it in his brother and his wife, despite the fact that the dragon had brought them together.

Last night was just fucking, Bren insisted — speaking to himself and Tynan. He wouldn't allow himself to feel anything more than desire for the woman — it would make it all the more difficult to leave when the conference of kings was over.

He would have to avoid Cissa. If he didn't see her or speak to her, there was no way to increase his attachment to her. Tynan grumbled inside his head, obviously not liking the direction of Bren's thoughts. The dragon would never accept or understand Bren's reason so he didn't bother to explain.

Though he couldn't release the dragon today, he hoped the peaceful setting would give him a few minutes of rest.

The crack of a twig behind him threw his senses into full alert. He spun around. Tynan instantly magnified his ability to see and hear, searching for any threat.

"Bren?" The flower-soft voice floated from the pathway, followed seconds later by Nerra herself. She smiled hesitantly, stepping forward.

The battle tension that had prepared his body slowly faded and he straightened to his full height. The tightness in his groin quickly faded as she drew closer.

"Nerra. What are you doing here?" He'd walked to a far corner of Ashure's lands. Where had she come from?

"I followed you. Or I started to." She blushed and laughed softly. "And then I got lost. I was sure I was going to wander

77

around these woods forever." Wide blue eyes stared up at him, looking hopeless and sweet. It was the look that had originally melted his heart and never failed to make him long to protect her.

Except today. Today his thoughts were elsewhere.

Besides, the path was clearly marked and she couldn't have wandered too far off the trail. Her slippers were still relatively clean and the bottom of her dress dust free.

She walked forward and held out her hands. Bren accepted them and kissed the back of her fingers. He drew in a deep breath. The light floral scent of her perfume was pleasant but gave him no pleasure.

"Perhaps you could escort me back." Her eyelashes twitched becomingly. "I hadn't meant to be gone this long." She lowered her eyes and turned her head away. "My husband will no doubt be worried."

"Then we should return you to his side."

She smiled softly and looked up. "And we can talk on the way back. I've missed you."

"I've missed you, too." He said the words out of courtesy and tried to find some truth in them but there was little. When she'd left to marry Herenson, Bren had put her from his mind. He'd loved her but she was out of reach—wife to another man. There was always work to do so he'd quickly immersed himself in his duties to the realm and Nerra had become a memory.

"It's strange, seeing you like this…and knowing that it's wrong to feel what I still feel for you," she confessed as they began to walk toward the castle.

Courtesy seemed to demand he respond in kind but he could not. He'd been in love with Nerra five years ago. He'd reveled in her smiles and served to please her. But now, the depths of that emotion seemed shallow when compared to—

He drew his thoughts to a halt. There was no emotion in what had happened last night. It had been sex—pure and simple.

Only it hadn't been that pure or that simple.

And the memories cluttered up his head—not only the pleasure but also the surprised look in Cissa's eyes as if the sensations had been new to her as well.

"Yes, it is unusual," he agreed. He lengthened his stride forcing Nerra to hurry to keep up with him. He searched his mind but could find nothing to say. His relationship with Nerra had been strictly romantic. Now that he couldn't rely on discussing her beauty, he was at a loss.

Dull. No spirit.

Tynan's interjected assessment made Bren walk even faster. He needed to return Nerra to her husband...and perhaps he'd have time to nap before the evening's banquet. Though he wasn't normally the type of person to nap, last night's fucking and today's mental battle with his dragon had drained him. A few minutes of blissful unconsciousness would be perfect to renew his energy. After dinner tonight, King Ashure would again escort them to his brothel. Bren's cock swelled again. *Return to my mate...find her and fu —*

"Why are we walking so fast?" Nerra snapped. The pleasant, airy voice was gone. She sounded out of breath and irritated.

Bren pulled to a sudden stop. He'd forgotten she was there.

"You said you had been gone longer than you'd intended," he pointed out. "And I'm not sure it's proper for us to be alone in the forest."

Her eyes grew wide. "I know, my love, the temptation is difficult to resist."

"I'm sure your husband wouldn't be pleased to find you here with me."

"You're not afraid of him are you?" She sounded almost excited at the possibility.

"No."

"Oh, I didn't mean to offend you." Her lower lip trembled. "It's just so hard sometimes."

Bren nodded but turned and started walking again. He'd come into the forest for few minutes of peace and solitude. He'd found neither.

Quickly, they reached the forest edge. Bren grimaced when he saw Herenson striding toward them. So much for her husband not finding out.

"Prince Bren. Nerra." Herenson bowed his head in greeting but the hard glitter of his eyes told him he wasn't happy about finding his wife with another man. Probably with Bren in particular.

"Lord Herenson," Bren acknowledged, returning the nod.

Herenson looked at Nerra. "I returned to our rooms after my meetings but you'd disappeared."

"I went for a walk and became lost." She sighed and smiled adoringly up at Bren. "Prince Bren came to my rescue."

"Wasn't that kind of him," Herenson said, though his voice indicated he believed it anything but.

"It wasn't much of a rescue," Bren responded truthfully. He didn't mind clashing with Herenson over important issues but he wouldn't let the man think he was dallying with his wife. "Lady Herenson had already found the correct path on her own. No doubt, she would have returned safely without my assistance."

He waited for Nerra to laugh or agree. Instead, she widened her eyes and shook her head—and if Bren hadn't been in the forest with her, he would have thought she'd been in real danger. She looked frightened and helpless.

"Oh no. The path was quite dark and I'm sure there are wild beasts in the forest."

The sunlight had easily illuminated the trail and they'd seen no sign of any animals. Bren looked down at Nerra's dainty figure. What game was she playing? Was it to make her husband jealous? Or did she just view herself as the damsel who needed rescuing—no matter the situation?

"Well, then, I'm glad Prince Bren was able to assist you." Herenson held out his hand, silently calling Nerra to his side. "Shall we go in? You'll no doubt want to rest this evening."

"Of course, my lord. Prince Bren, thank you again for your kindness." Her eyelashes twitched again and she held out her hand. He placed the perfunctory kiss on the back of her fingers and stepped away, allowing Herenson to guide his wife into the castle.

"Oh, and Prince Bren—" Herenson stopped and looked back. "I would like to continue *our discussions*. You seemed distracted today during our meeting." The smirk on his lips was designed to taunt Bren but he ignored it.

"My answers won't be any different but yes, we can talk again."

Herenson nodded sharply and turned away.

Bren stood on the path and watched them enter the castle. Though they walked close together, there was no comfort in their postures. As they turned the corner, Nerra looked back— her eyes filled with longing.

Bren was stunned by his own lack of emotion. Five years ago, every hint of pain in her gaze had made him ache. She was so fragile and delicate, he couldn't help but feel the need to protect her. But now, it seemed faked—to claim helplessness. She'd been in no danger in the forest.

Dull.

"Yes," Bren said aloud. "I know your opinion on the subject."

A gardener, kneeling in a flowerbed beside the walkway, looked up. "I'm sorry, Your Highness. Were you speaking to me?"

"No."

He turned on his heel and stalked in the other direction, Tynan's irritating chuckles following him as he went.

* * * * *

Keene peeked through the curtains watching the banquet, focusing her attention on the prince. He sat at the head table, his serious lips flattened into a tight line as one of the servants approached, her breasts barely contained by two jeweled ropes. She rubbed her tits along his arm as she stretched forward to refill his chalice. Keene felt a nasty sort of satisfaction when Bren shifted subtly, moving away from her touch.

Essentially, he was just what their reports had told them: humorless, sexless, boring.

But they hadn't been in that chamber last night, she thought. Her thighs still ached from his pounding...but it had all been worth it. She'd slept like the dead throughout the day. Her body desperately needing to recover from the hours of loving he'd indulged in. Unable to help herself, she licked her lips as she watched him slowly stand and straighten his emerald green doublet. She knew what that long waistcoat hid—a thick, long cock that felt wonderful in her pussy. And her mouth. Cissa had been right. She'd loved sucking his cock and wanted more. But if all went as planned, she'd never get the chance again. They'd finish their assignment in a few days and return to the Guild, leaving Prince Bren and his delicious cock behind.

The core of her body began to ache as if mourning the separation. Keene sighed and slowly rocked her hips from side to side, the slow build of warmth and moisture between her legs reminded her how dangerous Prince Bren was. Something about him weakened her control.

Though she knew it only made the desire worse, she continued to watch him, fascinated by the admiration and fear on the faces of those near him. The grim set of his jaw seemed to keep many people from approaching as he walked among the tables. Even when some called out, he ignored them, stopping only to talk to specific people.

At first she thought it was rank—that he only greeted those equal to or higher than himself—but then she saw him stop at one of the lower tables and greet a man dressed in obviously worn, inexpensive clothes. Bren listened intently as the man spoke, first haltingly and then with passion as the prince nodded. From her hiding place, she couldn't hear the conversation but she could tell from the expression on Bren's face that he was not only listening but thinking about what was being said. A warm emotion that had nothing to do with fucking settled into her heart. Bren shook the other man's hand and walked away. The stunned look on the gentleman's face as he watched Bren leave matched Keene's reaction. Prince Bren was arrogant and demanding but he'd given the other man his honest attention. *Maybe he's not as shallow as I thought.* Even as the idea formed in her brain she brushed it away. It didn't matter who or what Prince Bren was…he was her target, nothing more.

"Is he there?" Risa asked, peeking around Keene's shoulder.

"Uh—yes," she said shaking off her musings.

"Drunk?" The hopeful sound in Risa's voice made Keene sigh.

"No."

"Too bad. That would make it so much easier."

Keene nodded. Risa had the potion in her hand. If he drank it tonight, they'd be halfway to completing their mission. And then they would go home, she thought sadly. It's for the best, she reminded herself. After the way she'd behaved last night, she knew she should stay as far away from the prince as she could.

She'd been a member of the teams for more than six years and had never had a reaction to a target like the one she had toward Bren. Something about him wasn't normal. She'd touched him all through the night and still she couldn't read him. With their bodies as intimate as they had been, she should have been able to absorb a glimmer of the man but there was nothing. It was almost like he wasn't human.

But no, that erect cock and the skilled mouth had definitely been all man.

"The king is standing," Risa said. "We'd better take our places."

Keene nodded but didn't immediately follow Risa. She watched Bren for one more moment. Watched the strange light in his eye as King Ashure called all the high-ranking delegates to his side.

No, there was something definitely not normal about Prince Bren.

Keene let the curtain fall and straightened. She didn't care. She wouldn't care. Her job was to complete the mission—not fall in lust with a surly, grim prince from another land.

* * * * *

For the second time in two days, Bren stepped into the elegantly appointed salon—only tonight his chest was tight, his shoulders bound with knots. He'd spent the last two hours fighting the dragon. It had made dinner conversations extremely difficult.

The dragon had worn him down. If he was going to get anything done over the next few days, he was going to have to satisfy Tynan. And that meant finding Cissa. Despite his resolve earlier to avoid her, he was coming to the realization that he had to see her.

Tynan was screaming for release, screaming for his mate. The shouts of "mine" and the steady pressure in his groin had given Bren a raging headache.

And a raging erection.

The headache was the perfect excuse to give King Ashure for rejecting his "gift" for the evening but Bren knew, tonight of all nights, he couldn't. He had to see Cissa. Or Tynan would start tearing down walls to find her.

Though he had no intention of bowing to the dragon's wishes on his choice of a mate, Bren respected the dragon's strength and knew the animal's control was at its limit.

Madam Jaqis once again glided into the room, the filmy sleeves of her gown floating gently behind her. She nodded to the occupants as she headed toward the king. Bren had to intercept her. He hurried through the crowd, intersecting her path toward King Ashure.

"Mistress Jaqis, may I have a moment?"

She was too well trained to refuse a prince's request so she stopped and smiled. "Of course, Prince Bren. How may I help you?"

"The woman you gave me last night—"

"Cissa."

"Yes."

Concern infiltrated her eyes. "She didn't please you?"

"No, no. She pleased me well. Very well."

Her smile brightened and her eyes grew round. "You mean, she finally was able to—" She gazed dropped to his groin but she snapped it right back up. "I'm sorry, Your Highness. It's just in my excitement I…never mind…you simply must tell me what she did that…" she lowered her voice. "That pleased you."

She smelled right, Bren mentally answered, but knew that he couldn't share that with the madam.

"Perhaps we can discuss it later," he suggested. "I was hoping you could assign her to me again tonight."

The light dropped out of her eyes. "I'm sorry, Your Highness, but the assignments have already been made and Cissa has been given to another gentleman for tonight."

Tynan's internal roar weakened Bren's knees as it vibrated from his skull down to his toes. Bren grabbed the back of a chair to hold himself upright.

"Isn't there something you could do? I'm willing to pay extra."

"That's very sweet—and very generous—and I'm sure Cissa will be pleased to know that you asked after her but we have a policy of not allowing the same woman with a client for more than one night in a row." She looked sad and sympathetic. Jaqis stroked her fingers along his jaw line. "It's too easy for men to fall in love with our girls."

"Madam Jaqis—"

She shook her head. "I really can't, Your Highness. Now, I must go hand out assignments before the others become restless." With that—and a gentle, sympathetic smile—she left him.

He stared at the empty space on the carpet where she'd stood, his thoughts battling for dominance over Tynan's shouts. *We'll find her*, he assured the dragon. Anything to calm the beast. *Once we get into the back, we'll leave the chamber and find her.*

The idea had merit, he realized. Surely someone behind the main door could be bribed to tell him where Cissa was working tonight.

Tynan's cries turned to grumbles and the dragon settled.

Moments later, Madam Jaqis approached, holding out her hand. The sympathetic look on her face made Bren want to growl. The madam clearly thought he imagined himself in love with one of her pleasure workers. Perfect. His only consolation was that King Ashure's brothel was so well run Bren didn't have to worry that Jaqis would spread stories about him. No one would know that he'd acted like a lovesick swain. And he wasn't lovesick. Maybe fuck-sick. His cock twitched at the mere thought of Cissa. It had done it all day and it was getting damned irritating.

"Prince Bren, if you'll come with me?"

Jaqis greeted him again and indicated the large man next to her.

"Dardan will take you back to Vixi's rooms."

Bren nodded and followed quietly behind him until they'd walked through the door separating the lounge with the women's chambers.

"Do you know Cissa?" he asked, hoping to add a touch of casual inquiry that had obviously been lacking when he'd spoken with Jaqis.

"Of course, Your Highness. She's a lovely woman."

"Do you know where I could find her?"

Dardan shook his head and Bren saw a flicker of sympathy in his eyes. Damn, the entire brothel was going to think Bren had fallen in love with the first pleasure worker he'd fucked. He had no doubt that after his previous reluctance to touch any of the women, the fact that he'd fucked Cissa would be all over the brothel.

His escort led Bren into a room very similar to the one from the night before but, where Cissa's room had been decorated to appear exotic—scarves and shawls draped over chairs, pillows mounded on the floor—this room screamed power. And leather. Lots of leather. The woman who operated out of this room was clearly someone who liked to be in charge.

"Vixi will be with you in a moment. May you find pleasure in this chamber."

"Yes, I'm sure it will be fine. Now, about Cissa—"

"I'm sorry, Your Highness, but I'm not allowed to discuss any of the women with clients. Perhaps tomorrow Madam Jaqis will be able to assist you. Have an enjoyable evening, Your Highness." And he pulled the door shut, with Bren inside.

Mine?

I'm working on it, Bren mentally sighed.

He turned, looking around the room, waiting for the arrival of the woman who was assigned to him for the evening. Mayhap she would know how to find Cissa.

He didn't have to wait long. The door that led to the bedchamber opened.

His breath locked in his throat—trapped by the insane hope that Cissa would walk through the door. The courtesan entered…and never had he seen a woman more opposite the one who'd serviced him last night. This woman was tall—near to his height he was almost sure. Tight, red curls tumbled in riotous locks from the top of her head to just below her shoulders. And where Cissa had been dressed to convey youth and innocence, this woman was dressed for power. Her outfit matched the room around them—leather. Black leather.

A short skirt hung just barely beyond her sex, creating a wicked shadow between her legs that tempted a man to explore it. The skirt was so small Bren was sure that if she turned sideways the lower curve of her ass would be visible at the back. Long strong legs extended from that covered area. He followed the sleek, bare path to her feet encased in black high-heeled shoes. She didn't need to add to her height but the shoes completed the commanding picture she presented.

Even knowing he was staring—probably with his mouth hanging open—he couldn't look away. Her top was also black. Tiny strips of leather stretched across her skin, revealing more than they concealed, pulling tight against her large round breasts, crisscrossing over her chest and circling around back, conveniently hiding her nipples.

Bren felt his hands clench in anticipation. He wanted those tits in his hands. His mouth watered with the thought of sucking and biting on her nipples. Yes, this woman would enjoy a rougher touch.

It took only a moment for Bren to realize his cock was hard. But that was impossible. The dragon made it impossible.

He shook his head. It must be some lust lingering for Cissa.

"Good evening, milord." The woman's husky voice coiled around his cock like a fist making him even harder. It didn't make sense. He quickly pushed aside the strange desire, focusing on the fact that this woman, like Cissa, got his rank wrong.

"My name is Vixi. I'll be servicing you tonight. May I fix you a drink?" She held up a glass that was obviously filled with *burgenda*. The heavy black liquid was hard to miss.

He nodded and moved down the steps, still watching the courtesan. There was something about her. Something familiar. The strange tingling in his spine, moving through his body to his cock, reminded him of last night. He started to sit on the short leather couch but stopped. The memories of Cissa were too strong. They'd been on the couch when she'd sucked him off and he'd licked her. And he'd taken her for the first time there. His cock grew even more. He adjusted the end of his doublet to cover his growing erection and instead chose a nearby chair with high arms and a stiff back. It looked sufficiently uncomfortable that he wouldn't be inclined to relax and indulge in his memories.

He didn't understand it. The rooms, the women, the atmosphere were completely different but he felt the same need as he had last night.

"Here you are, milord."

Bren accepted the drink Vixi handed him and politely nodded. The courtesan smiled and turned away, her rounded ass swinging in a seductive rhythm as she strolled back to the bar.

Mine!

Bren flinched at the dragon's shouted reminder. Tynan was growing impatient.

"Vixi, do you know one of the other courtesans named Cissa?"

Vixi twitched and she hit her hand on the underside of the bar. Bren cursed himself as a fool. It was probably bad form to ask about one courtesan while he was in another's chambers.

Before he had a chance to retract his question, Vixi turned. Her smile was more of a smirk. "Of course, I know her. Why do you ask?"

Though he'd never considered himself a snob, the fact that a courtesan was mocking him made his teeth ache. He stared her down, keeping his face impassive. "I need to find her. Tonight."

She poured another drink—a lighter, sweeter liquor—and sipped it as she strolled across the room.

"But, milord, you haven't even given me a chance." She bent forward, making her breasts strain against the leather strips, and placed her glass on the low table in front of him. "I'm sure I'll be able to please you equally as well as Cissa." A wicked smile curved her lips as she reached over and slipped her hand up under the edge of Bren's doublet. She skimmed her fingers across the top of his thigh then curled her hand over his erection and squeezed.

The blatant, aggressive caress should have startled him but all he could do was stare at her. She ran her tongue along the inside edge of her mouth. "She told me just what you like." She leaned forward and placed her mouth against his ear as if she was sharing a secret. Bren felt a red haze cross his mind as a curled lock of her hair brushed his cheek. "She said that you liked to have your cock sucked and you *love* to eat pussy." Her voice was almost a purr. "And that you like to fuck hard and long."

Bren drew in a deep breath, trying to figure out what was happening to his mind and his body. He was rock-hard and her fingers were still stroking him. By all previous experiences, the dragon should have made his cock go limp when any woman besides his mate touched him.

Mine!

Her teeth nipped his ear lobe.

"I'm prepared to give you whatever you want." She pulled away, removing her hand and her lips. Bren shook his head, waiting for his thoughts to catch up with what his body seemed to understand.

Mine, the dragon said again…and Bren realized Tynan wasn't nagging him to find Cissa. He was claiming this woman.

Chapter Five

Vixi stood up to her full height, which put her pussy dangerously close to Bren's mouth, but stepped away before he could reach for her. With slow practiced moves, she sank down onto the edge of the couch that Bren had avoided. Her tight skirt crept higher as she sat and he knew her cunt juices were dripping onto the leather cushions.

Damn, how did he know she was aroused? That she was wet. He could smell the heady fragrance and knew Tynan was focused on the woman sitting across from him.

Mine, the dragon insisted.

But that's impossible. You claimed Cissa was yours.

Mine.

The dragon seemed almost as confused as Bren did.

"But before we get to the fucking," Vixi said with a throaty laugh. "Shall we sit and enjoy our drinks?" She picked up hers and raised it in salute. Bren automatically did the same. He let the liquid barely touch his mouth. The strong scent of the *burgenda* interfered with the delicious perfume of her cunt.

He looked over the rim of his glass. She'd crossed her legs, allowing him to see more of the curve of her backside. She was definitely bare beneath that tiny skirt.

Mine.

This time Bren nodded in agreement.

"Now, milord—"

The section of his mind that still thought like a prince flinched at the incorrect address. Did none of the courtesans know he should be addressed as "Your Highness"? Did it really matter when she smelled so delicious? His mouth began to water. It would take so little effort to have her on her back, legs spread.

"Tell me about yourself," she said, her voice low and commanding.

But the noise inside Bren's head made it difficult to concentrate. His own mind was trying to figure out how he could want this woman when he'd so clearly wanted and fucked Cissa last night. And Tynan wasn't helping. He created image after image of Bren and Vixi. The bedamned couch would make the perfect location to spread her open and lick her. And then he could roll her over and feel that curvy ass against him. He wanted to enter her from the front and feel those legs wrapped around his waist—wanted to take her from behind and slam his cock into her. The long strong muscles of her thighs told him she could hold on no matter how wild the ride.

This couldn't be right. Bren threw himself out of the chair and strode across the room toward the bar with the vague idea of pouring himself a different drink. One that might dull his senses.

"Milord, are you all right?"

"I'm fine," he said without looking back. He gripped the cushioned ledge, holding himself still—hoping it was enough to keep him away from her. There had to be an explanation for this—he just hoped he found it soon. Tynan was pushing him to return to Vixi and Bren was losing the strength to fight him. Strangely, he felt as if he was betraying Cissa by desiring Vixi. It was stupid, of course. Cissa wasn't expecting loyalty from him.

"I think I know what to do," she said.

He released his grip on the bar and turned around. Vixi stood and smoothed her hands down her body. She bent forward, arching her back and pushing her backside out as she picked up his drink. The leather pulled tight across her ass molding to the full curves and revealing the shadow between her legs. After a long moment, she straightened.

Bren tried to make himself look away but he couldn't fight the vision as she swung around and walked toward him, her hips rocking in a low, loose manner.

"This will help you relax," she whispered, placing the glass back in his hand. She reached up and teased the tips of his hair with her fingers, stepping close to him. Face to face with her, he realized he'd been right about her height. She was barely two inches shorter than he was. The full mounds of her breasts brushed against his chest as she looked expectantly at him.

She was waiting for him to drink. He didn't want it. He wanted her.

He looked into her eyes. Despite the dragon's reaction to her, there couldn't be two women more different than Vixi and Cissa. Cissa had seduced with innocence and sensuality. Vixi was sexual and almost daring him to fuck her. The bold stare that penetrated his was aggressive. She was used to being in charge. Used to commanding the men who came to her.

"Drink up, milord. It will ease you and then we can get on with the night's activities."

He took a step back and placed the glass on the counter. Vixi's eyes darted toward his drink and then back to him. The line of her jaw tightened for a moment. She didn't like to be disobeyed. Bren folded his arms across his chest and stared at her.

A new idea took shape—with Vixi tied to his bed, legs spread, her body writhing and whimpering under his mouth, his cock. Spread out and constrained he could do with her what he wanted. Spend hours between her thighs and she wouldn't be able to resist. She wouldn't want to resist. She'd want him.

Mine, Tynan said mentally smacking his lips at the thought. Though Tynan preferred oral loving, he found pleasure in Bren's fucking as well.

"Turn around," Bren ordered. A hint of defiance flickered through her eyes and for a moment he thought she would refuse. Then slowly she turned. "Bend forward and grab the bar." Again she hesitated but finally followed his command. That delicious backside was now before him and Bren's hands began to tingle with anticipation. He reached out and smoothed his palm down the curve, the leather hot beneath his touch. He stepped forward until his cock rubbed against the tight material, teasing himself and her. His fingers skimmed along the lower edge of her skirt and slipped up the front. Her moisture greeted him long before he'd reached her pussy.

"You're wet, already. I haven't even touched you yet and you're dripping. You want to be fucked, don't you?"

"Yes, milord."

He traced the feminine liquid up her thighs to the source and slowly skirted the tight hole that beckoned him. The concern that he was fucking the wrong woman faded as her liquid coated his fingers. This was no faked desire. She wanted this. Her cunt was begging for his possession. His cock twitched at the idea. He dipped his finger into her pussy. She sighed and he pushed deeper. Heat surrounded him. It felt like home. This was where he belonged. He pulled his finger out and dragged the leather skirt up until it bunched up around her waist.

"Spread your legs," he commanded. Slowly, she lifted one foot and moved it out, about three inches. She glanced over her shoulder. Arrogance in her eyes dared him to make her do more. He speared his hand between her legs and cupped her pussy, reminding her that he was in control. Leaning forward until his mouth was against her ear, he whispered. "Spread your legs like a good girl…or you'll get no cock."

A tiny whimper she tried to conceal was the only sound in the room. She hesitated for a moment, then opened her legs wide, presenting her ass to him properly.

"Very nice." He continued to stroke her skin, slipping his fingers between her cheeks and down to tease her sex. "Arch your back so I can better see the cunt I'm going to be enjoying all night."

A shiver ran through her body. No doubt, Cissa had warned her that he could and would fuck her until dawn. Slowly, she pushed her hips back and pressed her spine forward. He stepped away. The wet pink flesh of her pussy glittered in the pale candlelight and Tynan was fairly screaming with the need to taste her. The dragon's senses were overwhelming him—every delicious scent, every subtle increase of her need flowed into his body and curled around his cock. The desire to fall on her and feast on her pussy raged inside him. And for that reason he fought it. He'd lost control last night. He wouldn't do so again. But neither could he resist the urge to taste her.

He took a deep breath to collect himself and drew in the heady fragrance of her desire. Almost unconsciously, his hand slipped down and stroked his cock, anticipating the pleasure of sinking into her sex.

"Do I please you, milord?" The merest hint of a tremble in her voice drew him back into himself.

"Yes, my lovely, but your slowness to respond to my commands is disappointing. I believe you need punishing." She snapped her head to the side and looked at him over her shoulder. He could have sworn he saw a moment of fear in her gaze. Surely she knew he wouldn't actually harm her. Jaqis' instruction in the sensual arts had given him ideas—tempting images that he longed to explore with Vixi's lush, curved body. He smoothed his hand across her rounded backside.

He'd never had sex before last night but he knew enough of love play to know this was part of the game they'd chosen for the evening.

Only it didn't feel like a game. He had the sudden image of being with Vixi for years to come and having to repeatedly punish her. To both their pleasures.

"Don't you feel you are deserving of some punishment?" he asked, giving her an out. This was her moment to withdraw. He would still have her. There was little chance he was going to make it out of this room without fucking her at least once but he could move to the bed and take her in a more traditional manner. "Answer me, Vixi. Do you think you deserve punishing?"

Her breath pumped in and out of her lungs three times before she answered. "Yes, milord." Vixi's words, few though they were, were laden with sensuality and drenched in desire.

Bren slipped his hand down her bared ass and between her thighs. She groaned as he flicked his finger across her drenched skin.

"Milord, please."

"I am your prince for the evening. And I will do as I please. Do you understand?"

"Yes, my prince."

Pleased with her answer, he pushed his finger into the very tip of her passage. Vixi sighed and pumped her hips backward, as if trying to take more inside.

He could read her desires. She wanted him deep inside and he would eventually get there but now, he pulled back, teasing her with light touches, watching her until she began to relax beneath his touch. Again, he pulled his hand and smacked his palm across her ass. Her head snapped up and back. The glare she directed at him was a mixture of fury and surprise. Something didn't feel right. The room, her clothing, her attitude, they all spoke to the truth that she understood and enjoyed bondage games.

"Shall I stop?"

She licked her lips and he could tell she was considering his question. Slowly, she shook her head.

"Tell me."

"I accept my punishment, my prince," she whispered. She stared at him for one additional moment then turned back. To test the honesty of her words, he touched her again. The thick liquid flowed heavily from between her legs.

He spread her moisture across her skin filling the room with her scent.

"Relax, my lovely," he whispered. "I won't hurt you beyond what you'll enjoy."

She didn't answer but nodded, lowering her face between her arms and resting her forehead against the cushioned edge of the bar. The tension slowly faded from her body as he stroked her. Again, he slapped his palm against her ass, two quick strokes. She gasped but didn't pull away.

"That's better." He followed the taps with a quick finger into her pussy. A promise of what was to come. "Very nice. You are dripping wet." He continued the pattern—spanking her, then teasing her cunt. Soon, her ass was pumping up and down, quivering with each stroke. Each sensation—harsh or soft—produced a delicious muffled moan, as if she was biting her lips to keep from begging.

Taste.

Tynan had hovered near the edge of his mind, never seizing control but guiding Bren with his dragon's desires. Bren knelt down behind her. The perfume of her sex flooding his senses. He scraped his finger up the inside of her thigh, silently asking her to open more for him. Her back arched, spreading her cunt lips wider. With a whisper of approval, he stroked his tongue from her clit all the way to her wet dripping hole, capturing the warm spicy taste of her pussy.

She whimpered but the sound was crushed. Bren smiled. He had no intention of letting her come this way but he would enjoy her. Giving the dragon more control, he let Tynan lead, knowing the dragon could draw the hot luscious juices from her sex.

Tynan's cravings became his.

He lapped at her juices, the heated cheeks of her ass pressing against his face. Tynan growled his satisfaction while Vixi panted her need. She rocked her hips, silently begging for more. He circled her clit and fluttered his tongue along the side.

She spread her legs and pushed against his mouth. She was so far gone she wasn't controlling her movements. He pulled back.

"No!" she cried. Then as if she remembered her instructions for the evening, she lowered her head. "Please, my prince, don't leave me."

Bren felt himself smiling. She would get her pleasure but making her wait would make it even more delicious for her.

He rose from the floor and jerked his hose down. His cock jutted out from his body. He didn't take time for preliminaries — knew that neither of them wanted them. The tip of his erection pressed against her opening and slipped easily inside. Her tight walls clung to him as he gripped her hips and thrust forward, driving fully into her sex.

Her shout filled the room and power rose up in Bren. He needed her, hard and fast. The control he worked for all his life struggled to remain in charge but hunger and desire were strong opponents.

More.

The dragon's voice urged him on. He pulled back and drove back into her, fucking her hard and deep, filling every inch of her cunt. Her cries blended with those in his head until he couldn't tell which voice was in command.

He wrapped his hand around her waist and pressed his heel of his palm against her mound. She rubbed against it, moving in frantic time to his cock sliding in and out.

"That's it, baby, come for me. Come."

Her body seemed to hear his command. She screamed as he plunged into her, still hard and needing to feel the sweet contractions as she came. His heart pounded through his chest. He couldn't stop. There was more. He needed to give her everything inside him, bind her to him with his body.

He grabbed her hips, holding her for his heavy thrusts. She braced herself against the table and pumped her ass back against him, her body not slowing with the climax she'd reached. Bren thought his mind would shatter at the pleasure. The red haze that warned of the dragon's control brushed the edges of his soul but his body was trapped in the need for more and more of her.

"Please, my prince, please." Her low, begging voice penetrated the fog that threatened. Her body was tight and close again to climaxing.

"Come for me," he ordered again, slamming into her as he massaged her clit. The multiple assault made her cry out. Her cunt gripped his shaft as her release flowed from her sex onto his body. He thrust into her one more time, holding himself deep. Feeling every inch inside her. His seed shot from his body, filling her warm, welcoming cunt.

Energy drained from his body and he sagged forward, burying his face in her hair, grabbing the bar beside her hands. Sweat dripped down his back and his knees were starting to tremble. Vixi rested her head against the bar while she gasped for air.

They stood there for long minutes, neither finding the strength to move. As his heartbeat returned to a normal rate, he lifted his head and took a deep breath. The hot fragrance of Vixi's cunt mixed with his seed and flooded his senses. Buried inside her, he realized his cock was still hard. The dragon's power gave him more stamina than a normal man. He pulled out and slowly sank back into her pussy. Her soft moan and the gentle roll of her hips told him she was willing to take him again.

More.

"More," he said as he straightened and pulled out of her sex. "You may stand," he announced. She pushed herself upright and Bren was pleased to note she wasn't as steady on those impossibly high heels now. She swayed for a moment clutching his arm to stabilize herself. Bren felt the edge of his mouth pull up. The tough arrogant courtesan looked stunned. She shook her head as if to clear it. Strange urges entered his head—to pull her against him and hold her, tease her gently about coming so hard, tell her how much he loved feeling her come around his cock—but he resisted. He might have given in to his body's needs but he wouldn't let it become personal. Hating the intrusion but needing the distance, he reminded himself that he would never and could never accept the dragon's mate for his own. There was too much at risk.

This was about fucking, pure sex, pleasure. That's all it could ever be.

Surprisingly, Tynan didn't object. Bren listened closely but the dragon was focused on the woman before him.

The logic and control that had carried Bren through his life tried to assert itself—pointing out that it was most wise for him to leave now, before he became any more entwined.

But he couldn't do that to Tynan, he told himself. The dragon would have few chances to enjoy the woman he'd claimed. The least Bren could do was indulge the beast with another taste of her sex and the pleasure of her orgasms.

The sound of the dragon's chuckling made Bren wince. Even in his own mind he didn't believe it. He was staying because he wanted to fuck this woman, wanted to leave his imprint on her body.

He stepped back and skimmed his eyes down Vixi's body. Without speaking, he reached out and untied the two straps that held the complicated crisscross of leather on her chest. The mesh fell to the ground. Vixi arched her back, lifting her large breasts.

The tight straps had left thin red lines across her skin. Her eyes filled with arrogance, she lifted her hands and massaged the heavy mounds as if soothing the day's pain away.

Bren refused to give in to her blatant attempt to seduce him. Ignoring her, he reached around her and undid the snaps holding the waistband of the skirt closed. It was too tight. There was no way it would fall off.

"Remove it," he commanded, daring her to disobey him. She notched her fingers into the waistband and began to shove it down. The leather clung to her, making every inch a struggle. Her breasts shimmied with each wiggle. The tight nipples stretched long and Bren could almost feel them in his mouth. Only the soft thud of her skirt hitting the floor drew his attention away from the tempting mounds—down to her almost bare pussy. A light dusting of hair hid her final secrets. She lifted one foot and the other, stepping out of the skirt. Bren stared at the beautifully naked body. She was more stunning than he'd imagined.

Every night. We could have this every night, Tynan urged.

Just tonight, Bren replied, silently shaking his head.

"Get on the bed," he commanded.

She lifted her gaze, coyly fluttering her eyelashes at him. A hint of a smile marked her lips. The little witch was laughing at him. *Hmmm.* He'd have to find another way to punish her.

He smacked her ass one more time, making her straighten.

"Get on the bed," he repeated, adding force to his words. She tossed her head back and strolled across the room, letting her hips sway with each step. When she reached the side, she looked over her shoulder as if to make sure he was watching, daring him to look away, then slowly kicked off her heels and crawled onto the mattress. He followed her like a dog panting after water on a hot day.

Pausing in the center of the bed, she knelt on all fours and presented her naked pussy. Damn, but the little witch knew she was pushing him to his limits.

He pulled his gaze away from the captivating vision and found the solution to his problems. Fur-lined cuffs hung from the right bedpost. Twin chains were clipped to a bracket above the headboard, providing the perfect location to secure her.

"Onto your back, my lovely." She rolled one shoulder back and slowly slid onto her opposite hip, lengthening her body as she paused on her side. She watched him for a moment, taunting him with her eyes, then continued until she was on her back. Though his body was screaming its approval, Bren ignored her silent dares. "Reach above you," he said, keeping his voice cold, suppressing the desire to moan at the sight before him.

She slowly stretched her arms over her head. An odd flicker of apprehension flared in her eyes—so opposite from the sensuality that flowed through her muscles. Excitement quickly smothered the concern in her gaze and Bren knew he could continue. He attached the soft bands around her wrists and connected them to the chains bolted to the wall. A firm tug told him she was bound tight. A quick inspection revealed ankle cuffs connected to the outer edges of the bedframe. He captured her foot in his hand and pulled it wide until the band reached around her slim ankle. He repeated the process on the other side until she was chained before him...and exposed. Her puffy pink cunt shone with the moisture of her need. His seed trailed from her slit.

Mine. The dragon's claim blended with his own.

Bren stared down at the woman before him and knew he'd never seen a more intriguing sight. His woman, helpless and hungry before him.

He didn't lift his eyes to hers but could feel her stare as he walked around the end of the bed. She wasn't about to let him out of her sight. Good.

Stopping beside her, he finally met her gaze. "You look delicious spread out before me—mine to use as I please." Her nipples puffed up even more. He reached out and gently tweaked one sensitive point. She groaned and arched her back, pushing her breast closer to him. "I shall enjoy all of you and if you're good, perhaps I'll let you suck my cock." He palmed the full breast, squeezing lightly. "Would you like that?"

"Yes, my prince." Her answer was difficult to hear through the groan dragged from the back of her throat.

Bren couldn't believe the words that were coming out of his mouth. He had a fair understanding of sexual relationships but never would he have imagined himself granting a woman the right to suck his cock as a reward. Still, Vixi seemed to agree with the prize.

Sliding his hand down her stomach to the neatly trimmed hair around her sex, Bren kept his eyes focused on hers — wanting to see her desire as well as feel the hot liquid pouring from between her thighs. "Shall I fuck you again?" he asked almost casually. "Would you like that?"

"Yes." She said it with such an agonized whimper that Bren decided not to correct her for not addressing him properly.

He teased the top edge of her pussy, sliding one finger into her heat, teasing her clit until she rolled her hips in a silent plea for more. Her eyelids fell closed.

He jerked his hand away, waiting for her. Her eyes snapped open and for a moment she looked like she was going to protest. He raised his eyebrows, daring her with the silent look of retribution. She closed her mouth but she wasn't happy about it. Her lips formed a mutinous line. That was fine. She didn't have to like what he did but she had to obey him.

"Very good, my lovely. You're learning that when I give you a command you will follow it. Now watch me. I'm going to undress and I want your eyes on me at all times. I want you to see the cock that is going to be inside you all night. Do you understand?"

"Yes, my prince."

Bren nodded. He didn't really understand why this was important, only that he wanted Vixi to see *him*. To know he wasn't like all the other men she'd fucked.

He unlaced the green doublet he wore. Air circulating through the room washed over his sweat dampened skin, cooling his hot body. Knowing she watched, he denied her his gaze and stripped the doublet and shirt off his chest. He'd left his medallion in his room tonight. There was little risk of anyone attacking him in Ashure's brothel. He folded his shirt, sensing Vixi's intense focus as he undressed. Women had admired his form before but none had mattered before tonight. He wanted Vixi's approval. Last night he hadn't given Cissa time to look at him. Tonight the urge to fuck was less desperate—still strong but Bren knew he could take his time and enjoy the sensations.

He watched Vixi from the corner of his eye. Her mouth hung slightly open. Fear and desire battled in her eyes but she didn't shift her gaze. He placed his hands on the waistband of his hose. Her eyes followed. The soft wool hose were stretched to the extreme by the press of his cock. He pulled the material away, dragging them down his legs. When he straightened, he faced her.

"Do you see me, Vixi?"

"Yes."

He reached down and grasped his cock, still damp from being inside her. "You see how hard I am?"

"Yes, my prince." She sounded breathless.

Once again her eagerness was overcoming her worries. "You know I will need to fuck you long and hard tonight to satisfy my needs." She nodded and swallowed. "I will spend hours filling you, making you come, riding deep between your thighs and penetrating your sweet wet cunt."

Pushed to her limits, she yanked on the chains. "Damn it, get on with it."

Bren folded his arms and watched her. He could see when the awareness of her demand came to her and she sighed. "I apologize, my prince," she said though there was little contrition in her voice.

"I understand," he said with false sympathy. "Your desire pleases me, even if your demanding ways do not." He trailed his fingers up the inside of her thighs, skipping past her pussy to her stomach, her breasts. He rubbed his palms over the tight straining nipples, loving her delicious moans. "Perhaps I will punish you later. Right now, I am in need of this cunt."

Yes. Bren heard Tynan's voice and let the dragon's cravings fill him. Keeping a tight control on the beast but allowing him to feel their pleasure, Bren crawled up onto the high mattress until he knelt between her legs. He placed the tip of his cock to the entrance of her passage. It had been only moments but it seemed like hours since he'd been inside her and he was hungry for the feel of her wrapped around him. Her sweet groans urged him on. His own desires reacted to her scent and the pretty pink sex before him, clawing at his insides and demanding satisfaction.

His cock slipped easily into her wet hole, hot liquid smoothing his way as he pushed into her. It was a long hot glide into her pussy—each inch stretching and filling her, each inch of her passage opening to him. He settled himself deep, driving the last inch of his cock with a sharp thrust. She arched her back and cried out. Her breasts shook and he couldn't resist the temptation any longer. He leaned forward, placing his mouth over one tight nipple. He circled the areola with his tongue before sucking lightly, pressing the tight nub against the roof of his mouth. The sweet sound of her moan reached him as the delicate contractions of her sex massaged his cock. Bren smiled against her skin. He'd primed her body to the point that she would come with the slightest touch.

She blinked and stared up at him as if she was as amazed as he was.

He pushed up to his knees, lifting her hips high on his thighs. His fingers gripped her flesh, holding her still. With her body suspended before him, he punched his hips forward, driving in deep and fast. She gasped and twisted, lost in her body, in the physical pleasure he provided to her—that only he could give.

"That's it, my lovely. Take all of me."

"Yes, my prince." She spread her legs wider.

He pulled back until just the tip of his cock remained inside her. "Shall I leave you?"

Her eyes snapped open and a sensual fear heated their blue depths. "No! Please, my prince, don't stop."

Despite the drive to fuck her hard and satisfy his own needs, he smiled. Trained courtesan she might be, but she was begging for his cock.

More. The dragon's mental urging made Bren grit his teeth, fighting the desire and assuring himself that he was in control. He wouldn't let Tynan dictate how he fucked her.

But then Vixi whispered, "Please, my prince."

The drunk and dazed look in her eyes only heightened the power of his desire.

"Shall I fuck you, my lovely? Make you come?" He stared down at where their bodies were joined and circled his fingertip around her clit.

"Yes, my prince!" she cried, her back arching with each stroke.

"Shall I pour my seed into your pretty little cunt? Fill you with my cum?"

"Yes, my prince, come inside me."

The dragon hadn't weakened his control but there was no way Bren could resist her desperate hunger for him. He thrust his hips hard into her, strong and powerful, each stroke driving them to new heights. His body was caught in a battle—wanting to come but fighting it, unwilling to give up the pleasure of watching her writhe beneath his touch. He worked her clit, teasing and rubbing as he pounded into her.

"That's it, lovely. Reach for it." Her body was stretched tight as she pulled on the chains binding her to the wall. "Feel all of me."

With a final cry, she tossed her head back and came. The beast inside him boiled up. He roared his pleasure and drove into her one final time, exulting in the tight clasp of her pussy and letting his own climax take him.

His teeth clenched and his fingers still gripping her hips, he fought to regain his breath. His body felt like it had been invaded—conquered by a power and need stronger than him, stronger than the dragon. He couldn't stop. Even now, still buried inside her, he needed more. The primal urge to fuck her and come inside her drove him on.

She looked up at him and Bren found himself speaking, unable to stop the word from escaping. "Mine," he whispered.

* * * * *

Bren stared down at the woman beside him. The lure of sleep tugged on him but sunrise had just passed. It was time for him to go but he was reluctant to leave her. As hard as it had been to leave Cissa's bed, it was doubly hard to force himself away from Vixi's. She'd amazed him with her stamina, her strength. Her willingness to allow him the control he desperately needed. He'd fucked her until he was sure she would be sore but when he tried to stop, she'd begged for more. Wanting to be taken hard and deep.

Finally, his cock needing a rest but too addicted to her pleasures to stop, he'd washed the seed from between her legs and loved her with his tongue. What a demanding lover she'd been—wrapping her freed legs around his neck to hold him in place until she was satisfied. And when his cock had gotten hard again as he'd licked her pussy, she'd asked permission to suck him, saying she'd behaved as instructed and wanted her prize.

It stunned him even now.

She's good at her job, the cynical voice deep in his mind said.

No, it was more than that. Damn it, it had to be. He rolled onto his back, mocking his own thoughts. *Why did it have to be? Because you want it to be?* Opposing voices battered the inside of his head. None of it made sense. Two nights, two different women. Tynan claiming them both. The scrambled thoughts were further hampered by foreign emotions that seemed to be invading his body, trying to bind him to the woman.

Maybe Tynan's gone crazy and decided any woman will do.

He peeled Vixi's arm off his chest and slid out of the bed. It was time for him to leave. Though his body demanded he crawl back into bed, he forced himself to walk away, focusing on his reason for being there. Early meetings required his attendance. Support for the dragon hunting prohibition was growing but he had two holdouts. It was doubtful that Herenson's mind would be changed but the advisor to King Englet was also undecided. He, Bren knew, could be convinced.

Vixi moaned as she rolled over, smoothing her hand across the empty space he'd left, almost as if she was reaching for him. His shaft hardened and Bren cursed the beast inside his head. He should be exhausted. After the past two nights, he should be unable to become aroused *for months* but Tynan was creating feelings his body couldn't fight.

Damn, another uncomfortable day ahead.

He dragged his wrinkled clothes, comforted in knowing that half the men who left the brothel this morning would look as bad or worse than he did. He glanced in the mirror near the door.

"Most of them probably got some sleep," he told his reflection. He'd dozed a few times during the night but he hadn't been allowed to rest. The dragon had stayed alert, constantly driving Bren to mount Vixi again.

Mine.

Bren didn't bother to respond but he didn't mentally lock away the dragon either. He sent a mental query to Tynan, returning to the question of two different women. Tynan didn't understand it any more than Bren did. He just knew that Vixi was his mate. Just as Cissa had been his mate.

He laced his doublet closed while he considered the idea that he could have any woman. Maybe he'd somehow become like other men without restriction from the dragon. It didn't seem possible but then experience told him that having sex with two women wasn't possible.

With a last hungry look at Vixi's ripe form, Bren reached for the door. The bag hanging from his belt jingled, reminding him that he needed to tip Vixi.

The wrongness of it all assailed him again, as it had with Cissa, but he fought the feeling and pulled out the contents, dumping the entire amount on the table. He didn't bother to look at how much was there. The need to escape pressed hard on him.

The halls were filling with people as he stalked back to his rooms and tried to plan the day ahead of him. Yesterday had been a loss. He had to focus today. The kings would be arriving in two days. Everything needed to be settled by then.

He was scheduled to meet with Ashure and Marda, Englet's chief advisor, in two hours. Sleep tempted him but he fought it. He had work to do. People to convince. And when he had a free moment he had to see if someone could explain how a dragon could have two mates.

Tynan's surly growl weakened Bren's resolve to stay awake. His body was on the verge of exhaustion. If he became too tired, the dragon might be able to seize command. Bren couldn't allow that. He decided to take a short nap before his first meeting. Something to strengthen his resistance. If Tynan grew frustrated enough and Bren let his guard down, the dragon would take control and go searching for his mate.

But which woman would he go after?

Chapter Six

Keene stood in the back of the room, clutching a water pitcher and watching Prince Bren. She didn't know why she'd come here. It wasn't necessary. In fact, it wasn't wise but she'd wanted to see him—dressed that is. Even knowing it would make her job more difficult, she'd come needing to see more of him. The memories of their time together were so intense that with the light of day, she thought she'd imagined them. But now, seeing him and feeling her body's response, she knew the memories were true.

He was still stunning—not just handsome, though he was certainly that. It was more that he radiated strength and conviction. She listened to the timbre of his voice as he talked about dragons. He made them sound like noble creatures instead of the ruthless killing beasts of legend. She'd never actually seen a dragon but she'd heard the tales and seen the broken bodies—both male and female—after a dragon attack. Still, listening to Prince Bren, she found herself sinking under his spell, nodding along with the other men at the table.

The subtle movement jolted her from her thoughts and she had to suppress a quiet laugh. She wasn't the only one to fall under his spell. King Ashure and three other gentlemen who looked to be from a different court were listening intently. Bren was a very persuasive man. Something about the way he carried himself made one believe him. Keene watched as he leaned forward, listening to a question brought up by one of the others. She'd seen Guild leaders mimic the same pose but Bren's seemed real—not something put on to indicate concern. He seemed to be listening to and absorbing the man's question.

When he spoke again, his voice was too low for her to hear but she could see his listeners smile and nod as if he'd relieved their fears. Intrigued, Keene slouched against the wall and watched him. He fascinated her—his strength, his almost inhuman stamina, the hungry look as he'd stared down at her while buried deep inside her body. She felt her core heat and she unconsciously swayed her hips side to side. It happened every time in the past two days when her thoughts had turned to Prince Bren.

"Girl! Wine!"

King Ashure's command jolted Keene upright. She hurriedly put down the water pitcher and collected the wine jug. With her head lowered and eyes to the floor, she carried the wine to the table and began filling the five chalices. She didn't look up as she moved around the table but she could feel Bren's stare. When she reached across the table for his chalice, he waved her hand away and reached for her instead. She snatched her arm back and spun around, racing for the door. Her heart pounded in her throat. What had she been thinking? He'd almost caught her. Of course, it was impossible. He couldn't have recognized her.

Slightly out of breath, she slipped into a linen closet, set down the wine jug, and changed out of her clothes. Her hands shook as she pulled off the maid's costume. Was it possible that he'd seen through her disguise? Taking deep breaths and shoving the incident from her mind, she managed to calm herself by the time she'd returned to the team room. Triant was the only one inside.

"Did you sleep?" he asked.

"Some."

"You'll need to rest. You're on again tonight."

"I know."

"What's wrong?" Triant's talent, beyond the obvious, was to read people's emotions.

She shrugged, not sure she wanted to have this discussion. The Guild didn't allow members to question their instructions. "This one just doesn't feel right." She couldn't think of another way to explain it. Maybe it was that Bren was so close to succeeding on his dragon proposal and she hated the thought of ruining it all for him.

Or maybe it's just that you liked fucking him.

"Watch yourself," Triant warned. He didn't ask any questions about what she meant. She knew it didn't matter. It was a Guild mission and they would complete it. "I'm serious. Don't get too close to a target."

"It was kind of hard not to," she felt compelled to point out.

"You know what I mean. There's fucking and then there's more. It was just your body that he touched and your body serves at the will of the Guild. Don't let emotion play into it."

Keene knew he was right. It was silly to attach emotions to what had happened between them. And besides, she didn't know anything about him except that he liked to fuck and that he cared about dragons. But while she mentally agreed with Triant she felt a tiny whisper inside her resist it. When she'd seen the money on the table in the morning, she'd almost cried. He'd paid her to fuck him. *What did you expect? It had just been fucking to him.* It was strange but she'd felt like it was more than just sex between them. She mentally slapped herself. Romantic dreams.

"Are you going to be able to do this?" Triant asked and she could hear the seriousness of his question. He would have Risa pull her off the team.

"Of course. I serve at the will of the Guild."

She said the words but felt her heart shudder. She stared at Triant. He didn't look convinced either.

"I'll be fine," she said, giving the words more conviction than she truly felt. "Tonight. I'll get him. I'll be standing there with a drink in my hand when the eunuch brings him back to my rooms. I won't fail."

* * * * *

Bren ignored the food in front of him. He wasn't hungry and, despite the fact that the single hour of sleep this morning had been the only rest he'd gotten all day, he wasn't tired. Impatience was the primary emotion cycling through his brain. His foot bounced impatiently as he watched the crowd. How much longer was this bedamned banquet going to last? He needed to get to the brothel. Between meetings and discussions, he'd considered his dragon's attachment to two different women but had come no closer to an answer. There had to be something about those two women. He needed to speak with Madam Jaqis. She might have some explanation. Perhaps a new perfume the courtesans were wearing confused the dragon's senses.

The scent of his mate seemed to be everywhere. He even thought he'd sensed it coming from a maid during his meeting with Ashure. She'd disappeared before he could talk to her. He'd considered searching for her but if his suspicions were true and Tynan was accepting any woman, finding the maid would make no difference.

Mine. Tynan had been staunch in his commands—demanding Bren find the woman—but the dragon had had nothing to offer to Bren's musings.

"Your Highness, may I refill your chalice?" He turned at the husky, feminine voice and was greeted with two large breasts inches from his face, barely contained in a tight, jeweled bodice. He looked up at the serving wench. She pushed her shoulders back and winked in blatant invitation. Testing his theory, he leaned forward, near her cleavage, and sniffed. The woman's individual scent—even the hint of arousal—entered his body with no reaction from the dragon.

"No, that didn't work," he muttered.

"Your Highness?"

He winced at the confusion and worry in her tone. Great, now word would travel through Ashure's castle that Prince Bren sniffed women.

He held up his chalice. "Yes, more wine please."

He drank deeply from his cup but left the food on his plate alone. He couldn't wait for this banquet to end.

Finally, plates were cleared away and the occupants drunk enough that King Ashure called his special guests to follow him. Bren—feeling some effects from the wine he'd consumed—jumped up from his seat and was the first in line. Ashure smiled at his eagerness and Bren inwardly cringed. He had to resolve this issue before he became the laughing stock of the Kings' Council.

He looked around at the crowd, not really absorbing any of the other faces, though he did notice Herenson was also in the group. For the third night in a row, he'd left his wife in their chambers to use the courtesans provided by the king.

Normally the thought would have enraged Bren but tonight he had his own concerns and they centered on the women in this brothel. Tapping his fingers impatiently against his thigh, he followed King Ashure into the sitting lounge to await his assignment for the evening. He lurked near the door from whence Madam Jaqis had appeared the past two nights. Moments later, she walked inside. Bren reached out and snagged her arm before she could walk two steps into the room.

"Madam Jaqis, I must speak with you."

She looked down at the bold touch and then raised her eyes to him. It was a visual reprimand but Bren didn't release her. Instead, he smelled her. He leaned forward and inhaled, gathering her perfume, the sweet womanly scent beneath it. No hint of arousal.

"Prince Bren, are you all right?"

"I'm fine. I need to ask you about the women you've assigned to me."

"Your Highness, perhaps we could discuss this tomorrow."

"But I—"

"I'm sorry but I really must go. The assignments have been made and Cissa and Vixi are with other men tonight."

He nodded and backed away, finally releasing her arm when he realized he was pulling her with him as he moved. He had to get control of himself. He was going to embarrass himself and his family. Returning to his corner, he watched as Jaqis told the others of their assigned women for the night.

He waited, listening for who was assigned to Cissa or Vixi. Jaqis approached a young advisor of King Wehan's. Bren heard the soft lisp of Cissa's name as the eunuch led the man away. Bren clamped down, preparing for Tynan's volatile response. There was nothing. Tynan didn't react. A dragon's awareness of names was minimal. The creatures knew humans by sight and smell but rarely assigned names to them. They didn't care enough except for the one selected as their mate.

"Prince Bren?" He looked up at Madam Jaqis' call. "Bardo will escort you to Tacy's rooms for the evening."

Bren nodded and followed the eunuch down the hallway, almost racing past him. The answer was somewhere in these rooms. It had to be. How could a dragon choose more than one woman? It was unheard of. Or he hadn't heard of it. Perhaps his mother had. She'd studied dragons. Still, he wasn't quite comfortable telling his mother he'd fucked two different women and asking her opinion on the subject.

They were an open family—it was difficult to be overly modest with a dragon as the head of the household. When Nekane wanted to fuck, he wanted it then. His parents had been as discreet as possible but all three children knew what happened behind closed doors—and knew better than to enter a room without first knocking.

Still, he didn't know how he felt about the previous two nights. Or what was in store for him tonight.

The eunuch stopped at the last door in the hall and opened it. "Tacy will serve your needs tonight. May you find pleasure it this chamber."

Bren nodded and rushed by his escort. There she was. Different from either of the other two women. Maybe it won't happen tonight, he thought, but he had to find out.

Tacy was medium height, somewhere between Cissa and Vixi, with long brown hair that shimmered with golden highlights. Her clothes were much more modest than either of the other courtesans. She wore a green scoop-necked gown that merely hinted at the full curve of her breasts. The dress almost reached the floor, clinging softly to her rounded thighs.

She looked cool and serene as she stood beside the bar. She held a glass of *burgenda* in her hand and a gentle smile on her face.

Bren didn't take time for preliminaries. He stalked across the room.

"Good evening, milord."

"It's 'Your Highness'," he corrected absently.

She smiled and, just as with Vixi and Cissa, it felt like she was laughing at him. "I apologize, Your Highness. My name is—"

He stopped in front of her and inhaled.

Mine!

"Oh Gods, not again," he muttered, feeling his cock harden.

"Are you all right? Maybe a drink would help." She pushed the drink into his hand but even as she did he could smell her arousal. Just like the previous two nights only worse—stronger, more seductive.

He slammed the drink onto the counter and dropped to his knees. Tynan screamed his need as Bren flipped up her skirts. She was bare beneath the modest gown. He groaned as she instantly spread her legs, shifting to open herself for him.

The tangy flavor of her sex warmed his tongue and he plunged in, feeling the dragon fight him for control. He'd limited Tynan's access to Vixi's cunt the night before, giving him only samples when he would have feasted. The dragon was having none of that tonight. As Tynan battled for command of their human body, Bren felt his strength fading. He had no power left to resist him. Tynan took the moment and seized control. With a promise that Bren would get to put his cock in this sweet pussy, Tynan began to tongue fuck her, driving his tongue deep inside her passage.

Bren—still distantly aware of the dragon's actions—heard the woman's gasp and tasted the flood of her moisture on his tongue. With the part of his mind still able to think, he realized she'd come very quickly. As if she'd been thinking about his mouth on her sex as well. She'd accepted him, welcomed him.

Tynan howled his pleasure and Bren sank deeper into the dragon's senses, absorbing every flavor and nuance of her taste. He didn't understand what was happening but neither could he resist another night of fucking the woman he desired.

* * * * *

Bren stumbled out of the room seconds after the sun arose. Tynan had kept his promise. After sating himself of the juices between her thighs, he'd retreated and Bren had returned to control. By then his cock had been so hard, he'd spent the rest of the night fucking her on the floor of the chamber. They'd never made it to the bed. The only time he hadn't been in her cunt was when she'd had her lips wrapped around his shaft. She'd been as greedy for that as he had.

He placed his hand on the wall to hold himself steady as the memory assailed. His legs were weak, his cock limp, and his mind more confused than ever.

Tacy had been more than he'd ever imagined—a heady combination of the most intriguing elements of the first two women: Cissa's innocence and love of cocksucking and Vixi's strength and energy.

Fighting the desire to return to her, he forced his body to walk away. Before anything else happened, he had to figure out what was going on.

He needed help. He needed to talk to someone who might have answers.

He ignored the greetings of the early rising servants as he stalked back to his chambers, his steps gaining strength as he moved. The door slammed behind him and he raked his fingers through his hair to smooth the ragged tips before he reached beneath his shirt and gripped the medallion he habitually wore around his neck. He closed his eyes for a moment and concentrated on his brother.

The world shifted around him—a feeling not unlike the change into dragon form—and when he opened his eyes he was standing in Rainek's bedchamber. The blankets were alive, twisting and rolling with the two forms beneath. After a moment, Rainek must have felt the burn of his amulet and whipped the bedcovers back. The blonde head of his wife popped up as well. Along with her naked shoulders and the tops of her breasts.

"Damn it, Bren, what are you doing? Can't you see we're busy?"

Bren grimaced. "You two have been 'busy' since the moment you met." His form was almost transparent as he stood in his brother's chamber but Tiana, Rainek's wife, would be able to see and hear him. "I apologize, Tiana, for the intrusion but I'm in need of Rainek's counsel."

Rainek scraped his shoulder length hair back and sat up, making sure his wife's body was fully covered. "What's wrong?" Rainek, for all his teasing, knew when to focus and be serious.

"Is it possible for a dragon to have more than one mate?"

"At the same time?" Rainek stared at his blankets for a moment before shaking his head. "Not that I've ever heard. Nekane or Denith have never shown any interest in women beyond their one mate. Why?"

"Then something's wrong with Tynan because I've had sex with three different women in the past three nights."

"What?" Rainek straightened and sat forward. "How is that possible? What does Tynan say?"

"You had sex with three different women?" Tiana asked sounding slightly appalled.

"I'm sure they were women in a brothel," Rainek explained. "It's what King Ashure does for entertainment during these conferences." Then he looked at his brother. "But you've never been able to fuck any of the women before, have you?"

"No, but this time, he's given me three different women and I've had each one. Repeatedly. And Tynan doesn't seem to understand this any more than I do. He just looks at each one and screams 'mine' and then next thing I know I'm on my knees with my mouth—"

His brother's wife squirmed on the bed.

"I apologize, Tiana."

"Not necessary," she said with a low laugh. "Just talk quickly."

Bren actually felt his own cheeks warm.

"Yes, well, that's my problem. Somehow my dragon has chosen three mates and the Gods only know how many more women out there might interest him. I'm not sure I'll survive it. This can't continue."

"Maybe they're all the same woman," Tiana suggested. Rainek squinted at her. "You know, different colored wigs, different make up and clothes. Maybe it's the same woman just in a different disguise every night."

"Not possible. One was as short as you. The other almost my height. And they weren't wearing wigs." He'd had his hands buried in their hair enough times to know it was real. He shook his head. "No, the only way these three were the same woman was if she was a—" The truth hit him moments before the words reached his lips. "Oh my Gods."

"What?" Rainek demanded. "What is it?"

"A shape-shifter." His words faded away as he considered the possibility. That had to be it. Someone had sent a shifter after him. The question was why? He looked at his brother.

Rainek leaned forward. "A shifter is after you? Someone must have hired her. Or him."

Bren nodded. Very few shifters existed outside the Shifters Guild. If the rumors were true—and Bren knew too much about the truth of gossip to discount these stories—the Guild was a mercenary organization willing to do whatever the client wished. They never worked for themselves but hired their services to anyone who could pay.

"That has to be it," Bren said. "It's the same woman. That's why Tynan keeps recognizing her."

"Has she harmed you?"

"No."

"What could they want? Just to keep you busy?"

Bren shook his head, barely hearing his brother. He needed to think about this and decide what he was going to do.

"I'll let you know what I find out."

"Wait. This means your mate is a shape-shifter! I love it!"

Rainek's howls of laughter echoed in Bren's ears even as he released his amulet and let the image before him fade.

A shape-shifter. What did she want with him?

Bren stared at the empty space before him. He would find her and force her to tell him who hired her and what she wanted. His mouth curled up into a mocking smile.

He knew the best way to torment this particular woman.

Chapter Seven

Keene felt like she was carrying around shoulder bags full of stones as she stopped in front of the door. Beyond, her team waited for her arrival and the expected announcement of success. And she'd been close. She'd had the drink ready and waiting and then he'd flipped up her skirts and drove his tongue into her sex and all she could think was "Oh no, not again," quickly followed by, "Oh yes, he's doing it again."

And again. Her knees were shaking, her whole body ached, and her mind was like a sponge—soft, squishy and unable to hold anything for long. After three nights of steady sex with mind-expanding orgasms—for him as well as her, she thought with a slight smile—her body should have been sated but if he'd been there when she'd wakened this morning, she feared she would have climbed on top of him. She'd become addicted to his taste, his strength and the pleasure. Gritting her teeth, she pushed away the signs of renewed arousal. She didn't have time.

She had to go confess.

Bracing herself, she pushed open the door the team room. Risa, Marvis and Triant all waited. The room fell silent as Keene stepped inside.

"You didn't get it," Risa said before Keene could speak. "You failed again."

"Yes." There was nothing left to do but accept Risa's announcement. It was the truth. She'd had three opportunities and missed each one. *Just because the man had a wicked mouth and a long, thick, talented, totally unselfish cock…oh my Goddesses, I'm getting wet just at the thought.* She took a deep breath and tried to ignore the not-so-subtle pulses in her body.

"What happened?"

Keene decided if she was going to be interrogated by her own team, she was going to sit down while she did it. She dropped into the chair and stared them down.

"The same thing that's happened the last three nights. He pounced and I can't get away."

"It wasn't a difficult assignment. All you had to do was drug him and collect a small vial of blood. You've had three nights."

"I know." She couldn't defend her failure. Every explanation came down to the fact that she hadn't resisted Bren. She'd allowed herself to be seduced away from her mission. She'd had chances—she knew that—when she could have pulled away from him and plied him with a drink. But she hadn't done it. She'd stayed in his arms, chosen to stay. "I failed."

"Yes, you did." Risa shook her head and began to pace in front of the table. Marvis and Triant were silent. Keene felt the weight of their disappointment as well. Every part of a mission was important in the Shifters Guild. They had a reputation for being ruthless in completing any task they were hired to do. If the team returned to the Guild having failed, they'd be demoted and sent back to training until the Guild leaders felt they could be released into the world safely.

"We've got one more chance," Risa announced. "Tonight at the gathering."

"I won't fail this time," Keene vowed.

"You won't be involved this time. *I* will do it. Tonight's masquerade will be a mix of the men, their wives and the courtesans. I will take on the role of one of the courtesans and lure Prince Bren away from the crowd." Her lips tightened as she glared down at Keene. "He seems incredibly easy to seduce. I'll take him back to the rooms but I'll make sure he drinks the potion before he attempts to fuck me, since obviously whatever he does makes a woman incapable of conscious thought." The sneer and mockery in her voice made the hair on the back of Keene's neck stand erect. Not that the mockery wasn't deserved. She'd failed, choosing sex over her task.

Even if the team succeeded, Keene knew her behavior would be reported and she'd be reassigned and retrained. She shuddered at the thought. Retraining was a painful process designed to convince the Guild of the trainee's absolute loyalty to the Guild. She'd heard once of a female shifter who'd messed up a mission because she'd become attached to a target and had made love to him while on assignment. Her retraining had involved allowing every male shifter to fuck her until sex became so unpleasant for her that she wasn't ever tempted to stray from her mission.

Keene's insides clenched at the thought. More than being used by the other shifters, she hated the thought of her memories of Bren being destroyed. There was still time to save the mission.

"I think we should all be there tonight," Triant announced.

"Why?" Risa demanded. "*I* won't be distracted."

"You don't know that. We have to believe that there is something about this man or Keene would have succeeded."

Warmth curled in her chest at Triant's unfailing support.

"He's right, Risa," Marvis said. "Keene's good at what she does. There's obviously something different about the prince or we wouldn't be here in the first place. Triant would have been able to assume his identity back in Xicanth. I think having all of us there tonight is a good idea. You could still go in as a courtesan." He nodded to Risa. "Since he seems to enjoy them you have the best chance of succeeding. The three of us will go in as servants. That way, if you miss, we can get him."

"And one of us can follow you back to the courtesan's chambers to make sure whatever happened to Keene doesn't happen to you."

The thought turned Keene's stomach—that Bren would touch Risa, or any other woman, the way he'd touched her. But part of her almost wished he would. Then Risa would understand why he was so damned difficult to resist. Not that Keene had been able to pinpoint it. Just that whenever he was near, she wanted him. Part of it was the overwhelming sense of control he carried about him…and the knowledge that she could weaken it. He would lose himself in her body for a while.

"Fine," Risa snapped. "*We'll all go.* Maybe together we can defeat whatever magic dust the prince sprinkled on Keene."

Knowing better than to glare at the team leader, Keene lowered her gaze.

They would do this. She hadn't failed the Guild yet. She wouldn't do so tonight. They'd taken her in, protected her, become her world. There was no place for her except at the Guild and she would not fail them.

* * * * *

Bren reached into his purse and pulled out five *sentons*. He held his palm open and showed the coins to Dardan.

"It's simple enough. I just want to speak with one of them. Any will do. Cissa, Vixi or Tacy."

Dardan glanced around the parlor as if ensuring no one was watching.

"But it's forbidden for anyone but the workers to be in the chambers during daylight. Madam Jaqis will fire me."

"She'll never know. I need five minutes." He held up the coins in his palm. "Five *sentons* to you and five to the woman who speaks with me. And then I'm gone."

Dardan gnawed on his lower lip for a moment then nodded. "Cissa's usually awake at this time. I'll see if she's willing." He disappeared behind the door. Bren waited, his patience thinning. He'd never known an official so difficult to bribe.

It was a good thing his family was rich, he decided, or he'd be going broke from all the tips and bribes.

After his revelation with Rainek this morning, he'd spent several hours in Ashure's library searching for information on shape-shifters. Wrea was still looking. Bren decided to take a more specific approach.

Little was known about shifters. It seemed they were very careful about revealing any weaknesses. Of the documents he'd found, only one even mentioned a safe way to contain a shifter. All others just reported that shifters were too powerful, too changeable to constrain. Most of the advice was to kill a shifter immediately upon discovery. He didn't want her dead. He needed to figure out how to hold her while he got the information he needed.

"Your Highness? Cissa will see you."

Bren pushed his concerns aside and followed Dardan back into the Hall of the Courtesans. The doors were closed and the hall unnaturally silent. Dardan opened the door and bowed Bren inside. Cissa waited, her hair looking delightfully tousled. The tiny frilly nightgown she wore was almost see-through, allowing her pink nipples to push proudly against the fabric. She twirled her finger in her hair and smiled.

"It's good to see you again, Your Highness."

Her familiar greeting stopped him for a moment. Had he been wrong? Then he realized that she'd called him "milord" that night—as if she'd wanted to taunt him. He stepped forward, allowing Tynan to control their senses. The dragon drew in a full breath of air. Cissa's scent was delicate and floral but not familiar.

"You've never seen me before, have you?" he asked strolling across the room.

"B-but of course. The other night. You were here."

He shook his head. "But you weren't." She didn't back away when he stopped in front of her. He slowly bent down and sniffed her neck. His body, his dragon, gave no response.

"I don't know what you mean." Her voice trembled and she stepped away.

"Don't worry, I won't report you to Madam Jaqis. I just want to know who took your place and what she wanted?"

Cissa sucked the front of her lips between her teeth then sighed. "Her name is Keene. Beyond that, I can't tell you much. She said she could take my place and you would never know the difference."

"Why didn't you report this?"

"Well, she didn't seem dangerous, plus, she'd paid for my time and anything that happens with a paying customer is confidential." She waved her hand vaguely toward him. "At least until I might get in trouble for it," she said with a grimace.

Bren nodded, feeling little sympathy for the woman. He didn't blame her exactly but she was part of the plot, even unknowingly.

"Did she say why she wanted to take your place?"

"No. Just that she wanted to get close to you." Cissa's lips quirked up into half-smile. "And from the state of this room when I returned, it appears she was able to do just that." She wiggled her eyebrows up and down. "I'm glad to know my lessons were put to good use."

"What lessons?"

"Cocksucking lessons. She seemed quite eager to try it. I hope she got the chance."

Bren felt his shaft swell at the memory. And at the thought of Cissa instructing Keene on the finer points of sucking cock.

"I can see from the twinkle in your eye that she did. Good for her." Cissa chuckled and it sounded just like Keene's.

Mine, Tynan prompted.

Bren nodded. "Do you have any idea where I can find her?"

"No. She came to me here."

Bren handed her the promised five sentons. "Thank you for your help."

"Am I going to get in trouble for this?"

"No, just don't tell anyone else that she was here." He didn't want to reveal the shifter's presence just yet. He needed to discover her plan and his involvement in it. But at least now he had a name.

He left the brothel by a side door and hurried back to his chambers. The meetings occurring today were minor. Most of the final details would be worked out at tomorrow's session and then the following day the Kings' Council would meet.

"Bren?"

The soft feminine voice drew Bren to a stop. And he sighed.

"Nerra. Good morning." It wasn't the friendliest greeting. With his mind focused on other things, he didn't have time to cosset Nerra.

"You seem upset."

"I'm in a hurry."

She fluttered her eyelashes and smiled softly. "I was hoping we could walk in the garden."

Bren shook his head. "I'm sorry, Nerra. I have to go."

He bowed sharply and spun away. The strangled catch in her voice warned him he'd have to explain the next time they met. He'd deal with that then. Now, he needed to track a shapeshifter.

He burst through the doors of his chambers to find Wrea poring over stacks of books.

"Did you find anything else?"

"I think so, Your Highness." He grabbed a thin book with a pale blue cover. It seemed more like children's book than anything helpful.

"Well?"

"Most of it just repeats of what we found. I think the Shifters Guild must have members working as scribes because it appears any damaging information is cut out or changed. According to most of the sources, there is no way to capture or keep one. They can change into anything. Too strong for a regular man to fight."

"I'm not a regular man."

"Exactly, and this little book seems to have one item that might help us." He flipped open the pages to a drawing. "It's a pamphlet, really, of how to rid your village of evil and darkness." He grimaced. "They have a rather brutal section on dragons, by the way, but they also have these few paragraphs on shape-shifters. According to them, if a band is placed around the shifter's neck, they can't change. Into anything except their natural form, that is. They recommend using tension bands because they adjust to fit. Then if the shifter's natural form is smaller than the band, they can't escape. Once the shifter is in its true form, you're supposed to pierce its heart five times with a knife to ensure it is dead."

Bren's felt sick at the prospect. He didn't intend to kill Keene but he was going to find out about the plot. It seemed to have no purpose. His father ultimately made the decisions, unless the plan was for someone to take Bren's form and get close to his father. It didn't make sense. There were easier ways to kill a king.

"I don't understand this. I thought shifters could take anyone's form. Why keep coming back to me? As far as I know, there have been no reports of me wandering the halls at night so it can't be to keep me busy at the brothel but, for three nights running, the same woman has come after me."

"Maybe she's been sent to kill you," Wrea offered helpfully.

Bren grimaced. He couldn't imagine killing Keene and it irritated him to think she could kill him. "Perhaps. That seems unlikely at this point. She had opportunity. She could have stabbed me at any time during the night." Except he'd kept her busy during the nights, never letting her out of his sight. He smiled. He remembered the exhaustion in her body, the look of satiation on her face as she'd slept. That hadn't been faked. Shifter or no, she'd been as wrecked by their nights together as he had.

It was really too bad there wouldn't be more. Tynan grumbled his disapproval.

If she's after my father or plans to hurt someone else, she has to be stopped.

Tynan agreed but added that his mate wasn't a killer.

Bren hoped the dragon's intuition was right in this matter.

"So, we need to gather some equipment—"

"Including tension bands."

"If we can find them, yes."

"And you'll need somewhere safe to take her. According to the book, they don't work alone. There are probably several of them here."

"Wonderful," he muttered. "I have *a pack* of shape-shifters after me."

* * * * *

Keene smoothed the sturdy fabric of her gown. It was strange. After three nights of playing the courtesan, she was demoted to serving girl. At least she had a nice shape—nothing quite as sensual as Vixi or dainty as Cissa but still, her breasts were high and full. Keene knew by now how much Bren appreciated large breasts.

Not that you have a chance of getting near him, she reminded herself. She was merely there as support, to guide him into Risa's arms. Risa had the drug and, by tomorrow, their mission would be completed. King Kei was scheduled to arrive in the morning—with his wife arriving the next day. By then it would all be over and Keene and the rest of the team would have disappeared. The Shifters Guild prided itself on being a shadow organization that few believed actually existed. Every team was evaluated not only on their success in completing the mission but in hiding the presence of the Guild. *We can only continue to function if no one believes in our existence.* It was one of the many lessons Keene had been taught when she first arrived at the Guild and it was repeated during frequent "renewal" sessions where they reemphasized the mission and goals of the Guild.

When the job was completed, Bren would have no idea what had happened. A sick roll of her stomach made Keene wince. It shouldn't bother her. She was trained to do precisely what they were going to do but still, after having met Bren and spending so much time with him, it was hard to imagine following through with it.

She could only thank the Goddesses that Triant was designated to complete the final portion of the mission. She wasn't sure she could do it. She'd killed before but this was different. This was an assassination and the memories of this mission were already too strong. Trying to forget Bren's touch would be hard enough without adding the memory of a death on her hands.

"Menta, get moving with that tray. There are hungry guests to serve."

Quickly realizing the Chamber Master who oversaw the maids was talking to her, Keene bowed her head and picked up the silver platter piled high with bite-sized snacks. The servant she'd replaced had only been too willing to take the night off. With a tight smile to the Chamber Master, Keene carried her tray into the great hall.

Bren slowly sipped his drink—brought from his own chambers—and wandered the room. He wouldn't be able spot her by sight but Tynan would sense her, smell her if she came near, so he had to keep moving, encounter as many people as he could. She had to be in the crowd. She'd been stalking him the past three nights, surely she wasn't going to leave without getting what she came for. He just wished he knew precisely what that was.

He thought about the room he and Wrea had prepared. He would get the truth out of her. He would tie her to the bed, naked and splayed out before him. Tynan quickly picked up the scenario and inserted a woman into the image. Unfortunately, having no idea what she looked like, he simply chose a woman's body. Bren continued his steady stroll through the party, keeping his face set in a scowl. The people at this conference knew enough not to approach him when he appeared in a temper. Only the servants dared come near him--and that was more because they were afraid *not* to offer him something to eat.

"Bren?"

Nerra's sweet hesitant call was like nails down his spine. Crushing the irritation, he forced a smile and turned to greet her. The bow he gave was stiff and short.

"Nerra."

"I was hoping to run into you here." She fluttered her eyelids and then looked up at him with wide eyes. "My husband is off somewhere. I find myself quite on my own. I hope you will keep me company."

He battled common politeness with the need to find the shifter who'd been hunting him. And Tynan's need to find his mate.

"Nerra, I'm sorry about earlier today. I was —"

Mine!

Bren snapped his head up, inhaling to capture her scent. She was near. He turned — following the trail.

"Bren?"

"Uh, Nerra, I have to go," he said absently. He took a deep breath. Tynan identified her like a glowing lantern on a dark night. The serving girl in front of him — her tray almost empty of tiny meat skewers. Holding himself back, he knew he had to find some way of getting her out of the room — without grabbing her and tossing her over his shoulder. He deliberately looked past her. He wouldn't give her any indication that he recognized her but he wasn't letting her out of his sight either. As she moved through the crowd, he followed, casually, always keeping a few people between them.

"Prince Bren?"

He barely contained the growl as another person stopped him. Forgetting the manners his mother had trained into him, he turned his head. A beautiful, tall blonde woman smiled sensuously at him. Her see-through blouse designated her as one of the courtesans attending the event.

"Yes?" he asked brusquely.

"I'm Milne. I've heard great things about you." She held out her hand. Bren took it, watching over her shoulder as his shifter slid through the crowd.

"If you'll excuse me…"

"But Your Highness—" She sidled up to him and pressed her breasts against his chest. "I was hoping you would be willing to accompany me back to my suite. I've heard such delightful tales of your prowess."

Her final words drew him to a slow stop.

"From whom?"

She lowered her eyes in a mockery of modesty. "Cissa, Vixi…and Tacy." She winked. "Girls do talk you know."

But the real women who bore those names had never met him. Wrea had warned him that shifters traveled in packs. This was clearly an attempt to lure him away from the crowd. Bren did his best to return her sexual grin.

"I'm pleased to know I made the gossip chain." The woman's teasing laughter was almost drowned out by Tynan's comment that his mate was getting away. Bren lowered his head. "I really can't be seen walking out with you—I have a certain reputation to maintain—but if you'll meet me at the north entrance…" He nodded toward the door in the opposite direction of the kitchens. "I'll take you up on your offer."

It was almost amusing to see the triumph in her eyes. She thought she had him.

"I'll just head in that direction."

"Give me a few moments to say farewell to some people and then I'll meet you."

She nodded, and with a flick of her hair over her shoulder, she spun away. Bren watched her for a few moments and turned to follow Keene. He knew where to find her. She was playing the role of a servant, she would have to replenish her tray.

"I never would have expected it of you." The chilly voice pulled Bren to another stop. He looked to his side. Nerra waited, her fingers wrapped white-knuckled around the spines of her fan. "I knew my husband was incapable of fidelity but I thought *you* at least would stay true."

"What?" Bren couldn't believe what he was hearing—not only the words but the hard, bitter tone of Nerra's voice.

"You're off fucking those whores every night, aren't you? Even as you were courting me, you were seeing them. That's the real reason you rejected me, isn't it? Because I wouldn't perform wretched and disgusting sex acts for you."

The rising volume of her words drew the eyes of nearby delegates. Bren lowered his head and his voice. "Maybe we should talk about this somewhere else."

Nerra lifted her chin and sniffed disdainfully. "No, I don't wish to discuss it. I can only say I'm pleased I discovered your revolting tendencies before we were wed." With a quick flutter of her fan, she spun around and flounced away, leaving Bren more confused than ever.

Wrea popped out of the crowd, the ever-efficient assistant. "What was that all about?"

"I have no idea." He watched Nerra as she pushed through the crowd. She'd never behaved like that before. In fact, he'd never seen her raise her voice to anyone. And she was already married. Perhaps she was experiencing some delusion about their relationship. He would have to seek her out tomorrow and see how she was.

"Have you found her, Your Highness?" Wrea asked, distracting Bren from his concern for Nerra.

"Yes, but I need you do something for me. I just sent a blonde courtesan to meet me at the north door. I want you to go keep her entertained."

"Of course." The eager reply made Bren smile.

"She's a shifter."

"Oh." Wrea's lips flattened out.

"But don't worry. I think she'll continue in her courtesan role in the hope of catching up with me. Remember, it's bad form for an unclaimed courtesan to reject a man's offer. Tell her I've asked you to join us. See if you can lure her back to her rooms for a bit while I take care of my own little shifter problem."

Wrea nodded, some of the eagerness returning. Even if he didn't end up in bed with the woman, at least he'd get a few moments of adventure knowing he was serving his prince.

"I won't expect to see you until late tomorrow morning. If I do, I'm going to assume it's not you," Bren warned as he pushed through the crowd.

"So make myself known quickly if I need to find you."

"Exactly." He slapped Wrea on the back. "Have a good night."

"You as well, Your Highness."

The door to the kitchens was discretely placed behind a decorated screen. Bren moved along the side wall and watched the crowd for a moment. Tynan alerted him that Keene had come this way a short time ago. When Bren felt he'd sufficiently blended into the background, he slipped behind the screen and entered the noisy world of the kitchen. Keene's scent led him to the right.

"Milord, can we help you?" a voice called after him.

"No, I see what I want." He didn't give anyone a chance to stop him but walked boldly up to Keene as she stood layering her platter with more treats. "It's not a bad disguise, my dear, but you could do better."

Her head snapped up and her mouth dropped open, followed by a gargling sound as the shock choked her.

"Your Highness, how can I help you?" she asked recovering quickly.

"Come with me."

She shook her head. "I'm not allowed, sir. I must return to the ballroom."

Bren sighed. "I knew you were going to be difficult." He placed his hand on her shoulder and gave a sharp squeeze, finding the exact spot. Her eyes widened for a moment, then she sank gracefully toward the ground. Bren caught her before she hit, lifting her high in his arms. Tynan's joyous shouts blended with the servants' questions.

"What happened?"

"Is she all right?"

"She's fine," Bren reassured them, heading determinedly toward the side door. No one dared stop him. "I'm sure she's just overheated. I'll get her some fresh air and she'll be back in no time."

He didn't mind lying to the staff. The "real" maid was probably in her quarters and when they searched would no doubt be found healthy and whole.

He left the kitchen and strolled down the hall, feeling almost cheerful. For three days the mystery of this woman had plagued him and now he had the solution…and even better, he would spend the rest of the night teasing and tempting her until she was begging to tell him everything.

Chapter Eight

Keene came awake slowly, her mind drifting to awareness. She let her eyelids flutter open. And found Bren waiting beside the bed. His arms folded across his chest, his fingers tapping impatiently on his elbow. But it was the eyes that got her.

Arrogant, demanding and triumphant.

"Awake?"

Keene quickly thought back to the moments before she lost consciousness. Bren had come into the kitchen. She mentally slapped herself for her own reaction. She'd been stunned that he'd found her. How had he done it? He'd walked directly up to her without hesitation as if he could see through her disguise. Only it was much more than a disguise; she was a completely different person. There was no way he could connect her in this form with the women from the brothel. How had he chosen her? The question was left unanswered as reality crashed down on her. How he'd found her didn't matter, she had to get out of there. The team was waiting, probably searching for him…and to a lesser degree for her.

She twisted — hoping to ignore him — and realized her arms were immobilized. She tilted her head back and stared up at her hands. He'd wrapped tension coils around her wrists. And that wasn't all. The movement shifted the band that clung lightly her throat. Damn, he obviously knew more than she'd hoped. Few knew how trap a shifter but Prince Bren was obviously one of them.

If it had only been the bands around her wrists, she could have changed into a smaller form and slipped away but a band around the neck locked a shifter into that form. She was trapped in this body until she could free herself. She squirmed…and found her legs similarly tied. Only where her hands were bound together—her legs were spread apart. She lifted her head and looked down her body. Naked. Why had she expected anything else?

What made the matter worse was the moisture forming between her legs. She was tied up, spread-eagled, completely in his control. She should be terrified—or pissed, but instead her sex was preparing for his penetration. Three nights of almost constant fucking had trained her body to respond to his. Unable to stop herself she glanced down at his groin. The bulge in his hose revealed he wasn't unaffected by her position and form.

Maybe he didn't know who he'd captured. There was no way he could connect her to the three women from the nights before. Maybe he'd wanted a night of fucking and Risa hadn't found him in time.

"Your Highness," she said, trying to sound confused and frightened. "I think there's been some kind of mistake. I'm not one of the king's courtesans. I was just assigned to serve the delegates."

An arrogant smile curled his usually grim mouth. "Oh, you'll serve me well. And I know full well who you are. Or should I say—what you are. My dear little shifter."

Keene swallowed deeply and considered her options. Admitting what she was wasn't in her training. *A shifter never reveals herself to anyone outside the Guild.* Still, it was obvious he had some idea of her true nature. He'd specifically used the tension coils around her neck. He knew what he was doing. Testing their strength, she tugged on the bounds that held her but the bands tightened around her wrists. She hissed as they grabbed her skin.

"Relax and the bands will as well."

She glared in his general direction. She knew how tension coils worked. It was almost impossible to break them. She'd heard tales of prisoners fighting the coils and causing the bands to tighten, eventually cutting off the person's hands.

She took a deep breath and willed her arms to relax. She would need her strength later. When she managed to escape…and she would.

"So tell me, just what do you want with me?"

Staring up at the ceiling to avoid looking at him, she answered, "I don't know what you're talking about, Your Highness. I'm simply a serving maid in the—"

"Keene, despite being able to turn into any living creature, you're a horrible liar."

Keene snapped her head up. How did he know her name? Bren walked around the end of the bed, his eyes never leaving her.

"If you're going to tell a lie," he said as if instructing a subordinate. "You have to look the person in the eye—make sure they believe you." His fingers circled her ankle and skimmed up the line of her calf. "And you have to know when a bluff has a chance of succeeding." He traced his path along her skin. "You see, I know the truth. I know you're a shape-shifter, your name is Keene and you've obviously focused on me since you've posed as the three courtesans who've been assigned to me." The warmth of his palm moved upward, to her knee and brushed the inside of her thigh. It was difficult to focus on his words when he was touching her in such a delicate manner. "What I don't know is why and who? And that's what you're going to tell me."

Keene lifted her chin trying to ignore his slow caress, moving nearer to her sex with each long stroke. "You might as well let me go. I won't tell you anything."

He laughed softly. "Then we're in for a long night."

Bren recognized the truth of those words an hour later. He'd gotten no information out of her. She'd been staunch in her refusal to tell him anything about the Guild or why she was there. He'd asked a few questions about her personally and she'd answered those but they didn't give him the information he needed.

"Who sent you?" he asked again.

"I don't know."

He was starting to believe her on that point. It was likely that only the Guild Leaders knew who the client was.

"Why have you come after me? What do you want with me?"

Keene pressed her lips together and turned her head away.

"What was the purpose of coming to me each night?" Again, she remained silent.

If only he could bring himself to hurt her—add some pain to her torture but the idea sickened him. He was a failure as an interrogator. If would be simpler, of course, if he could keep focused on his objectives—if Tynan would stop feeding him images and descriptions of how wet she was and how her body was aching for his possession.

He looked down at Keene. Her brown eyes stared back. No. They weren't her eyes. This wasn't Keene. This was just another façade she'd taken on. The urge to see her in her natural form— to penetrate her in that shape—suddenly filled his chest.

Hoping to justify the plan forming in his head, he told himself that he could break her resistance down in increments and that the first step was getting her to change into her natural form.

The second step was fucking her until he could focus.

Her arousal hadn't faded in the last hour. He'd made sure that she'd remained aware of him by touching her as he circled the bed—a light brush of his fingers across her pussy, a tiny nibble on her breast. It served to keep both of them on edge.

Perhaps he could use that desire to get what he wanted.

"I think you like being tied up." He stroked his hand up her side, cupping her breast and thumbing the tight nipple. "You like being helpless before me. You like being commanded by me."

His cock throbbed at the idea, twitching inside his leather trousers. She was spread, open before him and wet. He could have her. Drive himself deep into her until she screamed her need for him.

But she gave nothing away.

"Let me go," she growled again.

Bren shook his head. He stepped back, though it was like stripping his skin from his body to do so. He had to stay in control.

"You're wet, aren't you?"

Keene tensed. He'd battered her with questions for the past hour but this was different. This question was full of lust and hunger and her body responded, heating and relaxing, opening to take him inside.

Fear wound its way around her heart. This kind of interrogation would be much harder to resist.

He crawled onto the end of the bed, kneeling fully dressed between her spread thighs. Keene tried to look away but the glittering black in his eyes made it impossible. "I can smell it. Your scent fills the room and I know you want to be fucked." He stroked his finger up the inside of her thighs, then brushed across her sex. "No matter what else you might want—and I'll find out what that is eventually—you want my cock. You want me to fuck you so hard you scream." He pushed one finger into her pussy. The hot wet warmth melted around his hand. Bren struggled to keep control. He wasn't fighting the dragon this time, he was fighting himself. He needed to be inside her.

But he wanted to be inside *her*. Not some woman she pretended to be.

"Remember what I feel like—buried inside you. Filling every inch of your cunt. I could take you now. This tight little cunt would just barely hold me."

Keene groaned as he whispered his promises. The memories of the past three nights were too clear. It was easy to remember how he filled her, stretched her. He pumped his finger in and out, all while he stared into her eyes. She tried to pull back, sought to use the training the Guild had given her to complete any mission even in the face of death. She would resist him. Fight him. He drove his finger in deep and brushed against the top wall of her passage.

Her breath caught in her chest.

"Yes, you like that, don't you?" He teased the same area again and Keene felt her mind grow hazy. "I can reach there, fuck you there, make you come so hard that you scream my name."

"Bren, please," she whispered, trying to wiggle out of his grasp.

He shook his head. "I want to hear you scream it." He pulled his hand away. She was almost able to control the whimper that crept from between her lips but a tiny trace of it slipped through. "Don't worry, baby, I'm not going anywhere. I want to hear you beg for my cock." The wicked smile that bent his lips sent a wave of fear into her stomach. "And I know just how to do it."

He shifted down, crouching between her legs until she had to raise her head to see him. He looked up, as if checking to make sure she watched. With no prelude, he buried his face in her cunt and began to suck. Keene arched her back and moaned. It had been less than twenty-four hours but it seemed like forever. She needed him right where he was—his mouth on her sex. Licking. Sucking. By every Goddess that protected women, he was good.

He pushed her hard toward her climax, using that wicked tongue to lick and circle her clit. Loving each stroke. Before she could come—seconds before she found release—he moved away, dropping to her opening and slipping his tongue inside. Not deep, just enough to promise more.

She rolled her hips upward. Bren felt his cock expand. His first response was to plunge into her, give her what they both wanted. Tynan fought for control, wanting his taste of her flesh. Fighting her desires and that of the dragon, Bren wrenched himself away, climbing off the bed.

"No!"

Keene sat up as far as she could, pulling on the cables that held her bound.

Her panting breath bounced her full breasts but what he was truly interested in was the glare in her eyes.

"Hmmm…" He let his triumph be heard in his voice because he knew it would push her even harder. "It looks like someone wants to be fucked."

"Bren…"

He shook his head. He hadn't succeeded in getting the information from her but he would win one battle.

He stared at the beautiful body stretched out before him. Her breasts were large and heavy and her hips slightly rounded.

Bren wanted to fuck her. He wanted to have her in every imaginable way. But more, he wanted the woman beneath the image. He needed to see the woman who'd driven him crazy for the past three days.

"Turn back to your natural form."

She whipped her head away, hiding her eyes from him. It was a strange, almost embarrassed reaction.

"Let me see you."

"Why?" She looked back, the defiance returning. "The answers will be the same no matter what form I take. I don't know who hired us and I won't tell you what was planned."

"I want to see you. I want to see the woman I've fucked for the past three nights."

Her eyes lit with a strange sadness. "They were different women."

He shook his head. "They've all been you." The urge to comfort her drew him forward. She looked sad, alone, but years of warrior training pulled him back. Sympathy would get him nowhere. He needed strength.

And he needed her.

Tynan rumbled through his head. It took a moment for Bren to focus the dragon's senses. The delicious fragrance of her arousal surrounded them. It had lingered in the air from the moment she'd awoken but now it grew. Bren crushed the urge to smile.

Her defiance, her anger, they weren't real. The truth lay between her legs.

"Turn," he commanded. "I will give you what you want— I'll fuck you. You know that's what you want—but I want to see you." He fluttered his first two fingers across her clit, giving her the promise of more to come.

Again she looked away. Bren shoved his fingers back inside her. Her hips punched up and she groaned. "That's it, baby. I can give you more." He leaned down until his mouth brushed against her ear. "So much more. I'll drive my cock so deep inside you, you'll think I've become part of you." He pulled his hand away from her pussy and dragged the fingers up, through the curly hair protecting her sex, up to her stomach. "You want that, don't you baby? You want my cock."

"Yes," she sobbed. He'd pushed her to the edge, he knew. Close to coming but never quite there. Her body was stretched tight and dripping with the need.

"Turn," he said again. "And you can have it all."

For one long, interminable moment, he thought she would refuse—and he didn't know how he would survive. Teasing her had made his cock impossibly harder. She grew still. "Turn, baby," he encouraged. "Let me have you." She stared at him and he could see the decision in her eyes. He leaned back, his innate curiosity forcing him to watch her transformation.

It was slow—almost dreamlike—as if the process flowed through honey before it was completed. The pretty blonde woman melted and melded, shrinking and growing, until the body before him found peace. The bands around her wrists, ankles and neck adjusted—changing to match the new body.

Bren stood up, stepping away from the bed. Keene raised her chin, the defiance in her eyes a weapon against him.

"You should have let me stay in that form," she said self-mockery filling her words. Her voice was different as well as her body. The sound was harder—without the deliberate huskiness of seduction. But it still curled around his cock.

He enjoyed the pressure in his groin as he looked at her body. This was her true form. This was the shape of his woman.

Bren looked at her, his cock pressing hard against his leathers, straining for release. She was lovely.

Nothing like the exotic beauties she'd portrayed as the courtesans, but lovely. Intriguing. She was almost plain except for the power in her crystal gray eyes. Her dark brown hair was cut almost as short as his—barely an inch from her head. Her small breasts were thin mounds, stretched almost flat with her arms pulled above her head. The tight nipples poked up and Bren's mouth began to water. He scanned her body, trying to hold himself aloof but knowing it was futile. The sweet curve of her hips, slight, almost boyish, called for his hands.

And her legs. He groaned at the thought of those long lengths curled around him. She'd played many roles in the last few days but none had sleek powerful legs like that. The dark curls between her thighs glittered with moisture.

"Damn it, just let me go," she said, futilely tugging on the coils that bound her. "You don't want me."

Bren felt his mouth curl up in a smile. "That's where you're wrong."

Knowing that she watched him, he stripped off his shirt, standing topless before her. She'd seen him naked, of course, but this was different. This was her—just her—with no illusions between them. And him—his cock hard and desperate to feel her.

He ripped open the placket that held his leathers shut, freeing his shaft. He'd bucked tradition tonight and worn the heavy protective leather trousers. He hadn't known what to expect when he'd planned to find the shifter. Now, the leathers slipped easily down his legs until he stepped free, leaving his body as naked as she was.

Keene swallowed deeply as she stared at him. Without the confidence of illusion, she stared at the thick cock and wondered how she would take it. How it would fit inside her? But even that concern didn't weaken her desire.

She shouldn't want this. She should be resisting but the will to do so was nowhere in her soul. All that remained was the need to have him—to feel him inside *her* body instead of that of a stranger.

Her own shape was almost foreign to her. She spent so little time in it, having served the Guild since she was eight. The first thing they taught her was that her body did not belong to her— it served the Guild. Shifters were taught to change and maintain a variety of shapes, never becoming too attached to a specific form.

She couldn't even remember what her face looked like. It had been years since she'd seen her own reflection. But with Bren staring down at her, watching her with eager eyes—she wanted to know what he saw. She knew enough. Her breasts weren't large and her hips didn't have the rounded curves so many men seemed to prefer—that *he* preferred. She'd been the other women he'd fucked and knew how much he'd loved their lush forms.

Bren stood beside the bed, completely naked, his cock still hard. She took shallow breaths through her mouth trying to stay calm. He was actually going to fuck her.

Dread was instantly pushed from her thoughts by desire. She would have him. He would have her. Even as the thrill coursed through her body she knew the truth—she would fail in completing her task again. And without this piece, the entire mission would fail. The thought didn't make her stomach clench as it should. It was strange but after so many years in the Guild, she found herself reconsidering their need for unswerving, unquestioned requirement of loyalty to the mission. No matter the cost.

Bren was the cost and she wasn't sure it was a price she could pay.

The soft whisper of his fingers on the insides of her thighs spreading her open just a hint wider nudged at her concerns, pushing them farther into her subconscious. How could she worry when such delightful pleasure was being given her? She let her eyes fall shut and let the sensations surround her. The light teasing touches soothed her but gave no chance of release.

"Now, let me come inside you."

It wasn't a request or a plea but a command…and Keene moaned her acquiescence. Before the sigh was out of her mouth, he was there, slowly pushing into her—each inch of cock electrifying the sensitive tissues of her passage. Pleasure and pain increased in increments as he eased his hard flesh deeper.

The sensation of taking him inside her was new once again. Every form a shifter took came with its own memories and responses—and the shifter felt the world through that form's senses. But this was her—*her* body, *her* pussy…and *his* cock. She took a deep breath, trying to hold back the whimper that threatened.

"Shh. You know I fit." But even as he slid the first few inches of his cock inside, he knew it was different. She'd been playing the part of other women each time before. Now she was truly herself. "Let me in, baby. Let me feel you." Her sweet groan rewarded him and he pulled back only to thrust farther, just a little deeper. She was so blasted tight, wrapping around his shaft like a virgin's cunt.

"That's it. Take more." He rolled his hips pulsing inside her and stopped. A thin membrane covered her passage. He lifted his head and stared into her eyes. She *was* a virgin. Tynan roared with the possibility that he would be her only lover. The urge to thrust fully into her, to claim her, surged through him, driven by Tynan's need and Bren's own possessive nature. But he held himself still. "Keene? You're a virgin?"

"Don't be silly." She turned her head away as if she couldn't bear for him to see the truth. It wasn't necessary. The blush that crept up from her chest told him all he needed to know.

"I can feel it, Keene. How is this possible?"

She swallowed and the muscles along her jaw tightened and clenched. She was a strong, confident woman and here and now she was vulnerable. He lowered his head and gave her a quick kiss.

"Tell me, baby."

Her gray eyes turned stormy and he could see her gathering her courage.

"We don't exist in our true forms. We take the form of whatever is needed. I've never had a lover in this body."

Bren nodded and slowly drew his hips back. Unable to pull completely away without her express demand that he do so, he sank slowly in, stopping after a shallow thrust.

"Should I stop?"

Keene couldn't believe she was hearing the words come from the prince's mouth. *Stop? When had he ever stopped?* He'd fucked her legs out from under her for three nights straight and now he was asking her if she wanted him to stop. Then she realized the truth. He didn't have the same lust for her in this form as he'd had for the other bodies she'd inhabited.

She lifted her chin, conscious of his cock still partway inside her. Still hard. At least he hadn't gone limp with the thought of fucking her.

"Is that what you want?"

He laughed. The sound was harsh and grating, liked metal spikes dragged along a stone floor.

Damn it, he was penetrating her body and he laughed at the idea of fucking her. Tears she never would have allowed herself to shed crept into the corners of her eyes. Damn, she wished she was free to throw him off her.

"You bastard. If you don't want me, then just get off," she snarled and pulled against the cords that held her to the bed.

That stopped his humorless laugh. "Not want you?" His cock twitched inside her passage and for the first time she noticed the tension in his muscles—his arms holding him above her, his thighs pressed against hers. He pushed up, sitting back until he was back on his heels. His cock slid out, almost escaping her pussy. They both gasped as if neither could bear to lose the connection. Bren stared at the place where their bodies were joined. Keene couldn't see it but she could see his reaction. Finally, he lifted his head. The hot fire in his green eyes burned into her soul.

"I want to fuck your body in every way possible. I want to drive my shaft so far into you that you'll never forget what it feels like to hold my cock in your passage. I want to have you so often, so deep you'll feel empty when I'm not inside you." He rubbed his thumbs across the top of her sex, massaging deep. Renewed heat warmed her cunt. "But I won't take your maidenhead unless it's what you want."

Keene shivered—at the thought he was giving her a choice, that he might actually leave her. And the slow steady press of his thumbs closer and closer to her clit.

"I'll still love you with my tongue, make you come until you're screaming my name but I don't need to take your virginity for that."

She shook her head. She needed him inside her. Needed this man to come inside her.

"Fuck me," she whispered.

His eyes shimmered and for a moment they looked black before returning to that vibrant green.

"Be very sure, because once I take you, you'll belong to me."

The words sounded so final. So permanent. Keene ignored the joyous leap in her chest. He didn't know the truth. His desire would be turned to disgust when he found out what was planned.

But she needed him one more time, needed one more memory to sustain her.

"Come inside me, my prince."

His eyes flared with dangerous fire and he entered her in one long hard thrust. She gasped and tipped her head back, biting her lip to counteract the stinging pain between her legs. *By my Goddesses, he's big.*

"I've hurt you."

She felt him withdraw and reached for him. The bands around her wrists gripped her flesh and she stopped, reminded of her bondage. He looked up at the tension coils and she knew he was considering releasing her.

At this moment, she didn't care if she was freed or not. She dared a look into his eyes waiting for his decision.

"Shall I stop?"

She shook her head. She wanted him. With her body, the body she was born with. To know how his mouth felt against *her* breasts and the warmth of his cum exploding into *her* sex.

She curled her legs up as far as the bands around her ankles would let her. She pressed her knees against his hips, holding him, her body relaxing a little around his shaft. She offered a tentative smile and waited for him to begin.

Bren felt her ease. He didn't want to hurt her so he moved slowly, pulling back and sinking in one long fluid stroke, loving the way she held him and the knowledge that this was truly her body. This was the woman Tynan had chosen. Part of him still resisted falling for the dragon's chosen mate but Keene was a strange mix of bold and shy and the combination was too much for a man of his temperament to resist. He wanted to draw her out when she was shy and control her when she was bold.

He strained to keep his penetration slow and gentle, easing into her newly breached sex. But his body would only allow him so much before its demands grew intolerable. He needed to have her, needed to claim the body that belonged only to him. He bit his teeth together and fought the slow steady massage of her cunt around his shaft, struggling to restrain himself.

"Bren—" Her low moan gave him the signal he needed. She could take more. His thrusts grew faster, harder, taking him deeper until there was no inch left untouched.

And Keene was with him, twisting and punching her hips up against him. He stroked his hand down the sleek line of her thigh, loving the tensing of her muscles as she fought to take him. His bollocks drew up, ready to explode. Bracing himself on one arm, he slipped his free hand between their bodies and pressed lightly against her straining clit even as he thrust into her.

Her shout vibrated his eardrums and the sweet contractions of her pussy along his shaft triggered his own orgasm. He pulled back and drove one final time into her sex—letting his body release inside her.

As the strength faded from his muscles, he collapsed on top of her and a foreign sense of contentment crept into the corner of his chest—quiet and unassuming, going almost unnoticed. Bren lifted his head and looked down into her eyes. They were gray, like a heavy sea fog that warned of a storm beyond the horizon.

As he stared at her, he realized it wasn't done. Their loving had been incomplete—wild and passionate but some part was missing. He bent down and placed his mouth on hers. Her lips opened softly, tentatively. Bren responded in kind, kissing her gently, reveling in her taste and letting it flow through his senses. The contentment swelled inside him. He needed this— this tenuous connection to her.

Still inside her, he lifted his weight off her chest but didn't release her mouth. There was no urgency in their kiss but neither wanted to stop. It was a wet, seductive melding of lips and tongues, gentle nips of teeth and long slow breaths.

His cock swelled inside her but he made no move to fuck her. There was time for that later—she belonged to him.

* * * * *

The soft tap on the door drew Bren from the bed. Keene groaned as he left her. He smiled. That hadn't changed. In all four incarnations of women she'd been, she hadn't liked it when he pulled away. Masculine arrogance swelled in his chest. He looked back at her body, spread and open for him. He would get rid of whoever was at the door and return to her. There was more to be had.

Mine.

Bren listened to the dragon's growl. It was a mix of satisfied pleasure and still needy desire. *What will she think when she meets Tynan?* Bren thought reaching for the window latch. The question drew him up short, inches from peering out the viewing port.

Was he planning on keeping her? His vow to never accept the dragon's mate held firm but did he really think he could keep Tynan away from her? His control over the animal was strong but eventually the beast would break free and find her—and then the Gods only knew what would happen. Memories of the broken body in the dragon's lair when he'd been a child slammed into him. That's what happened when the dragon lost control.

Never hurt, Tynan insisted.

"I know you wouldn't mean to…"

Another tap on the door, this one louder and slightly more insistent, halted his discussion. He would have to think on this. On the best way to satisfy the dragon's needs and keep Keene safe.

Bren peeked into the viewing port, expecting to see Wrea. Instead, it was Johen, his father's personal bodyguard—though why Kei needed a bodyguard no one had ever been able to figure out. Bren had decided years ago it was for appearances. Johen had sharp political mind that Kei relied on.

Seeing Johen sent Bren instantly into alert. How did he know it was Johen and not a shifter come to rescue Keene? Still, his father was scheduled to arrive this morning. If the rumors were true, a shifter had to touch a person before turning into their form. How would a shifter have gotten to Johen?

He knocked again. Keene sighed but didn't wake. He had to answer—if it was Johen, he was here because something had happened to his father. Unlikely but Bren couldn't ignore the possibility.

He pulled the door open by inches, keeping his body hidden.

"What are you doing here?" he asked.

"Wrea told me where to find you. Your father's been stabbed."

Tynan was instantly alert inside his brain. In a strange way, they were his parents as well.

Bren ripped open the door, unconscious, uncaring of his naked state. Perhaps his father had been the target all along and they'd gotten to him while he'd traveled—while Bren had been fucking Keene.

"What happened?"

"We were riding and King Kei…"

Bren froze. That wasn't right. Johen didn't call his father that. They'd known each other too long.

Even as the realization struck him, Johen lifted his hand. He blew air across his flat palm and white powder exploded into Bren's face. His eyes stung, instantly watering as he gagged, choking on the dust filling his nose and throat.

He blinked and the body before him changed, shifting from the massive black haired guard to an equally massive blond god.

"Keene, get up. We've got to get out of here."

The words fluttered through Bren's quickly fading consciousness. Tynan screamed but the body they were in was trapped in the spell of the drug. The strength to move was gone. He couldn't lift his arms or turn his head. His knees weakened and Bren felt himself falling.

"Catch him," Keene commanded.

Strong arms snagged him moments before he hit the ground. His mind was surprisingly clear despite the paralysis of his body.

"I apologize, Your Highness, but I'll make this as painless as possible."

He heard the masculine voice seconds before the world turned black.

Chapter Nine

"Did you have to hit him so hard?" Keene asked, lying on the bed, straining her neck to see where Triant had dumped Bren's body. Triant looked at her and quickly evaluated the scene. She was naked, still chained to the bed at two points. Bren had released her legs in the middle of the night but her arms had remained bound and the band was still molded to her neck. Keene felt her cheeks flush as Triant stared at her. It shouldn't bother her—Triant had seen her naked before. Well, not actually *her* naked. He'd seen her in other forms and they'd been naked. He'd even been one of the men assigned to her as her lover but that had been in another's body.

She was intensely aware of her natural form. The Guild emphasized that no one should ever see a shifter's natural shape. Never having a specific identity based on looks allowed a person to more comfortably change into other forms. And it reinforced the fact that the body belonged to the Guild.

But for some reason, Keene wasn't in a hurry to change. Bren had seemed to enjoy her natural shape, even though her breasts were small and her hips a little too slim. She knew from three nights of fucking that he also enjoyed the rounded shapes, but last night, he'd loved her body as if it had been the most beautiful he'd ever seen. She shivered lightly—from the memory and from the cool air without Bren to warm her.

"We have to move quickly and I didn't want to worry that he was listening the whole time. That powder just weakens the body. It allows the mind to stay fully awake." Triant reached over and released the tension coils that gripped her hands. Freed, she sat up and removed the band around her throat. "You'd better dress quickly. We've got to get going. Risa is screaming down the Goddesses to bring you back. We'd better walk in there with what we need."

Keene couldn't quite decide why she was hesitating. This was it. She could complete the mission. That's what mattered. That's all that mattered. *The Guild is everything in your life. You live to serve it as it serves and protects you.* She'd heard the words since she was a child. Eight years old and sent away when her power was discovered.

But for the first time she wasn't sure she could do it. It didn't seem right. To take Bren's form. To force a piece of his soul into someone else just to satisfy some vague political desire.

"Keene?"

Triant's prodding call snapped her back. He stood before her—in one of his favorite forms. Tall, blond and gorgeous. She'd never seen his natural shape.

He was her friend, her partner and a fellow Guildmember. The Guild had protected her when no one else would. When others had wanted to stone her, when her own mother had shoved her into the street, the Guild had saved her. She climbed off the bed, moving quickly, suddenly very aware that she was naked and in her own body.

"Are you all right?" he asked, turning slightly away. She knew he was trying to give her some privacy.

"I'm fine. He caught me—I don't know how—as I was serving. Then somehow, he knocked me out and brought me here. He obviously knew something was happening."

"Yes. We'll have to figure out how that happened later."

Feeling as if they were getting back on their normal footing, Keene relaxed a bit. This was her world and she would do what needed to be done.

"How did you find me?" she asked, pulling on the gown she'd worn into the room. It hung on her natural frame like an oversized potato sack.

"We started looking as soon as we noticed Bren was gone." Triant dragged the prince onto the bed. The cords that had held her were conveniently still hanging from the frame. Triant glowered at the bonds and Keene knew he was imagining her being tied up. He just didn't know the pleasure she'd received while she'd been in that position—and she wasn't going to tell him. Not now.

"It took us a while to figure out Risa wasn't with him. She ended up spending half the night with the prince's personal assistant before she could finally get free and tell us the prince had escaped again."

"We can use those to tie him up," Keene suggested. They had to hurry. Having seen how quickly Bren's cock recovered, she feared the paralyzing powder would wear off too soon. She didn't want to be there when he woke. He'd be furious. "Let's just get this done." She grabbed the tiny purse she'd had looped around her waist, pulled out her dagger and stroked the knife across Bren's fingertip. Blood poured from the wound and she caught it in a tiny vial. Squeezing his finger to force the blood to flow, she filled half the glass container then stoppered it. "I've got enough," she announced.

Triant waited beside the bed, having made no move to tie Bren's hands. Keene reached over and did it, pulling his arms high above his head and coiling the cable around his wrists. Like her, she bound him so he couldn't escape but not tight enough to hurt him. When she moved toward his legs, she realized Triant still hadn't moved. "What's wrong? We need to get out of here."

"We can't leave him like this," Triant said pulling his eyes from Bren's unconscious body and staring at her.

"Sure we can. He's not hurt. Someone will find him tonight. By then we'll be gone. Mission accomplished."

"No, we can't leave him alive."

"What?" Pain shot through the center of her chest.

"He knows about you." He waved to her body and the silver band that Bren had placed around her neck. "He'll figure out that the Shifters Guild is behind this and then everything we've done here will be for nothing. We kill him now. I'll take his place and, by tomorrow, when they find his body, they'll just assume he couldn't bear the guilt of what he'd done."

The pain expanded filling her whole body and Keene shook her head. "No. We can't do it." She'd killed before. It was part of her job, but this was different. "We've knocked him out. By the time he comes to, he'll be confused. No one will believe him. They'll think he's crazy. There will be no sign that we were ever here."

Triant sighed. "Keene, we can't…"

"Please. Don't do this. I messed up, all right? And I'll take my punishment when we return to the Guild but don't make him pay for my stupidity. If I'd done it right the first time, we wouldn't be in this position. He doesn't deserve this." She saw Triant's jaw tighten. He was her one true friend in the Guild and since she only ever saw Guild members, he was her *only* friend. And her only hope. "Please."

"Fine. We'll just tell Risa that we found him and knocked him out." Again he scanned her body. "No mention of how you spent your night. You'd better change back into the maid's body."

Keene closed her eyes and willed herself into the woman's form. Her body expanded, turning her curves round and her hair blonde.

"I wonder how he recognized you," Triant said absently. "We'd better go. The sun is up and they have sent advance scouts to greet the king."

Keene nodded and stepped outside the room. "Check to make sure he's tied tight. We don't want him getting free before we're gone."

Triant quickly checked the coils and then nodded. "He's fine." He pulled the door closed behind them. "Let me have the vial."

Keene hesitated, even moving her hand toward his then snatching it back.

"Keene, this is our mission. This is what we were brought here to do." The sympathy in his eyes made her stomach flip-flop. "I know what it's like to get too close to a target. That's why they tell us to keep ourselves separate."

"I tried, somehow he just got closer than I expected."

"I know. I'm sorry but we have a job to do. Our loyalty is to the Guild. We owe everything to them. Give me the vial."

She knew he was right but, damn it, it just seemed wrong. With a sigh, she held out the vial and let it fall into Triant's hand.

"If it's any consolation, I'll make sure you're not around when it happens."

She nodded her thanks. Perhaps the memories would fade.

"Let's go."

They ran down the hall together. The early servants were rising and going about their morning tasks. Triant and Keene ignored them and hurried to the team chamber. They knocked and slipped inside, instinctively closing the door without a sound. Risa stood before them, her hands firmly fisted on her hips. The pose matched the glare in her eyes.

"Tell me you have it," she commanded.

Keene nodded.

"It's about damn time. Where were you last night? You were supposed to guide him to me, not take another night for yourself."

"I didn't have a choice. He pulled me from the room. I could hardly say no."

"You could have picked a less attractive form," Risa snapped.

Keene glanced down at the maid's body. It was true. There had been other choices but she'd instinctively known that Bren would like this one.

"Well, it's done and that's all we have to worry about, right?" Keene said, ignoring Risa's anger.

She wanted to get this over with. The primary target would be arriving in less than an hour. They all needed to be in place. "Besides, part of the goal was to keep the prince busy while we finish this and we've done that. He won't interrupt." Keene thought about the tension coils that they'd bound him with. She knew from experience that he was staying there until someone freed him.

"Let's do it." Triant pulled out his knife and held it out over his palm.

"Wait," Risa said. "I think Keene should do it."

"Me?" An invisible weight slammed into her chest.

"Risa, it makes more sense for me to do it," Triant objected. "It's easier for a male-to-male shift and I've had more experience."

"Then I think it's time Keene gains some experience." The hard edge of her voice warned Keene that there was little hope Risa would change her mind. "She knows him. She's spent so much time with him in the last three days, she'll know his movements and attitudes." She lifted her chin. "Give the vial to Keene."

Keene's fingers trembled as she reached out for the glass container. This was her punishment for getting too close to Bren.

She was going to have to shift into his form…and kill his father.

Marvis and Triant stared at her with trepidation. They didn't think she would do it. But with Risa daring her, Keene couldn't back down. This was her mission as well. It was the Guild's assignment and she would complete it.

The glass vial felt warm as she gripped it. Willing hands steady, she accepted the knife Triant offered her and sliced the blade across her palm. The skin separated and blood flowed. She wiped her hand on her skirt then emptied the vial into the open wound. Quickly, she closed her fingers over her palm, sealing the cut. Staring defiantly at Risa, Keene grit her teeth and focused on moving his blood into her body, blending his lifeblood with hers. Fire burned across her palm as his blood combined with hers. The pain crept up her arm to her shoulder and settled into her chest.

She held part of him inside her now. She could feel him, swelling, flowing within her. The room began to spin.

"Keene, are you all right?"

Triant's voice came from a distance but she nodded.

She'd never done a blood shift before and wanted to ask if the searing pain was normal but didn't. She had to get this done. This was what she'd been trained to do. She would be strong. Within the Guild, weakness was destroyed; strength survived.

She would do what was needed.

Increased noise in the corridor alerted them that their target was arriving. It should be a simple thing. All she had to do was request a private audience with King Kei and then slip a knife between his ribs. Keene tried to visualize the killing.

All she could see was Bren's face.

"We'd better get into position. *Our* target will remain in the brothel for another hour or so," Risa said. The team was splitting up at this point. They would meet again at Guild headquarters. "Are you ready?"

Triant looked to Keene. She nodded again and turned away. Stepping into the second chamber, she quickly slipped out of her borrowed dress. The maid's full breasts hung heavy, weighing down her shoulders. Standing naked, she took a deep breath and imagined Bren. She pictured every detail, every strand of hair, each line around his mouth. The tight shoulder and chest muscles and the slim, strong stomach. She knew his body well and it was outrageously simple to create the clear mental picture she needed. Once it was set in her head, she poured herself into the image. She felt her body changing—growing and expanding. Her muscles felt strong. She squeezed her fingers into a fist just to enjoy the sensation of making his body work.

She rolled her shoulders, trying to get used to the power that flowed through him. With no mirror to judge her appearance, Keene quickly donned the clothes Triant had gathered. She pulled on the black hose that she'd seen Bren strip off his body on several occasions and dragged on the crisp white shirt. She smoothed her hands down the front placket. The thick cock fluttered beneath her touch. She shuddered and jerked her hand away. It felt like Bren's body but she was on the wrong side of it.

Closing her eyes, she took a mental inventory of the form. It was strong and powerful but the fire that had started when she'd poured his blood into her hand continued, searing her insides. Needing to get this done, she stepped outside. Triant was alone.

"How do I look?" The sound of Bren's voice coming out of her mouth made the pain in her chest even worse.

"Just like the prince. How do you feel?"

Keene listened to the body. It was strange. She'd taken other forms before but this one didn't seem to fit right. The room began to sway around her. She placed her hand on the back of the chair to keep herself steady.

"Keene? Are you all right?"

"I'm fine." She looked at Triant. "I'm ready."

"Risa and Marvis have returned to the brothel to take out their target. We just have to do ours. Let's go."

Triant had changed back into the form of the king's bodyguard. He explained that Marvis had arranged a distraction for the guard that would allow Triant to slip in and assist Keene if she needed it. They left the team room and walked to the west side of the castle.

"I'm going to check on Kei's status. You stay here. Kei's apartments are through those doors, connecting to Prince Bren's. I'll be right back."

Keene nodded and tried to maintain Bren's stoic attitude. The hallway extended long to each side of her. The walls that had been turning in a slow circles began to speed up. She silently cursed Risa.

Keene should have been doing the advance work but instead it was Triant and she'd been assigned the assassination. Servants walked by, bowing their heads when they saw Bren's form standing in the hall. Keene ignored them. It would help their cause if several servants could claim they saw Prince Bren lurking outside his father's apartments.

She stood there, trying to keep her head from exploding until Triant returned. "The king's just arrived," he announced. "I'm going to go in." Keene nodded but was only half listening to what he was saying. The noise inside her head was incredible. Pain, loneliness, and power bombarded the inside of her skull. She knew a blood shift could cause a person to pick up trace emotions from the original form but these seemed unusually strong.

She approached the door to Bren's chamber and took a deep breath. With any luck, the mission would be finished in an hour and she could escape—hopefully leaving the memories behind.

The door swung open as she reached for the handle.

"Your Highness, you're back. How did it go?" The small wiry man asked eagerly.

"How did what go?" she snapped.

"With the shifter? Did you manage to discover her plot? Who is the target?"

Keene's stomach fell away. They were more exposed than she'd realized. If this man knew about them, then he would have to be killed as well. She fingered the knife in her hand. It would fit the image of a prince gone mad if his trusted servant was found dead as well. She took a deep breath and—

"Bren!"

She whipped around at the feminine cry and was instantly enveloped in a welcoming embrace. A light floral scent wafted over her as Queen Lorran hugged her son. Keene wrapped her arms around the queen and gave her a quick squeeze—all the while silently cursing to herself. No one had said that Queen Lorran would be here. Only Kei was supposed to arrive today. Lorran was scheduled to arrive tomorrow.

"Mother, what are you doing here?" Keene asked.

"I couldn't wait to meet her." She stepped back but still held his hands. Then she shrugged and shared a knowing smile that Keene didn't understand. "Besides, you know Nekane. He gets so restless if I'm not around. It's just safer for everyone if I travel with your father."

Keene nodded but was trying to place "Nekane" in the family. None of her information on Bren's family had mentioned that name. Of course, the information on Bren and his use of courtesans had been outrageously incorrect as well.

"That's a good idea," Keene finally said.

"Rainek and Tiana are also here. Kayla stayed home to help with the planting. We just couldn't wait. Where is she?"

"She?"

"Tynan's mate. Your future bride." Lorran's face held a mixture of frustration and amusement. "Please tell me you're not still planning to reject her just because Tynan chose her. They have an excellent record of picking women."

From the sound of it, this was a conversation between mother and son that had been going on for some time and Keene didn't know how to respond. But she did latch onto one phrase—"your future bride." Bren was planning to marry? The room around her swayed and wavered.

"Bren?"

Keene blinked and forced her attention back to Lorran's question.

"Uh—well, I'm not sure."

"Hey, Bren, where is she?"

Bren's brother and sister-in-law walked in from the far door as well.

"Uh, she's not here."

"Damn, I was hoping to find you two in bed. Thought it would be suitable revenge."

His bride punched his shoulder lightly and laughed. "When can we meet her?" Tiana asked. "I can't believe you met her in a brothel. That's going to be a great story for your grandchildren."

Lorran laughed. "Yes, that will be interesting, won't it?"

Keene's stomach did a double flip. All this talk about mates and brides and…they seemed to be talking about her. A foreign red haze drifted across her eyes. Mated to Bren. Belonging to Bren. A desperate hunger billowed up from inside her chest and spread through her body, weakening her knees.

It wasn't possible. His family was obviously mistaken. Bren didn't want her. If he *did* want her now, he certainly wouldn't after she killed his father. He, of course, would know she was responsible, even if no one else believed it.

The weight of the knife suddenly felt heavy in her fist. She had to move. Her mission needed to be completed. She had to return to the Guild. If only the damned room would stop spinning.

"Is Father around? I need to speak with him." Her question was notably abrupt but she couldn't stay here any longer and listen this family—the way they teased, the obvious love between them. It made her life at the Guild seem beyond cold.

Lorran raised her eyebrows but nodded. "He's in our chambers finishing up some business. But don't expect him to be any more sympathetic than I am," Lorran warned and the teasing smile was back. "We want to meet her."

Keene nodded and started toward the door.

"And be prepared…" Rainek's cautious tone drew her to a stop. "Nekane and Father are both incredibly concerned that a shifter would be after you. Did you ever find out what she wanted?"

Keene's chest seized up. They knew about her. His whole family knew about her and the shifters.

"Yes, it was nothing," she said, hoping for a casual tone to cover the panic that bound her chest. "I'll talk to Father about it."

She whipped around and almost sprinted from the room. The plan to kill Kei and place the blame on Bren was crumbling around them. His family knew. They would immediately suspect the Shifters Guild. The spinning grew worse. It moved from her head to her stomach. All she wanted to do was lie down and close her eyes, maybe then the world would stay solid. Instead, she gripped the knife handle and stepped into Kei's chamber. The king was reading a document and nodding as his "bodyguard" explained the notations.

"Oh, there's Prince Bren now. He'll be able to explain more fully." Triant, in the guard's form, stared directly into Keene's eyes. He nodded slightly.

Keene shook her head, trying to convey her concerns. There was no way this plan could succeed. Not without revealing the Guild's involvement. They'd have to kill Bren's entire family, including Bren.

"Bren, how has everything been going so far?" The greeting was a mixture of fatherly affection and kingly inquiry.

"Fine." She stepped forward. "Everything's well."

"And I hear Tynan's chosen a mate…"

He left the statement hanging, waiting for Bren's confirmation. "Uh, yes."

"When do we meet her?"

Bren moved closer.

"Later tonight, probably."

Kei nodded and stared at her. His eyes turned black for a moment—the way Bren's did when he was inside her. The pressure from his gaze didn't alter but he tipped his head to the side. "Bren?" There was a new quality to his voice—low and gravelly.

"Yes?"

Kei shook his head and took a step away. "You're not Bren."

Triant grabbed the king around the neck and jerked him back. Kei growled and dug his fingers into Triant's thick forearm. With one furious pull, he ripped free of Triant's grip. Kei shoved him out of the way—sending him flying into the wall—and stalked forward, the black in his eyes reminding her of Bren's. Keene pulled out the knife and held it before her.

"Where's my son?" Kei demanded.

She wasn't going to lie. There was something about him and Bren that made them able to see through her shifting.

"He's fine." She circled him, putting her back to the outside door and closer to Triant.

"And who are you?"

"That would be Tynan's mate." Bren's quiet voice filled the room.

Keene snapped her gaze from his father to Bren. More bodies pushed into the room behind Bren—his family had come to the rescue. Her vision began to darken as if the curtains had suddenly been closed. All she could see was Bren's fury. Blood dripped from his wrists. "The trick to escaping tension coils is being strong enough to break the wires before they snap your wrists," he growled. The blood marking his skin made the nausea rise to her throat.

Bren didn't notice. He stared down at the knife in her hand.

"So this was your mission all along? Kill my father?"

Bren stepped closer. Keene shook her head to clear it and held up the knife. "Stay back."

"It's uncanny," Rainek announced, walking boldly between them, looking first at Bren and then at Keene. "But I can tell now that this is the shifter." He sniffed the air. "She doesn't smell right."

Triant stood behind her, pulling her toward the door. Keene followed the silent command and inched backward. "We're leaving now," Triant announced.

"Oh, no. You're not going anywhere. Especially not her," Rainek announced.

Bren shook his head. "Let them go. They'll never tell us who hired them, even if they know."

"But Bren, that's your—"

"She's nothing to me."

Worse than the mission's failure was the brutal cold in Bren's voice. She had no doubt he meant each word. The desire to apologize—to try to explain—filled her but there was no way he would understand.

At Triant's urging, she stepped outside. As the door swung shut behind them, he dragged her forward. Keene didn't know why they were rushing—Kei and his family weren't going to come after them.

The nausea that had threatened earlier rose again. She pulled her arm out of Triant's hold and slowed to a stop, taking in long, deep breaths. The world shifted around her spinning and sliding away.

"Keene, what's wrong?"

She heard his cry as if from the end of a long narrow tunnel. Blinking, she looked up and realized she was on the floor.

"Are you all right?"

Unable to speak, she knew the answer to that and slowly shook her head. Something was very wrong. As the realization came to her, black covered her mind. Silence should have followed but a voice was there to greet her.

Mine?

* * * * *

Bren stared at the closed door, gritting his teeth as Tynan shook the walls with his bellow.

"Are you sure you don't want to go after her?" Kei asked.

"She tried to assassinate you," Bren pointed out.

"Yes, but she is your mate."

"She's a hired killer."

"Which begs the question…" Lorran said walking to Kei's side. He immediately pulled her against his body. "Who sent the shifters after you?" She looked into her husband's eyes with concern and fear.

The gentle affection sent a new pain into Bren's chest. He was never going to have that. But he'd made his decision. Tynan had been wrong. The woman he'd chosen had betrayed them both.

"Any number of people could want him dead," Bren announced. The whole family looked at him. His mother raised her eyebrows as if offended for Kei. "Well, it's true, isn't it? He's a king. He's bound to make enemies."

"Yes, but this wasn't a normal assassination," Rainek said, stepping forward. "They could have used anyone's form at any time but they chose to take Bren's shape. The other shifter was in the room with Father for ten minutes and didn't try to kill him. Why become you to kill our father?"

Bren thought about Rainek's words and nodded. "I think I was the primary target. You were supposed to die, of course, but someone was out to frame me for killing you."

"Who hates you enough to do that?"

One name sprang to mind instantly. "Herenson." The man had been aggressive and antagonistic since they'd met but was it possible that Herenson hated Bren enough to kill a king? "I should go see him and Nerra."

"But it could be another shifter trap," Rainek pointed out. "And if Herenson did try to frame you…"

"I'll be fine. He won't try anything while others are around." The concerned faces of his family stared back at him. He spun on his heel and stalked from the chamber before any of them could stop him. Their concern and sympathy was too much for him to handle on top of his own ragged emotions. Part of him had died when he saw Keene, in *his* form, wielding a knife and pointing it at his father. Identifying her had been easy. He'd instantly recognized her scent.

The pain of her betrayal united Bren and Tynan. The dragon was silent as Bren walked the corridors but he could feel the beast's rage welling up from deep in their souls. A dragon's one fear was that the chosen mate would reject him. Now that Keene had chosen her people over Bren, Tynan was fighting that pain with fury.

And Bren was glad that Keene was gone. There was no way to predict Tynan's reaction to her now.

Bren looked down the hallways and realized he'd arrived at Nerra's rooms.

A maid with sad eyes greeted his knock.

"I'm sorry, Your Highness, but Lady Herenson is not accepting visitors today. We're mourning the great tragedy."

"I don't understand."

"I'm sorry, Your Highness. I thought you knew. Lord Herenson was killed last night."

"What?"

"Merka, is that Bren? Oh, Bren, it's just awful." Nerra hurried to his side, her eyes red and a damp handkerchief clutched in her hand. "He was killed at that horrible place."

"What happened?"

"I don't know. They found his body this morning in that brothel. But Bren, it's worse than anything." She took his hand, dragged him over to a lounger and sat down. "They think you did it."

"What?"

"People have noticed our affection for each other." She blinked up at him. "And Herenson's jealousy. Of course, I told them it wasn't true. That you would never do anything so terrible." She dropped her voice despite the fact that they were essentially alone in the room. The maid hovered at a respectable distance. "I believe we should tell them that we were together."

"I'm sure that's not necessary."

"But if you have no one to prove your location, they could easily accuse you of killing him."

"I'm not worried. I have someone who can prove I was nowhere near the brothel."

Nerra's eyes tightened. "What? You were with someone else?"

"Yes."

"But that's impossible." Her voice squeaked, making him flinch.

Why? Bren leaned away and looked at Nerra. The tight lines around her mouth indicated more irritation than grief.

The door opened and Kei walked in. Bren stood and looked curiously at his father.

"Your mother got worried and sent me after you."

"You're supposed to be dead," Nerra said. Her head tilted in a delightful impression of confusion—only Bren didn't think she was joking.

Bren stepped between Nerra and his father and stared at the woman he'd once hoped to marry.

"*You* sent the shifters after us."

Nerra didn't deny it.

"Why?"

"Because I was supposed to be a princess. You were supposed to marry me. And then I got sent away—the mere wife of a royal advisor. I was supposed to be a princess," she repeated. The insanity in her eyes knocked Bren and Kei back a step. "But I decided if I couldn't be a princess I'd be queen." She smiled and held out her hands, silently calling for Bren.

"And you were going to be my alibi for my father's death."

"I knew you'd be grateful and then we could marry. I'm the perfect wife for you, Bren. I'll rule by your side with a strong firm hand. It won't take much. We just have to kill your father and then we can be together. I've already taken care of Herenson." She smiled sweetly up at him, her eyes still blinking with that wide, innocent stare.

"What do we do now?" he asked his father quietly. Nerra didn't seem to notice that he'd spoken.

"I think we make sure she doesn't leave the chamber and we call King Ashure and let him deal with her."

"Good idea. Nerra, I have to go see King Ashure for a moment."

Her eyes lit up. "Oh good. Give him my best and won't you share my tragedy with him. I'm sure he'll want to come give me his condolences. And maybe he'll preside over our joining."

Bren had no answer for that. He merely backed out of the room and gave orders to her maid to watch over her. The maid nodded solemnly and said she'd call one of the footmen to assist her.

"Excellent idea," Bren approved as they closed the door.

"And that's the woman you wanted to marry?" Kei asked.

"Yes."

"Hmmm. Perhaps you were better off with Tynan's choice. She was at least sane."

Bren stared at his father's back as he walked away.

"She tried to kill you," he called out. "Why doesn't that bother anyone but me?"

Chapter Ten

Bren leaned back into the wicker chair and stared out into the gardens that backed up against the apartments his family was using. The Kings' Council had met as planned, though Herenson's death and Nerra's arrest had cast a strange pallor on the proceedings. Still, in the end, the dragon hunting initiative was approved unanimously. Bren at least had that satisfaction. But now it was time to leave. His family had been stalling, delaying for days with the explanation that Tiana was too tired to travel, given her delicate condition. Bren, at first concerned about his sister-in-law and the child she carried, no longer believed their excuses. He'd heard Rainek and Tiana rolling around their bedroom for more than half the night. She can't be that delicate, he thought. Not if she could make those sounds come out of Rainek's mouth.

Frustrated by the delay, Bren had finally demanded that his family prepare to depart this morning. He knew why they were stalling—they hoped he would go after Keene.

For some reason it didn't seem to upset his family that she'd attempted to kill Kei and have Bren framed for the murder. All mattered was that Tynan had chosen her. Tiana even sounded sympathetic, saying she'd heard that shifters were forced to follow Guild instructions.

Bren was having none of it. Keene had made her choice clear when she'd left him tied to the bed they'd shared. His fingers curled compulsively around the arm of the chair and he heard the wicker crack beneath his grip. It was definitely time to return home and return to his daily life. He would forget what it felt like to be inside her. To hold her body next to his.

It was ironic. His greatest fear in life was that he would lose control and someone would end up being hurt. He'd never imagined that someone would be him.

She'd betrayed him. She'd chosen her people and her mission over him.

And all the passion, all the desire had been planned and faked. It had seemed so real.

More than anything was the pain. It hurt. Somehow, amid all the lust, he'd found some kind of emotion. He wasn't sure what it was, wasn't sure he loved her. Hells, he didn't know her well enough for it to be called love but still the dragon's innate connection to her made him feel close to her, even when most of their encounters had been purely physical.

"Thinking about her?"

Bren looked up at his mother's entrance and nodded. "Thinking about it all actually."

"Are you sure you won't go after her? Tynan could probably find her."

That made Bren laugh softly. "I have no doubt about that but no." He sat forward, letting his hands dangle between his knees. "I know Tynan chose her but for once the dragon's intuition was wrong. You wouldn't want me to be with someone I couldn't trust."

"Of course not," his mother said with the dedicated motherly support Bren hadn't relied on in years. Now he needed it. He needed her strength to help him fight the desire to find Keene. Somewhere, she still called to him. "But I can't stand to see you hurting."

"I'll recover," Bren said with the confidence of a man used to controlling his world. He would get over this. Forget Keene. Maybe then the pain would leave him.

Voices in the inner chamber drew him to his feet. It sounded like the rest of his family was awake and ready to move. Good. He wanted to be gone. His father wandered into the garden and immediately went to Lorran's side. It was expected. Even after almost thirty-five years together, Nekane liked to be near his mate at all times. Rainek and his wife walked in moments later. Sexual satisfaction surrounded them like a glowing sun.

Tynan and Bren both growled in frustration. He didn't begrudge his brother his happiness but it was still painful to watch. Bren turned that pain into irritation.

"Are we ready? I'd like to get started before the sun is too high in the sky."

All parties agreed but no one moved.

"Then let's go," he encouraged, waving toward the door. Finally, as if they accepted he truly wasn't going after her, they moved.

The slow shriek of a lone hawk drew the group to a halt. Bren stopped and looked up, Tynan going on full alert. There was something not right about the sound. Kei and Rainek tensed as well and Bren knew they'd heard it. As a unit, they turned.

A full-grown red hawk dived toward them at full speed. The bird streaked across the sky, plummeting to earth, finally pulling up into a graceful landing on the back of the chair Bren had so recently been occupying.

As Bren and his family stared at the bird, it began to shimmer and expand. Bren tensed. He'd seen the same movement when Keene had changed. A shifter had come to them. But not Keene. Slowly, the form took shape, growing into a human. A man. He stood up, brushing long blond hair away from his face. He was naked and stepped behind the chair as if to cover himself. He looked vaguely familiar. It took Bren a moment to identify where he'd seen him before—he'd bumped into him in the hallways on one of the first days.

"What do you want?" Bren demanded. He placed his hand on the sword at his side and noticed his father and brother did the same. All three stepped toward the threat, putting their women behind them.

The shifter glanced at the placement of Bren's, Kei's, and Rainek's hands and held up his own.

"I'm not here to hurt you," he announced to the group. He looked at Bren. "My name is Triant. I'm a friend of Keene's and I need your help."

Bren shook his head. "Get out of here. We have nothing to say to you." He turned away and was pleased to see his family moved with him.

"Keene's in trouble," Triant called out.

Pain pierced Bren's chest but he'd spent years controlling his emotions. He could control this as well. "It doesn't matter to me what happens to her," he said without looking back. "She made her choice."

"She's a warrior, what would you have had her do? She was sent here to do a job and that's all she was trying to do."

"She tried to kill my father," Bren said, taking time to face Triant. "That's a little more than a job. That's someone's life."

"And you've never killed in service to your king or kingdom?" Triant dared him to deny it. Bren couldn't. "She was doing nothing more than any soldier would do."

The truth of the shifter's words stopped him. She'd been on a mission—sent to complete a job ordered by her leader—and she'd done it. Would he have expected anything less of someone he'd sent? Of course, he didn't order executions on his enemies.

Bren dug deep inside his flagging strength, looking for the power to continue walking away.

"It's all she's ever known," Triant pressed. "She's been trained to be a part of the Shifters Guild since she was a child. You can't blame her for doing what she was trained to do."

Logically, Bren knew that was true but his heart still ached with the betrayal. A betrayal even Tynan recognized. He took another step away, forcing his body to reject the need to help her.

"They're going to execute her."

Bren whipped around and without looking knew his family had circled around him.

"What?"

"The Guild Leaders are planning to kill her. Early next week."

"Why? Because of what happened here?"

Triant shook his head. "No. We've failed missions before. Rarely. Keene's one of the best." If that thought was supposed to comfort Bren—that he'd been seduced by one of their best—it didn't. "Something's wrong with her. Ever since we left here, she's not behaving normally."

"Why would they kill her for that?" Lorran asked, placing her hand on Bren's arm as if to tell him she was there.

"Shifting is a very powerful talent. That's why almost all kingdoms allow shifters to be executed upon discovery. The ones who keep it quiet find their way to the Guild and the Guild trains them." He stared at Bren. "Becomes their family and friends." Bren heard the underlying message—that Keene wouldn't have known how to betray the Guild. "The Guild can't allow an unstable shifter to wander about. They are too great a risk—for the world and the Guild's reputation. Since there is no way to contain a shifter for long, they'll kill her unless she returns to her normal self."

"So, why come to me?"

"Because something here caused whatever sickness is affecting her." Triant began to pace and Bren felt a moment of sympathy for the man. "Almost as soon as we escaped she collapsed and fell into this feverish trance. When she finally recovered, she hasn't been herself. She won't let anyone near her. She has fits of fury—" He flicked his eyebrows up. "She screams your name a lot during those moments. But then, at other times, she seems perfectly normal. Just scared." He shook his head. "I don't know how to explain it." He stared at Bren. "But I think it has something to do with you or your blood."

"*My blood*? What does that have to do with any of this?"

176

Triant took a deep breath and Bren could tell the man was deciding whether or not to explain. Finally, he sighed. "For most people, a shifter merely has to touch them to gain their essence. Once we have that, we can turn into that person whenever we want. But some people have mental shields or some kind of protection about them that makes it impossible to gain the essence just by touch. The Guild's never been able to figure out what it is exactly, just that some people have it." He nodded to Bren. "You have it. I met you back in Xicanth. I was sent to take your shape so when the time came here, I could assume your role."

Bren waved his hand brushing away the rest of the story. "I don't understand what this has to do with Keene and my blood."

"For people with these shields, the only way for a shifter to turn into that person is to collect some of their blood and draw it into the shifter's body. To literally make you a part of the shifter. It's called a blood shift." He started pacing again, seemingly forgetting that he was naked and there were ladies present. "Keene collected your blood—"

"And injected it into her body?"

"Yes."

"And then she got sick? Almost immediately thereafter?"

"Yes."

He looked at his mother and then up to his father.

"She fell into the healing trance," his mother said. Lorran turned to Triant. "Was Keene in this trance for about three days?" Triant nodded. "And she's been out of it for four more. She won't make the full transition for another few weeks but it's started."

"She'll be hearing the dragon's voice already," Kei added. He'd been through this process himself. Bren and Rainek had been born this way so they never knew life without a dragon as part of their soul. "The dragon will be panicked and confused. So will Keene because she has no idea what's going on."

"I've got to get to her," Bren announced. Betrayed or not— Hells, he could almost understand why she'd done it. He couldn't say he wouldn't have done the same thing. But he couldn't leave her out there…not while she was nearing the final transition from human to dragon.

"Dragons? Wait, what are you all talking about?"

"We know what's wrong with Keene and we can help. Bren will go to her and bring her back to Xicanth." Lorran turned to her oldest son. "That will be the safest place. She can't make the transition near the Shifters Guild. Too many memories."

Bren nodded. "I'll get her."

"They won't let you near her," Triant protested. "She's isolated and under constant guard."

"I'll get her," Bren said again, knowing he wouldn't fail. Tynan wouldn't let him. Bren stalked into the garden. He needed an open place to change.

Mine?

Yes, we're going to get her.

"Are you going to hurt her?" Triant called out. Bren could tell the man was a few paces behind him.

"No," he replied, not stopping. He had to get to her. Somehow when she'd injected his blood into her body, she'd reacted like someone bitten by a dragon. The three-day trance followed by a slow steady decline into madness.

"She didn't want to do it, you know," Triant said.

Bren pulled up short and spun around. "What?"

"All Keene was supposed to do was collect your blood."

"That's what the nights in the brothel were for."

"Yes. She was supposed to drug you and collect a vial of your blood, then she would give it to me and I would take on your form."

"Then how did she—?"

"Our team leader decided Keene needed to prove her loyalty to the Guild—thought she was a little too sympathetic to the target."

"Me."

Triant nodded.

"Where is the Shifters Guild?" Bren asked.

"You'll never find it. They've hidden it too well."

"I'll find her. You'll just make it easier by telling me which direction to go."

"South, near the Adrik Mountains. It will take days to ride there…Where are you going?" Triant finally demanded.

Bren stopped. The area around him was free of trees and out of sight from the main castle. "Here." It would have to do. There was some chance that someone in the two west towers would see him change but he didn't have time to worry about that. He had to get to Keene. He hadn't lived through the transition himself but he'd listened to the tales from his father and Nekane. The dragon came into awareness confused and scared.

Bren had never heard of a woman turning into a dragon and had no idea if the transition would be different for her. The instant the beast had formed in her mind it would begin looking for its mate. By the Gods that protected him, he hoped her dragon accepted him as her mate or they were going to have some issues. Tynan would never let another man touch Keene.

Tynan roared his agreement.

"Damn it, tell me what's going on."

Bren looked at the hand on his arm and had to resist the urge to throw the man off. But he could hear Tynan's sudden change in emotion.

"Are you in love with her?" Bren asked.

"Who? Keene? No."

Bren focused with the dragon's senses and didn't detect any change in the man's heartbeat.

"I care for her," Triant clarified. "She's been a friend."

Bren squinted his eyes, seeing something in the other man that made him want to choke the life out of him. "You've fucked her."

"Yes," Triant admitted. "As part of her training. It's expected that a shifter learn that their body doesn't belong to them. It belongs to the Guild and if they demand you fuck a target, you do."

Bren's jaw tightened and his hands curled into fists. He wanted to pound someone. And Triant was close.

"But I can tell you, no one ever put the light in her eyes the way you did. Exhausted as she was, if she'd had a chance, she'd have crawled back into your bed at any time."

Bren couldn't help but smile. It was a masculine way to comfort Bren. If the circumstances were different, he might have been friends with Triant. If the man wasn't a shifter...and he hadn't had sex with Keene. That would always be a major sticking point with him. Of course, *Triant* hadn't slept with Keene in her real form. That pleasure had been reserved for Bren alone.

He looked up and saw his father and brother enter the clearing.

"We're going with you," Kei announced.

"She'll panic if three of us come after her. She'll trust me." *Maybe*, Bren mentally added, hoping some trace of the physical connection remained.

"We're just going to get you through the guards, then we'll pull back and you'll have to deal with her," Kei said.

"She's probably going to be pretty pissed," Rainek added with a smile.

"So I've heard."

"Wait," Triant stepped into the center of the three men. "It will be you against the whole Guild. You can't beat them. I'll go with you."

"You won't be able to keep up."

"I can turn into anything."

"*Almost* anything," Bren told Triant. "Now, step back."

"What is going on?" His eyes bounced suspiciously between the three men.

"You came to me to help Keene. That's what I'm going to do. Now, step back. You don't want to be this close. Particularly now that Tynan knows you fucked her."

Triant took two steps away but was still asking questions.

"Who's Tynan? What—"

That was the last Bren heard as he released his hold on the dragon and let him enter the world.

The dragon's trumpeting roar shook the leaves. He screamed and then swung his head around looking for the male. Bren was a rider in Tynan's mind now, aware but not fully in control. Triant fell onto his back, landing hard on the gravel path. The wide eyes and the rapid heartbeat gave Tynan the satisfaction that the human was sufficiently terrified.

Mine, he growled, sending his thoughts into the male interloper's head. *She's mine.*

"Uh, y-yes."

The dragon briefly considered biting the male but Bren drew him back. They had to get to Keene. At the mention of his mate, Tynan screamed again and leapt into the air.

Behind him he felt a second, then a third pair of flapping wings as his brother and father joined him.

South, head south, Bren reminded as the dragon flapped its powerful wings and sent them in search of his mate.

Triant stared at the creatures as they turned and flew south.

"Oh, I see you've met Tynan."

Triant looked over his shoulder. He recognized Queen Lorran from his visits to Xicanth.

"Th-those were dragons." He pointed to the empty sky.

"Yes, I know." She smiled serenely. "They tend to run in our family."

* * * * *

Keene stretched out on the cot and stared up at the ceiling. There was nothing for her to do. Her guards sat playing cards outside her cell. They ignored her for the most part—only looking up if she made noise—and they refused to talk to her.

She didn't understand why the Guild Leaders felt compelled to assign two guards to her. She was in a metal cell which was surrounded by unbreakable glass. And they'd attached a band around her neck. She couldn't shift. She was well and truly locked away.

Of course she knew the real reason for the guards. They were monitoring her "condition" and reporting back to the Guild if her status changed. If she somehow became normal again.

The precautions were silly. The Guild Leaders didn't seem to understand. She was content inside this cell. Safe inside it.

There was no way to explain that whatever was happening to her, whatever was wrong, terrified her far more than it could ever frighten them. Keene pulled her lips back and growled at the empty space above her. She hated the fear and uncertainty that seemed to increase with every day.

The Guild was her life. The Guild was all she knew. The Guild had taken her in, raised her, trained her.

Some would say it had become her family but she didn't know what that meant anymore. They'd become her world. She knew that. And she'd failed them. She'd let them down and exposed their mission to the external world.

She should have let Triant kill Bren. That would have solved most though not all her problems.

Mine!

The dark feminine voice whispered, making Keene cringe. The sound slipped from inside her head down deep in her body, seeming to settle in her sex. Something very strange was happening to her. One Guild Leader proposed that her failure had simply driven her insane. That her loyalty to the Guild was so great that she had lost her senses when she'd failed her team. He'd been very supportive of her. Of course, he still called for her execution. Whether the reasons were valid or not, an insane shifter was much too dangerous. It was bad for business.

No one would trust the Guild if they couldn't control their own members. So if she didn't start behaving normally soon, they would kill her.

Keene sighed. She wanted to but something was stopping her—the voice inside her head that would scream for hours, alternately crying for and swearing at Bren.

And the smells of the men. She shuddered. No matter how much cologne they wore or how often they bathed, she could still smell them and it wasn't right. The thought of interacting with them, of letting any of them come near her made her wretch. Two days ago, during a rare visit, Triant had reached out and placed his hand on her shoulder—merely to comfort her. Her body had reacted, rejecting his simple touch. Her fist out had swung out, with power she didn't know she had, and struck him—sending him hard against the iron bars. She'd apologized but there had been no way to explain. No one had touched her since.

But they watched her. For some sign of what caused her descent or, in the case of some, any sign that she was recovering. She wanted to tell them but they already thought she was crazy. Telling them she heard a voice inside her head that didn't belong to her would only prove their point.

Bren. She rolled to her side and pulled her knees up, increasing the ache between her legs. Along with the foreign voice had come a powerful lust that she could barely control. She'd collapsed outside of Bren's door and didn't remember anything until she'd woken up three days later at Guild

Headquarters. She'd come awake with the desperate need to fuck. But none of the men around her smelled right. She needed Bren. Deep inside her pussy, the ache built again. She needed him—filling her, coming inside her. She groaned and slipped her fingers down between her legs. Through the thin material of her shorts, she rubbed her clit, teasing the sensitive flesh with light caresses. Shivers ran up her spine. She pressed harder, needing the release, the freedom of peace in her body. She spread her legs just a little wider, conscious of the guards just feet away. Pressing her lips together to keep herself silent, she slid her hands underneath her clothes. Wet hot flesh greeted her.

Raising her upper leg a little more, she teased the entrance to her cunt. *Bren.* She needed Bren. He'd been so wickedly hungry as he'd licked and sucked her pussy. She pushed her finger into her opening and couldn't hide the whimper. It wasn't enough. She needed him.

She closed her eyes and saw him. The picture perfect memory filled her head and a roar filled her thoughts. *Mine!*

"Yes," she groaned in response. She concentrated on his image, the way he'd felt pumping inside her, riding her so deep. Still driving her finger into her cunt, she rubbed her clit with her other hand, circling and massaging, using the dream of Bren to guide her. No longer caring if the guards knew or not, she pumped her hips against her hand. She was close. "Come for me, my prince," she whispered. The memory of his climax triggered her own. Tiny waves broke from her core and washed through her body. The pleasure seeped into her limbs making her drowsy and relaxed but it wasn't enough. It would never be enough.

A tear leaked out the corner of her eye. Her body ached—satisfied but empty.

* * * * *

"Now, let's try this again," Bren said, though it was difficult to speak with his teeth so tightly clenched. He knew if he let go of any bit of control, Tynan would take over. The anteroom they stood in didn't appear large enough to hold one furious dragon. And if Tynan appeared, so would Nekane and Denith.

Bren wrapped his hand around the guard's neck and squeezed. This was the third set of guards they'd been through. They'd arrived quietly, landing in the mountains and climbing down the steep slopes. They'd taken out the perimeter guards and received some vague directions on finding Keene. The two soldiers who'd stood beside the one Bren now held were unconscious beside the door.

"Where can I find Keene?" Tynan was ready to break down the walls to get to her and, while it was an option, Bren wanted to hold it in abeyance. He wanted the young man to know he was serious so he lifted him off the ground.

"I-I can't tell you that and I can't let you in." The young guard, larger than Bren almost by half, clearly hadn't expected Bren's strength.

"Tell me, have you ever seen the power of dragon? Seen the damage one of those creatures can do?" The guard nodded. "Now, imagine the worse possible damage from one dragon and multiply it by three."

The guard looked over Bren's shoulder. Kei and Rainek waited, arms folded, eyes black with dragon-fire.

"Lower level. Fourth door from the stairs on the left."

Bren nodded and let the man sink to the floor. "See, that wasn't too hard."

"She's guarded and locked in a glass cell. You'll never get to her."

"You think so?" Bren slammed the guard against the stone wall. His eyes rolled to the back of his head and he fell to the ground. "You'd be wrong," he said to the unconscious man. Bren grabbed the guard's sword. He wasn't sure how much help it would be against an army of shape-shifters but it comforted him to have to the steel blade in his hand. His father and brother had collected the weapons of the others they'd encountered.

"You get Keene," his father said. "Rainek and I will go have a chat with the Guild Leaders so you have a chance to reunite without interruption."

Bren nodded. He glanced at his brother. Rainek's amulet glittered in the bright sunlight. Made of magic, their amulets were the one item that survived the transition from human to dragon and back again.

Rainek touched the medallion around his neck and Bren felt his own heat. He nodded, letting his brother know he got the message—he could call for help if he needed it. Turning away, he stepped over the guard's body and through the main door. Relying on Tynan's senses, he started down the steps; Keene's scent grew stronger and it was all Bren could do to keep Tynan contained. The dragon wanted its mate. Even more now that he knew she was in danger.

Bren tried to temper the dragon's response, not knowing what they would find. He followed the guard's directions-- fourth door from the stairs on the left. Tynan pulled at him. Bren knew better than to restrain the beast too far. He would need the dragon's strength. He ripped open the door. Two men, one sitting, one standing, immediately faced him.

"What do you want?" the front one demanded.

"Her." Bren calmly announced tilting his head toward Keene's cell. Glass surrounded a metal cage and inside was Keene. She lay on a cot in the far corner, her head snapping up as he spoke.

"Bren?!" She leapt off the bed and ran for the door. Bren could see from the changing color in her eyes that her dragon was struggling for control and she probably didn't understand what was happening. His first task was keeping her dragon calm.

"I'm here, baby. I'm here. Don't worry. I won't leave."

A low animal growl to his left dragged his attention back to the two guards—one of which was now in tiger form. The tiger lunged forward, in direct line to Bren's throat. Bren waited until the animal was almost on him then grabbed it by the neck and swung. The tiger screamed as it flew across the room. It hit the wall with a thump and changed back into human form.

The second guard stayed human but swelled to twice Bren's size.

The guard came after him, fists at the ready. Bren drew back, again waiting for the attack. The dragon in him watched as the guard swung. Bren ducked and came up, jabbing his fist into the man's stomach. He quickly followed with a heavy punch to the jaw. The guard crumpled. Bren stared at him for a few moments contemplating more violence. They'd locked up his mate. If they touched her—

"Bren?" Keene's confused, frightened whisper left the rest of his threat unspoken. He had to take care of her. He looked up. Her gray eyes blinked at him through the glass and metal cage. Tears crept down her cheeks. Bren's heart skipped a beat. This wasn't the brave woman who'd faced him.

"I'll be right there," he assured her, dragging the first guard to the door. He dumped the body in the hall and went back in for the second. As he stepped inside, he heard Keene pounding on the glass. "I'm back, I'm back. Don't worry." He vaguely remembered his mother saying the same things to his father and Nekane when the dragon would start to worry that she had left. He'd been young when the dragon had finally believed that she wasn't going to leave him but Bren could still remember Lorran's soothing tone. "I'm here," he said again as he picked up the groaning guard and helped him out of the room. Neither seemed severely injured. More stunned than anything else.

Bren dropped him outside the door, closed it, locked and lowered the bar across it. He didn't know if his father and brother would be successful in convincing the Guild to leave him alone but he didn't want to be interrupted.

Keene and her dragon were going to take some soothing and the best way for a mate to do that was by loving her. His cock leapt at the idea.

"Bren, what are you doing here? What's going on?"

He turned around. Keene waited beside the door—waiting in her natural form. Her short shaggy hair stood up in spikes. She looked confused and lonely.

"I'll explain it all. Let me get the door open." There was no lock on the glass door, just a latch on the outside. He pulled open the glass and Keene's scent flooded him. Tynan howled and Keene whimpered. She reached through the bars, grabbing for him, clawing to get to him. Bren looked in her eyes. The clear gray was gone and black filled the space. "What's your name?" he asked knowing the dragon was in charge.

Andra.

Chapter Eleven

"Andra, I'm here," he assured the frightened dragon. Her desperation to reach him soothed one concern. Her dragon had clearly claimed him. "Don't worry. I'm here." He pulled away enough to grab the cell door and rip it open. As soon as it was free, Keene was on him. She wrapped her arms around his neck and her legs around his waist. He felt her grind her pussy against his erection and knew that the immediate needs of the dragon would have to be satisfied before he could talk to Keene and explain what was happening to her.

He carried her toward the narrow bed, the twisting clawing woman in his arms unbalancing his weight. They fell onto the mattress together, his weight landing hard on her. She didn't seem to mind. With her body coiled around his, he could barely move. Slowly, he rolled his hips against her clit. Her head dropped back and she moaned. Her hunger was a visible thing. The sight and sound ripped through him. Tynan joined him, screaming his desire for this woman. She clung to him, her arms and legs wrapped so tight he couldn't pull away to remove their clothes.

"I've got you, I'm here," he whispered over and over. "I'm not leaving you. I won't leave you." Even as he said the words, he tried to deny them. His self-promises that he would never accept the dragon's choice of mate nagged at him. But here, with Keene in his arms, he couldn't imagine not having her, not holding her. He pushed the concern aside. He'd deal with it later. Now, he needed to soothe the dragon—both dragons.

Fighting her growing strength, he lifted his hips away and tore off the loincloth that covered him, baring his cock to Keene. Triumphant, she screamed and pushed him over, climbing on top of his body. The remaining traces of his human control told him to slow her down but it had been days since he'd felt the sweet grip of her cunt around his cock. He had to have her. And from her reaction, she was in the same state. He ripped the thin shorts away from her body, grabbed her hips and slammed her down on his shaft. She was tight but wet, taking him deep with that one heavy thrust. Their matching shouts filled the cell, bouncing off the glass walls.

This was it, he realized. This was where he was supposed to be.

Keene sat up, the motion driving him deeper into her. Her hands pushed against his chest, her nails biting into his muscles. He loved the tiny points of pain. He watched as she began to adjust to his girth inside her. Her eyes fluctuated from gray to black as she struggled with her dragon.

"That's it," he encouraged her in a low voice. "Ride me, baby. Let me feel you."

The black glowed for a moment until the gray took control. She slowly pushed up, pulling almost off him before sinking down. "That's it, ride me. Let me come inside you."

"Bren?" Her voice quivered in confusion. He knew what was going on inside her head. The dragon alternately seized control and let it go, so her awareness was fading in and out.

"I'm here. Just focus on me," he commanded. "Feel me inside you. Let me fill you. That's it." He kept talking, speaking to the dragon inside her. Slowly, the animal retreated. He recognized the moment when Keene relaxed and settled into the rhythm of fucking him.

Keene felt the strange presence fade away. She didn't understand what was happening to her. Vague memories of Bren's arrival and of how she ended up practically naked on top of him teased her but the need to have him overwhelmed her reason. It didn't matter. He was here. Inside her. It wasn't enough to fuck him—she needed to be a part of him. She opened her mouth on his neck and scraped her teeth along the tight skin, loving the violent groan that erupted from his mouth. He raised her hips up and pulled her down, slamming her against him. The long heavy slide rubbed against her sensitized clit and Keene knew she would never find this with any other man. He filled her in just the right way. She gasped and swirled her hips, her body primed for a hard ride.

"I'm here," he said again. The simple words soothed something raw inside her. She didn't understand it but for now all she could do was accept it. Gripping his shoulders, she raised her hips and began to pump. The first thrusts were pure physical pleasure, satisfying her need to be filled by him again. He kept his pace slow as she enjoyed the steady massage inside her cunt. His voice, his hands and the hard push of his cock combined inside her mind and body and blurred the world around her. Sensations and memories battled inside her until she couldn't tell what was real. All she knew was the drive to release. Harder and faster until she thought her heart would explode.

Bren's words became groans and power welled up inside her in response. She picked up the rhythm, giving him the hard ride she knew they both wanted, unaware of anything beyond the desire for more. She dug her fingertips into his chest and held on. It was wild and wonderful.

The pressure deep inside her cunt began to shimmer each time she bounced down on him. Noise filled her head—her groans and his. And the demanding voice inside her, willing her to take him deeper. It built until the power broke inside her. She couldn't contain it. Tossing her head back, she sank down one more time and freed the delicious tension that coalesced inside her sex. As she cried out, hot bursts of his cum erupted inside her. Her passage clenched and held him, taking everything as her own orgasm consumed her.

Mine.

The voice was different this time—no longer the mournful lonely cry that had haunted her since her return from Ashure's kingdom. This was fully male and commanding. She lifted her head from where it had fallen against Bren's shoulder.

"How are you?" he asked. He rubbed his hand through her short hair, along her cheek and down her shoulder.

"I don't know." But even as she said the words, she felt a renewed ache in her sex. She rocked her hips, massaging him inside her. "More."

"Yes, baby, I'll give you more."

* * * * *

Keene collapsed back on the bed, her body limp. She'd lost track of time but knew it had to be hours—hours of pleasure. Hours when the voice inside her head had been silent. But as exhaustion crept into her muscles, she recognized their danger. Why had no one come to capture Bren? Surely the guards had alerted the Guild Leaders that Bren had broken in. And they had to know she was…was what exactly? Bren had made no move to remove her from the cell. In fact, from the moment he'd arrived he'd been focused on one thing—fucking her. As if he knew that was what she needed. Even more amazing, he'd let her lead—had simply made his body available for her use.

"Feeling better?"

Keene felt her cheeks heat. He'd seemed to understand her body's cravings better than she did. She nodded. What could she tell him? That the mysterious voice inside her head quieted when he was near?

"Can I leave you?" he asked. "Just for a moment."

Keene wondered about the unusual soothing undertone of his voice. Why was he so concerned about leaving her for a few minutes? But as the question formed in her head, fear and panic slammed into her skull making it almost impossible to concentrate. Keene forced the foreign emotions away and nodded. But as he pulled out of her body, she felt an internal scream she didn't recognize well up. *He was leaving her. Rejecting her.* The thoughts vibrated through her head, building and expanding as he walked across the room to the tiny sink. Keene didn't even have the ability to enjoy the sight of his naked backside walking away—her mind recycled the fear. *Leaving me!*

Even as the panic assaulted her, her logical mind rejected it. But logic couldn't break through. Her heart pounded loud, echoing in her ears.

She groaned in relief when she watched him return seconds later. She grabbed his arm and used his strength to pull herself up to sitting. "Bren? What's wrong with me?" The plea sounded pitiful to her own ears but she needed help. She clung to him as the only sane and calm thing in her world right now.

Cool wet dripped down her thigh snapping her out of the panic. He'd brought a washcloth and, before he answered, gently bathed her, wiping his seed away from her thighs, soothing the sensitive flesh between her legs.

He tossed the cloth into the corner and sat on the edge of the mattress. His face was serious as he turned to face her.

"I'll do my best to explain. The story starts about thirty-five years ago."

Bren told an incredible story. How his father had sustained a dragon bite and survived, learning to control the dragon enough so the human and dragon could exist as one creature. And that Bren himself was dragon spawn.

"You mean you turn into a dragon?"

He nodded. "And when you absorbed my blood into your body, you made the transfer as well."

"I don't understand." Her slow moving mind had made an outrageous connection between absorbing his blood to becoming a dragon. It couldn't be true. "Are you saying…" She let her question trail away.

"When you took my blood, you basically suffered a dragon bite."

"I'm going to turn into a dragon?" She was surprised that the words could find an escape. Her lungs were locked up and she could barely breathe.

"You already are. Her name is Andra."

"You know its name? How do you know that?" Ignoring the screams of her body to cling to him, she pushed away and threw herself off the bed. Her legs trembled as she stood but she forced them to stay strong.

"Those moments when you seem to lose consciousness? That's when Andra is taking control."

"I don't understand. This isn't possible. A dragon? I can't. I'm a shifter. It's what I do. I can't be a dragon."

"You won't live out your life as a dragon," Bren said in a soothing tone that just irritated her further. "It appears Andra has claimed me as her mate so that simplifies things a bit."

Mine.

The cry seemed to acknowledge Bren's statement.

"Why?"

"Because Tynan, my dragon, has claimed you."

Keene backed away. The voice inside her was growing louder. A dragon? Was that what she was hearing in her subconscious? A hollow pit formed in her stomach. This couldn't be happening. She shook her head, trying to reject the idea, but the truth wouldn't shake free. Bren wasn't the sort to joke or make up stories.

The remaining traces of air in her chest rushed out…and none moved in to replace it. The harsh pants of her own breath reached her ears.

She was turning into a dragon. A cruel, heartless creature destined to live in a cave and hunt humans.

But if what Bren said was true, *he* didn't live in a cave. He lived life as a human. It could be done.

Reality came quickly on the heels of this revelation. The Guild would never accept her. If the dragon was controlling her actions—and based on the way she'd pounced on Bren, Keene had to assume that's what was happening—they would never let her return.

"What am I going to do?" she asked aloud feeling truly lost for the first time since she was eight. "If I'm a dragon, I'm no use to the Guild."

"The Guild?" He slashed his hand toward the cell door. The sudden burst of anger set her back on her heels. "You'd really go back to those people?"

"They are all I have. They've raised and protected me."

"They were going to execute you."

"It is the way of the Guild," she said, calmly reciting the words she'd been taught since she was a child. "The Guild must protect itself."

"By killing their members?"

"It's better that one should die for the Guild's greater existence." The stunned look on his face told her he had no way to grasp the situation. "You can't understand. The Guild protects shifters. It is the only place we're safe. Can you imagine what would happen if I tried to live in some village?" She shook her head. "No one would accept me. I'd be killed, stoned in the first town I tried to stop in. The world isn't safe for shifters."

"I do understand. Believe me. I live every day with the threat that Tynan might seize control of this body. That's what has locked all those dragons away in caves. The human isn't strong enough to battle the beast, so I know what it's like to be different from everyone around you, to have power and strength they can't imagine. I know just what it's like but locking yourself away here isn't the answer. Not any more at least."

Keene looked away and Bren felt her loss. She been hit with so much in the last few minutes and now he was telling her she had to leave the only home she'd ever known.

"How did you ever come to the Guild?" he asked curiously.

Her lungs expanded and she took a deep breath. The rise and fall of her breasts momentarily distracted him but he forced his attention back to her words.

"My grandmother contacted them." Her voice faded with the memory. "I was eight and the lord who owned the large estate near our house saw me playing and offered money to my mother to take me up to his manor where I would 'serve' him. I don't know how much I understood then but I knew enough to see he was a foul human. My mother took the gold but when he came for me, I hid in the rabbit hutch." She finally looked over at Bren. "I was in charge of taking care of the rabbits." A faint smile curled her lips as if the memory was a pleasant one—but then her mouth flattened out. "I hid in the back corner, holding one of the rabbits, thinking that if only I could become a rabbit, he wouldn't be able to find me. And I changed.

"It's all sort of hazy but I remember he crawled into the hutch searching for me and I was surprised when he didn't grab me. Then I realized, he couldn't tell which rabbit was me." She flashed him a sad smile. "When he'd left, I willed myself back into my body and ran to tell my mother, thinking she'd be pleased at how clever I was."

"She wasn't."

Keene shook her head. "She called me a demon child and pushed me into the street saying if I didn't leave her house immediately, she would call the watch and have me stoned. I went to the only place I knew."

"And your grandmother took you in," Bren added.

"She didn't want me either but she contacted the Guild and three days later they rode up and took me away." She shook her head. "I have nowhere to go if I can't belong to the Guild." She lifted her chin and almost dared him to contradict her.

"Come with me. My father and mother have experience going through a dragon transition. They will help you."

Keene felt her defiance melt away. He sounded so confident and calm—a balance to the raging panic in her mind.

Not knowing what else to do, unable to think beyond everything Bren had told her, Keene accepted the shirt and trousers that he handed to her. She dragged them on, moving by habit with no conscious direction. Where seconds before there had been too much noise—now there was silence. A dragon. Was it possible?

Dragon? She mentally called to the creature in her head.

There was no response. Maybe Bren was wrong and Keene was just going crazy. Insanity actually sounded preferable.

When she was dressed, she looked at Bren. He was naked except for a medallion he wore around his neck. He was wrapping his thin cloth around his waist, covering the delicious cock that she needed. A red haze covered her mind and Keene started forward, needing to have him. She reached out and placed her hand on his thigh.

"Baby, we need to go."

Sharp stabbing pains shot through her chest. He was rejecting her, sending her away again. Keene knew these weren't her thoughts. The dragon—Andra, Bren had called it—was on the verge of panicking.

"Uh, Bren…"

He immediately pulled her against him, matching his body's angles to her curves. His heat crept into her bones. "Don't worry, I'm here." His sexual, soothing voice returned. "I won't leave you. I want you, want to be inside you and fill you, but we need to go. Once I get you someplace safe, I'll fuck you. I won't leave you," he repeated.

The words calmed the beast inside her and Keene felt the constriction around her heart ease. How was she supposed to exist with these random emotions assaulting her?

"Let's get out of here. My father and brother seem to have held off the Guild for now but we should go."

She nodded. There was no other choice to make. Not right now. This would take time to digest and she needed peace to do it.

"Here, let's get this off you first." Bren hooked his fingers beneath the metal band that encircled her neck. The Guild Leaders had welded the ends together. Only a saw would break the seal. She heard Bren's grunt and felt his body tense. The slow creak of metal ripping was loud in her ears. He pulled, separating the edges until finally the collar opened wide. He pulled the band away and tossed it into the corner.

"But how—?"

"Dragon strength. You learn to use it even while in human form."

Another fact for her to consider. Stunned by the constant barrage of revelations, she followed him to the door. He opened it cautiously and looked out. They were alone.

In fact, they met no one as they walked down the hall, up the stairs and into the main courtyard.

"I don't like this," she said as they stepped outside.

"Neither do I. Too easy." He looked to the skies. While he looked up, she scanned the area around them. There were people there. She could smell them, sense them, even though they were hiding themselves in the shadows.

"My father and brother are in the hills. We'll get to them and then decide the best way to get you home."

"Am I going to turn into a dragon?"

"Probably not yet. It usually takes a few weeks for the full transition to occur."

Bren stepped forward. Keene went with him. He let Tynan's senses control him, seeking out any signs of danger. As they walked into the open-air courtyard, movement caught his attention. Five people coming toward them. They moved in a line with the arrogance of warriors who knew they outnumbered their opponents. Bren's first instinct was to allow Tynan to take his corporeal form and defend Keene but he crushed it. He wasn't sure how Andra would react to another dragon's physical presence. And he'd prefer not to have to fight the entire Shifters Guild. He would, if it meant taking Keene back with him, but he hoped to find another option first.

"Keene, I don't think it's wise for you to be out of your cell at this time," the oldest gentleman in the group announced, ignoring Bren's presence completely. He looked at her neck and she knew he saw that the constrainment band was gone.

"Seheth." Keene bowed her head in greeting.

"These people have attacked us in our home," Seheth said. "We ask you to stand at our side as we protect ourselves from these invaders."

"She's leaving with me," Bren announced stepping forward, putting his body between her and the shifters.

Warmth curled into her stomach with the knowledge that he was prepared to defend her.

"I wasn't speaking to you, Prince Bren." Seheth dismissed him like a wayward servant. "Keene, the Guild Leaders are willing to reconsider your execution order but we must have time to observe you."

Keene felt her throat tighten. They would take her back. She could go home.

She would have to leave Bren.

The Guild had been the only home she'd ever known and now she was considering leaving it to go with a man who had to hate her. And how did she feel about him? The emotions surging through her were too volatile for her to decipher. But the thought of being separated from Bren was too painful to consider.

She moved to his side. He didn't have to protect her. She could defend herself, though she wanted to believe the Guild wouldn't hurt her.

"I'm going with Bren."

"I'm afraid the Guild can't allow that."

It all happened so quickly. Where five people had been standing, suddenly there was a menagerie of creatures. Two had chosen to remain human, doubling and tripling in size, and three had slipped into animal form—a tiger, a bear and a wolf.

"Damn, I hate hurting animals," Bren muttered.

"They aren't animals," she said, bending her knees and loosening her body to prepare for the attack. "They're humans in disguise."

Bren turned and smiled and she saw the wicked joy of triumph in his eyes.

"Well, that's okay then. I don't have a problem hurting humans who bother me."

The laughter that tickled the back of her throat was a complete surprise. They were outnumbered, about to be attacked and she'd just found out she was turning into a dragon. She shouldn't be laughing. Maybe hysteria was finally setting in, she thought.

"Let's take care of these guys so we can go home."

His deep growling voice sent shivers down her spine, re-igniting the tingles in her sex. Andra picked up on the emotion and heightened the memory of Bren inside her.

No, Keene silently admonished the dragon. *Later. When we're done, you can have him.*

The promise seemed to satisfy the creature. As Keene turned to face her former friends, she felt Andra's presence inside her. Energy filled her. Power flowed from her core. She was strong and dangerous. And these people were daring to threaten her mate. The strange possessiveness made Keene step forward and stand beside Bren. Side by side, they turned, so their shoulders were touching and they could see all but a small section behind them.

The tiger crouched low and began to creep toward Bren. Keene tensed. "I've got him. You worry about your two."

"How come you get three and I get two?" she asked.

"Because I've been a dragon longer than you have and because I'm a man and I said so."

"Oh, we are so going to have to talk about that attitude," she groused.

She didn't get a chance to hear Bren's reply but sensed his amusement.

Seheth, still in human form, lunged at her, his fist aimed at her head. The hand-to-hand training the Guild had given her came alive in her body—and was focused by the dragon's strength. She knocked Seheth's arm away and heard a quiet snap as the bone broke. The sound shocked her out of her defensive position. How was she able to break his arm with one punch? *Dragon strength.* Shaking her head, she looked up as the bear leapt forward. Keene reacted, swinging her leg out and planting her foot in the animal's massive chest. With one sharp push, the bear flew backwards, landing hard on its back. The image shimmered and the human returned, collapsing with a groan. She whipped around. Seheth was trying to change, knowing he could shift into a creature that wasn't wounded. She slashed her arm out and slammed the heel of her hand into his head. He crumpled into a heap on the ground.

She knelt down, placing fingertips to his neck. His heart still beat strong. Good. She'd never killed without specific instruction to do so and she didn't want this to be her first time.

"Aaah!"

Bren's cry spun her around. The human shifter flew through air and slammed into the rock wall behind them. The wolf and tiger were still on their feet. Blood dripped from deep scratches in Bren's shoulder from the tiger's claws. The tiger and the wolf separated until they were at Bren's sides. They leapt, attacking from opposite angles. Keene saw them land on Bren.

"No!"

The word burst from her mouth—a terrifying roar as the dragon recognized the attack on her mate. Keene had only a second to realize what was happening before she felt her body explode and a new creature was born.

Distantly aware that she was no longer in control and no longer in her own body, Keene felt her form stalk toward the intruders. How dare they hurt her mate?! She didn't know the

201

source of the emotion but the rage consumed her. She collected it, turned it to heat and released the flames.

Fire erupted from her throat. She heard the screams as it touched the weaker creatures but she didn't care. All that mattered was getting to her mate. Bodies scattered as she moved forward, clearing a path with her fire. Pain and loneliness during her years at the Guild added heat to the flame and she raised her head, searching for more to destroy.

"Andra!"

The voice penetrated her anger and she followed the sound to the source. Keene felt the tension ease as the dragon saw Bren standing before her. She stretched down and sniffed his body. The blood of his attackers was still on him but beneath it she could smell the warm masculine scent. Her tongue flickered out, stroking his thigh. The fight forgotten, the dragon instantly returned to her original focus—Bren. Trapped inside the dragon's body, Keene felt everything, the overwhelming desire that hummed continually through her veins, the fear that Bren would reject her and send her away. She licked closer to his groin and he tensed. Keene recognized the dragon's reaction. She thought Bren was pushing her away and wanted to scream with the loss.

He placed his hand on her nose. "Andra, are you with me?"

Mine?

"Yes." His deep serious answer triggered a response in Keene.

No. She took control of the dragon's thoughts, instinctively voicing the truth. *He doesn't belong to us.*

The memory of his discovery of her betrayal penetrated her awareness.

She's nothing to me. The hollow, frigid words settled in her chest. He'd sent her away. He didn't want her.

The dragon captured Keene's pain and multiplied it until she couldn't hold it inside. Andra tipped back her head and howled. The loneliness and fear grew until she could feel nothing else. She had to escape.

Bren didn't want her. He'd sent her away.

"Andra?"

Not mine!

The dragon's petulant, pain-filled cry snapped the final level of resistance. She had to get out of there. She crouched down and jumped. Massive wings captured her weight and propelled her into the air.

The animal's cry echoed off the rocks and Keene let the dragon consume her.

Mine!

Tynan's scream filled the small courtyard. Even some of Andra's victims heard it because they flinched as they tried to crawl away.

The dragon's anguish filled his chest. Bren endured the poison that seemed to seep into his heart and watched his mate fly away. She was a beautiful creature—pale purple scales mixed with the green ones that dominated Nekane's hide.

"So that's the woman who's going to be your queen?" Kei said, stepping up behind Bren's shoulder. He didn't know where his father had come from but it didn't matter.

"Yes," Bren said, for the first time feeling a definitive emotion. He wasn't going to lose her.

Mine! Gone? Find her. Bren grit his teeth. Trying to hold a conversation with Tynan storming through his head was growing increasingly difficult.

"Your mother will love her," Kei continued, unaware of Tynan's distress. "Just tell her the tale of how Keene's dragon came to your rescue."

"I didn't need rescuing," Bren's masculine pride compelled him to reply.

"I know. That's why Rainek and I didn't interfere. But we'd better get out of here. I think they are recovering from the shock of seeing one of their own turn into a dragon."

Bren nodded and followed Kei through the courtyard and over a low rock wall. They climbed back up the mountain and found Rainek waiting, dressed as they were in a simple loincloth.

"So she's already made the transition?" he asked nodding to the empty sky. "Isn't it a little early? I thought it took about three weeks."

"It does. Usually," Bren answered moving them deeper into the rocks. "I don't know if it's because she's a shifter and can taken on other forms…"

"Or if her anger is so intense it brought out the dragon early."

"Right."

Kei chuckled. "Your mother will probably tell me that women are just more efficient than men so it didn't take as long for her transition to occur. And she might be right. Are you going after her?" his father asked.

"I have to, don't I?"

"Yes, but I'd give her a little distance. She's a bit upset."

Bren noticed the trace of laughter in his father's tone. He might have found the amusement irritating if not for Tynan's cries reverberating through his thoughts. The dragon wanted its mate back. Fear and anger rose up inside him and he had to remind himself these were Tynan's emotions, not his. He took a deep breath and silently vowed to get Keene. The promise did nothing to calm the now panicking dragon.

"Don't let her stew too long," Kei warned. "She might decide to come back here and destroy anyone who's ever hurt her." Kei's upper lip curled up and he shook his head in disgust. "From what I've seen of the Guild so far, there would be plenty of targets for the dragon's anger."

Bren knew he had to find her but resisted. The dragon inside him was too strong, too hurt to go after her now.

Rainek and Kei continued to talk but Bren lost track of their words. Fire burned inside his chest, like Tynan was clawing his way out of Bren's human form.

Mine. Want mine. Make her love me.

Fear drove its way into Bren's heart. He couldn't release the dragon now. Keene was too frightened and confused to understand Tynan's need to possess her. She would back away and Tynan would react as his instincts led him. Bren clenched his teeth and fought to contain the creature inside him.

Mine. Need mine!

Bren could feel his strength fading. The dragon was too strong and its pain too great.

Mine!

"No!" Bren heard his own scream as the dragon rose inside him.

Chapter Twelve

Keene shivered in the darkness of the cave. It wasn't cold that assailed her. In truth her body hummed with warmth. Probably the fire of the dragon. She could still remember the flames leaping from her mouth and the cries of the shifters as the heat had touched them.

Another shudder ran through her body.

What was she going to do now? She'd attacked other members of the Guild. She couldn't ever go back.

Mine?!

She winced at the loud mournful wail inside her head. The dragon had been screaming that word for what seemed like hours. Sometimes it was a pitiful moan, sometimes a cry of anger.

The creature seemed to bounce between desire and anger—wanting Bren and hating him. A low ache built in her body and she stomped her foot in silent frustration.

How was it possible to become aroused when her world was falling down around her ears?

She looked down at her naked body. Her clothes had disappeared when she'd made the shift to dragon form. When she'd finally conquered the dragon's panic and been allowed to resume her natural shape, she'd been naked.

Keene pursed her lips together. The dragon was a part of this form—her natural body. But if she changed into someone else, would the dragon be left behind? Having never considered the philosophy of shape-shifting, she didn't know the answer but knew it was worth a try.

Fighting the distraction of Andra's voice and erratic emotions, Keene created the image of Cissa in her head. Of the women she'd been while she was with Bren, Cissa had been her favorite.

Mine!

The cry shattered the mental picture. Keene clenched her teeth together and started again, taking more care than usual to design the image. If she left any detail out, she could shift into something unrecognizable and potentially would be unable to return from the form.

She willed Andra's emotions away and focused until the precise picture of Cissa filled the space before her. She braced for the slow change and mentally poured herself into that shape.

Nothing happened.

She closed her eyes and tried again. But her body remained static.

Her heartbeat sped up as the implications of this hit her. She couldn't shift. She was trapped forever in this form. She stared down at her body—her too small breasts, her boyish hips. Bren had his choice of women. He would never want her, not like this. He'd said she could go with him to his castle. Meet his family. Now, with her mind calmer and reality facing her, she knew that was impossible. She'd been on the team assigned to kill his father. His family would never welcome her into their home.

That left her with nowhere to go. She couldn't live in a village, not with the dragon in charge of portions of her mind. She couldn't go with Bren. She couldn't return to the Guild. She was alone forever.

Andra wailed inside her head.

Keene looked around the cave. This would be her home, hidden away in the mountains.

The wind picked up outside the cave. The scratch of claws across stone whispered in the silence. Her heart leapt in her chest instinctively knowing what kind of creature would make that sound.

A dragon. Bren. He'd come after her.

She'd stared toward the cave's entrance. Why was he here? She knew from his impassioned conversations with the other delegates, he would do anything to protect dragons. Even come after her. He obviously was worried about Andra.

But it wasn't the dragon facing him now. Straightening, Keene ran her hand through her short hair. Having not seen her own reflection in almost twenty years, she'd yanked out a few strands to see the color. It was brown. Boring, bland brown. Conscious of her nakedness and the lack of curves she possessed, she slid one arm up across her chest—noting that she easily covered her breasts—and placed her other hand over the apex of her thighs.

He'd seen her naked before but this was different.

A shadow covered the entrance, blocking the evening light.

And Keene realized this wasn't Bren. This was his dragon.

Andra trumpeted her greeting inside Keene's head and the sound weakened her knees.

Mine?

She'd heard this voice before. It was…she tried to remember what Bren had called his dragon. Tynan, she thought.

Why cover yourself? The mental question was low, almost accusing.

"Uh—"

Even in the semi-darkness she could see the flicker of green in his black eyes. Crisp clear green that reminded her of Bren. He was somewhere inside that body but didn't seem to be in control of the beast.

Mine to have, Tynan asserted.

Keene shook her head and backed away. The dragon's deep growl stopped her retreat.

Andra seemed to pick up on Keene's agitation and began to rumble her defiance. Keene took a deep breath mentally trying to contain Andra. She couldn't handle one dragon, let alone two—and she wasn't sure the two creatures should meet just yet.

I'm fine. We're fine, she soothed Andra. *He won't hurt us.*

Oh please, Goddesses, don't let him hurt us.

The soft click of claws on stone now sounded loud in the rock cavern. She swallowed, forcing herself to remain still as his head stretched forward, stopping inches from her neck.

Mine?

He nudged her with his snout. Keene yelped and leapt away, tripping on a stone outcropping. She landed hard on her backside and groaned.

The dragon was there, his open mouth hovering above her.

Hurt?

"Uh, no." A little startled and she'd have a bruise on her ass but she would survive—the fall, at least. She didn't know whether she'd survive the dragon.

Have you. Need you.

Before she had a chance to process those words, a warm, damp caress slid up the inside of her leg. Staring at the open space between her thighs, she watched as his tongue flickered delicately across her pussy. Keene gasped at the sweet caress. She'd heard of the rampant sexuality of dragons and their hunger for human females but she'd never imagined this was how they used their victims.

He pressed forward, forcing her to either open her legs or push him away. She stared at the gleaming white teeth. They could rip her into tiny pieces with one bite.

Instinct snapped her knees shut. "No."

The dragon jerked his head back at her rejection. Fury and loss washed over her—emanating from Tynan, captured and magnified by Andra.

Tynan stood above her, watching her for one long moment, pain flaring in the black depths of his eyes. He was going to kill her. The pain was too great. She gasped, trying to force air into her lungs. He opened his mouth and screamed.

Keene curled into a ball, covering her head as the sound shook the rock around them. She waited—for the pain of his bite or the crushing blow of a stone falling.

And she waited.

Silence greeted her. She peeked her head out from beneath her arm. The dragon was gone. She sat up.

He hadn't gone far. Tynan was crouched into the far corner of the cave, snugged up against the wall, his head buried beneath one massive wing.

Mine? Andra's question came out as a sympathetic whimper. Keene stood.

Tynan hadn't attacked her. She'd felt his rage and his pain but the creature hadn't harmed her. He'd wanted to fuck her. Keene pressed a flat hand against her stomach.

"Tynan?"

He didn't react except to bury his head further beneath his wing. She had the distinct impression that he was pouting.

"Uh, Tynan, I'm sorry. I was frightened." By the Goddesses she hated admitting that.

Fear me?

She stepped forward drawing closer. The cave wasn't huge so she reached his side in six cautious steps. "A little."

As she drew near, Tynan lifted his head. Keene forced herself to remain still even as he leaned toward her, his snout six inches from her neck.

Want to love you.

"Uh, yes, about that, I'm not sure—"

His tongue whipped out and laved the tip of her breast. "Oh!" She took a deep breath. "It's just I'm not sure if—"

He swirled the tip his tongue around her other nipple, making it tighten even more.

Need to have you. Much pleasure. She held herself steady as he licked down her stomach, teasing the top of her sex. *Touch deep inside you.*

The delicate strokes and the dragon's seductive words weakened her knees.

Let me have you.

The sensual plea was reminiscent of Bren's commands. It appeared his dragon was no less demanding.

It was odd—when she should be terrified, confused and panicked—desire managed to work its way into her body.

Yes. Smell your desire. Need your sweet taste. He accompanied his words with a long caress up the inside of her leg. Taking a deep breath—knowing somewhere deep inside that she was binding herself to this creature with her actions—she lowered herself to the rock floor. This time when Tynan moved over her, fear didn't consume her. She slowly opened her legs, keeping her knees bent as she bared herself to the dragon.

A soft rumble from deep in his chest told her he was pleased with her acquiescence.

Andra seemed to be gone now—silenced as Keene faced Tynan alone.

The dragon hesitated for a moment then slowly dragged his tongue up her slit as if preparing his place. Heat flowed inside her and every nerve ending in her sex came alive. The long thick muscle slipped easily into her passage. Keene's gasp echoed off the cave walls and came back to her. Bren had been most attentive during his oral loving but this was a different caress. Tynan drove deep inside until he filled her and his mouth rested against her sex. She stared up into the darkness, amazed at the sensation. It was so alive and hot, not stretching her but setting her on fire with delicate brushes on the inside walls of her passage. He didn't thrust or pump, just let the tip of his tongue rub her, deep inside her pussy.

She'd never felt anything like it. The slow steady massage radiated tension from inside her sex to her chest, seeping out into her limbs—like her body was being stretched and pulled. Unable to control it, her hips began to roll, seeking to counter the dragon's touch. Tynan rumbled his pleasure. The sound vibrated through her clit—the lightest touch, just enough to release all the wicked pressure he'd created. Keene screamed, her hips arching up, pressing toward the dragon's mouth, silently begging for more. He pulled away, lifted his head and trumpeted his success.

Keene barely had time to recognize the triumphant sound before he returned, plunging deep inside her, one quick thrust before pulling back and circling this tongue around her clit, renewing the sharp spikes of need into her pussy.

The cave fell into silence with only the sound of her breathing—heavy and harsh as he licked and caressed her flesh. He was everywhere—lapping at her juices, dipping into her opening, teasing her clit. His touch was new but strangely familiar. The distant edge of her mind still capable of rational thought recognized his caress from Bren's oral loving in the brothel but her body wouldn't let her hold the concept for long.

Tynan's wicked tongue moved across her flesh in a random rhythm—exploring, licking, tasting. The desire that had overwhelmed her since she'd woken up from the trance slammed into her body. She groaned and punched her hips up. She needed more.

"Tynan." Her whimpered plea was soft but he heard her, driving his tongue into her, pumping deep inside. He drew back and nimbly massaged her clit while the tip slipped into her opening. The twin caress was too much for her to bear. She arched her back and let the climax come to her.

Yes. More.

She groaned as she stared up at the dragon, still lapping at the fluids between her legs. Her body was hovering on satisfaction but there was one thing still she needed. Bren.

Andra, blessedly silent while Tynan was loving her, awoke at the thought of her mate and growled her need for him.

"Bren," Keene whispered, needing to see the man, face him and have him inside her. Tynan drew back, lifting his mouth away from her skin. With one final lick, the image before her began to change. Moments later he was gone and Bren was kneeling between her thighs. He slowly raised his eyes to hers. Green alternated with black. Tynan hadn't released his hold. She watched, fascinated by the struggle, her own needs fading as she watched Bren. Tension radiated from his body. His shoulders rolled back, arching his spine as he fought the creature inside him. His hands curled into fists, clenched on his rock hard thighs.

He drew in one long, cleansing breath. When he looked at her, she could see the human was back in command.

"Are you hurt?" he demanded harshly.

"No." She accompanied the denial with a shake of her head.

"He didn't hurt you?"

"Tynan? No."

Some of the tension seemed to ease but the downward curl of his lips told her he wasn't happy.

"You accepted him then." It was a blunt statement, with no question in it but Keene felt the need to explain.

"Not at first. I think I hurt his feelings."

Bren blinked. "What?"

"I rejected him at first."

Bren reached out and grabbed her shoulders. He ran his hands down her body, inspecting her chest, stomach and legs. "And he didn't hurt you?"

"No. Just pouted," she said with an ironic smile. "Why would you think he would hurt me?"

He opened his mouth. Before he spoke, his eyes darkened and Keene could tell he was listening to Tynan. Bren shook his head. "I'll explain later." He looked down at her naked body.

Kneeling between her spread thighs, his gaze immediately fell to her bared sex.

And as quickly as the desire had faded inside her, it returned. Without speaking, he moved over her, positioning his cock at her entrance. Keene felt herself losing control of the body she so recently began to share.

Mine! Andra's cry was no less fervent than Tynan's had been.

Without any specific words, Keene realized Andra didn't want to be mounted—she wanted to ride her mate. She needed him on his back. Following the dragon's instincts, she pushed on Bren's shoulders. The dragon's strength moved through her body and her gentle shove sent him flying through the air. He landed with a thud and a groan.

Air locked her in throat like someone's fist around her neck. Keene couldn't move. What had she done? She hadn't meant to hurt him. Struggling to find a way to call out to him, she watched as he rolled over. The sharply raised eyebrow and half-smile eased some of her worries. Then he laid himself flat on his back and held out his hand.

"Come to me," he commanded.

Andra reacted before Keene could respond. As if she was a passenger in her own mind, she scrambled across the cave. The dragon gave neither of them time to prepare. She swung her leg over his hips and found his hard cock waiting for her. She wrapped her fingers around the hot shaft and groaned. He would feel so good inside her.

Keene tried to slow the beast but the dragon was having none of it. She spread her legs wide and placed his cock against her entrance. The moisture from Tynan's intense licking dripped from her sex, coating her hand and his cock.

"Put me inside you, baby," he urged. "Let me inside that sweet cunt."

The words settled into her core and she dropped her head back and screamed—the sound vaguely like Tynan's shout of pleasure.

Slowly, she looked at the man beneath her. His green eyes glittered in the weak light of the cave. He was hungry for her—needed her cunt. Power welled up inside her. *Yes. The man would serve her well—provide her all the cock she needed, give her pleasure whenever she wanted it.*

The foreign thoughts tumbled through her head. The dragon created images to accompany her words—pictures of Bren, kneeling before her, licking her pussy, or standing behind her pounding his shaft into her.

Lost in the fog of her own desires and the dragon's, Keene tightened her grip on his shaft and pushed it into the first tight inch of her sex. The thick head began to stretch her as it filled her. She hesitated, letting the tension between them rise—pulling Andra back when she would have shoved him inside.

"Keene, honey, if you don't fuck me right now, you're going to find our positions reversed."

She smiled, pleased to know she could inspire that hungry, commanding growl from such a powerful man. She pulled back, working the first few inches of his cock inside her. Wrapping her fingers around his shaft, she held him as she rode him, allowing only half his cock to sink into her. The shallow thrusts worked the entrance of her pussy, the same sensitive place Tynan had licked so eagerly.

"Damn it, Keene, take all of it." Bren's voice was hard and rough. But like the dragon, she knew he wouldn't hurt her. She tipped her head back and laughed, feeling joy along with desire. She'd never imagined loving could be like this. She lifted herself until his cock almost slipped out of her then, as she sank down, she pulled her hand away and drove him all the way inside her. The thick pole filled her, every inch massaging the inside of her cunt.

And suddenly she had no breath for laughter or words. Andra's needs pushed her on. She rose up on her knees and rode him, long hard strokes. Bren gripped her hips, pulling her down as he punched up, needing to go ever deeper.

Keene raked her fingernails down his shoulders. He shuddered and slammed her down. The hard, heavy penetration was the final stroke she needed. Her scream came out as a gasp as her breath was stolen. She held herself still, enduring the sweet release as it flowed from deep inside her core to the far reaches of her fingers.

She raised her eyes to his, felt a silly smile curve her lips…and collapsed forward.

Bren caught her as she fell, her body sinking as if the strength had been leached from her muscles. The slow contractions of her cunt continued to pulsate along his cock as she sighed. Bren growled, fighting his own needs.

"Keene? Are you all right?"

"Hmm?" She snuggled against him and didn't seem inclined to move.

She probably needed sleep, needed comforting at this moment, but Bren had his own cravings to satisfy. She'd had him, now he would take her, bind her body to his, reestablish their connection.

He grabbed her hips, holding her to him, holding his cock inside her, and rolled, putting her beneath him. Her eyes snapped open and he watched as the hazy fog of sexual satisfaction drifted away. He waited, mentally bracing himself if she pushed him away. He didn't know if he could pull away if she demanded it. The thought stopped him. Tynan hadn't hurt her. He'd managed to control himself. Bren could do no less. He started to pull back but Keene's legs whipped around his waist before he could move.

"More," she demanded. A shout of triumph, similar to Tynan's cry, crept into Bren's throat but he crushed it.

He crouched up on his knees and pulled her hips up, drawing her high up his thighs so he could feel her deep, feel every inch of that sweet pussy holding him.

"My turn," he growled and began to plunge into her. He didn't hold back. He let her have every inch, every bit of power that flowed through his body. He pounded into her and she took him.

And begged for more.

"Please, come inside me. Come in me," she whispered, her words echoing through his head.

Tynan hovered at the edge of his mind. Bren's instincts were to push the dragon away for fear if he took control he'd hurt Keene but then he remembered how she'd thrown him off her and ridden him like he was a stallion created for her personal use. Her body was strong—she had the dragon inside her. And Tynan would never hurt her.

Slowly, Bren let the dragon into his head, reveling in Tynan's exultant scream as they fucked her. Each thrust took him through the tight grip of her cunt. He lost track of time—his whole world became focused on riding between her legs. He was vaguely aware of her heels wrapped around his back, pulling him harder and deeper. And he did his best to satisfy her desires.

Mine.

He snapped his head up and watched Keene. It hadn't been Tynan's voice. It was Andra, claiming him…and he had to respond.

"Yes," he whispered, knowing the words were true.

Keene stared up at the dark cave ceiling and wondered briefly why she could see so clearly. By all rights she shouldn't have been able to see beyond a few feet but every rock and crevice was clear. The dragon's senses were growing inside her. Still and silent, she looked around the cave. Her predictions of spending her life in a place like this seemed less dire with Bren beside her. Actually on top of her.

He'd settled on top of her in an exhausted heap after coming for the third time. She smiled, stroked the back of his head with her fingertips and sighed. He looked up. "What was that for?"

"I was just thinking."

"About…" he encouraged.

"What happens now? We can't exactly stay here forever." Her stomach growled as if to agree.

Bren sat up, disconnecting their bodies. They both groaned as his cock slipped out of her but by silent agreement ignored the temptation of more.

"I thought we settled that. You'll come with me. To my family."

She shook her head. "That's a kind offer but I tried to kill your father. I doubt your family would welcome me with open arms."

He grimaced. "You'd be surprised. They want you to come. And it's for the best. Your dragon is going to be difficult to handle for a while and it will be wise if I'm nearby."

It made much more sense now. "Good Prince Bren—always thinking about what's best, what's good for your kingdom and good for the dragons of the world." She pushed herself up and turned to face him. "What about what you want? You're going to take me in—a woman you hate—because it's best for my dragon? The world doesn't work that way."

"I don't hate you."

"Don't lie to me, Bren. I saw it in your eyes when you sent me away."

"That wasn't hatred, it was pain. Betrayal. I don't know." He threw up his hands and stood, slowly pacing the length of the cavern. He knew they needed to talk about this but he didn't know what to say. How did he explain his feelings when he didn't understand them himself. Tynan remained remarkably silent. "I'll be honest—I don't know what I feel for you. I desire you. I want you…but I don't know you well enough to claim that I love you. My brother—you met him—he fell in love with his wife in less than three days. I'm not able to do that. I never expected to have a wife—I never expected to accept the woman that Tynan chose. I couldn't risk it." He could tell she wanted to ask why but he didn't pause long enough to let her interrupt. "But now I find myself unable and unwilling to let you walk away."

"But—"

"Please. Return to the Castle with me. Meet my family. Get to know us, me. And let me get to know you. I've always feared what would happen when Tynan selected a woman. I knew the dragon had such power that a fragile delicate female could so easily be destroyed."

"I'm neither fragile or delicate," Keene corrected and Bren had to smile.

"I know. Perhaps that's why I'm willing to try. I just know that if you leave, more than Tynan will feel the loss." He looked directly at her, hoping that one of his arguments would persuade her. Everything he said was true. His emotions were a jumbled mess inside his chest but one feeling was growing louder than all the others—he couldn't lose her.

He knew she didn't have many options at this time. He would work on convincing her. He pulled her to her feet toward the entrance. As they stepped into the streak of fading sunlight coming into the cave, he realized he was thinking of this as a permanent relationship. He'd done it. He'd accepted the dragon's mate. He didn't know what would happen but he knew he needed Keene with him. He stood up and held out his hand. "Let's go home."

She looked at his open palm. After one long moment, she placed her slim fingers in his.

Fear he hadn't even recognized faded away as she stepped forward and pressed her body to his. She was accepting him.

He'd found his mate.

Chapter Thirteen

Keene stared at the board and did her best not to let her mouth fall open.

"I won." The sound was more of a gasp than a triumphant shout but it worked. She lifted her head and stared at Bren. In the six months since she'd come to the Castle with him, she'd become very fond of their almost daily tri-level chess battles. She'd learned much about him…but she'd never beaten him. "I won."

Bren didn't look up for a moment. Almost as if he couldn't believe it.

Keene threw back her head and laughed. And laughed. She stomped her feet on the ground and giggled until she was weak. Finally, she sat up straight.

She might have felt guiltier about gloating if she hadn't seen the black flickers in his eyes. Tynan was obviously pleased. That's what came from playing tri-level chess topless. She should have tried the technique months ago. Maybe she wouldn't have lost every other game.

"I won," she repeated.

"You cheated," he stared pointedly at her chest.

"You've played without your shirt many times."

"That's different."

Keene smiled at Bren's righteous tone. He always assumed that arrogant attitude when he was losing a fight. It was just one of the many facets of his personality she'd learned to enjoy — his drive to succeed, to protect dragons across the lands. His serious nature punctuated by a strange sense of humor. And his lust, she couldn't forget that. His dragon's desire for her hadn't diminished, nor had Andra's for Bren.

Tiana had suggested that Keene play topless when Keene had been complaining that Bren always beat her. Tiana had sworn it would be enough to distract Bren…and it had worked. Keene still didn't understand it. After six months she'd become adapted to seeing *her* face and *her* body in the mirror. She knew that Tynan desired her. But Bren…she didn't know. Did his lust belong solely to the dragon?

Knowing that he still watched and loving his eyes on her, she leaned back in her chair and stretched her arms above her head. "Hmmm, it's amazing how good it feels to win." She stared at him. "Now, for my prize…"

"Well, then…"

He placed his hands on the arms of his chair and started to stand. The sensual look in his eye told her that if he made it to his feet, he would be on her and the morning would be spent in bed. Not that that idea didn't hold merit but she wanted a very particular prize.

"No," she said, leaping out of her chair and away from the table. "I want my prize *tonight*."

He sat back down and watched her. She could see his eyes—bright green and glowing with hunger—as he stared at her breasts. She knew just from watching him that he was imagining sucking on her nipples, biting the tight peaks. Her nipples tightened and poked forward. Bren licked his lips.

"Yes, that will be part of it. Now, you should go do your work but you might want to rest up."

Bren stood up, started to turn away and then turned back. "Your prize is going to require my *resting up*?"

Using the wicked smile she'd learned from him, she nodded.

"I'll go make sure my secretary hasn't put anything too strenuous on my schedule."

"You do that."

She waited as he scraped his fingers through his hair and put on the heavy velvet doublet he wore when he was conducting the King's business.

He turned toward the door and stopped, returning to her side. He leaned down and placed a quick kiss on her lips.

"Have a good day," she whispered.

"Take care," he replied.

It's what he said every morning as he left but it was the way he said it that made her shiver with need. The tone was low and dark with just a hint of warning. As if he was warning her not to get into any danger. Keene smiled at his back.

She dragged on her shirt, tucking the ends into the tops of her soft leathers. Bren's family had accepted her. They'd dismissed Keene's apologies for trying to kill Kei as unnecessary. His mother in particular made her feel welcome. Keene had learned, through experiments and talking with Lorran and Kei, to adapt to Andra's presence. She even found herself liking the dragon.

Her life was so different now. At first, she hadn't known what to do with herself but then Lorran had taken over, given her lessons about being part dragon. And slowly, she'd been given the duties around the castle. Though there had been no formal connection between Bren and her, his family treated her like a daughter-in-law. His family had become hers — with all the trials and joys.

She finished dressing and fluffed her hair. She'd tried to let it grow it long, noticing Rainek's admiration of Tiana's long flowing hair, but it had fallen in her eyes and required too much effort. The final solution had come when Bren had seen her raking her hair away from her face and asked why she didn't just cut it off. The concept of having a choice about her appearance was fascinating to her. Never before had it mattered. She'd spent so little time in this form that she'd never been concerned.

She'd taken a pair of scissors to it that night. And Tiana had helped her fix the ragged mess the next morning.

Ready moments after Bren left, Keene wandered down the hall and found Lorran in the small salon where she typically breakfasted. She joined Lorran for breakfast most mornings, spending the time learning about dragons and getting to know the queen.

It was strange. She'd spent most of her life alone. Even after the Shifters Guild had taken her, she'd spent much of her time on her own. It wasn't good to become too attached to people, the Guild preached. It interfered with the successful completion of missions. Keene knew that from experience.

But here, she was rarely alone, unless she specifically sought out solitude. And even then Andra was always there.

"Good morning, Your Majesty." Keene bowed formally. Even though Lorran insisted on a relaxed relationship, Keene greeted her every morning as was fitting of her rank.

"Good morning." Lorran looked up from her papers and smiled her welcome. She watched Keene for a moment then her eyes squinted. "You looked decidedly cheerful this morning."

"I beat your son at tri-level chess for the first time."

"How did you do that? He's a brilliant player."

"I played topless."

"Ah." Lorran nodded. "If he's anything like his father you're lucky you made it through the game."

"I played on his competitive spirit every time he tried to move toward me."

Lorran laughed. "What's your prize? I can't imagine you don't get some kind of boon from Bren from this."

"I've got something in mind," Keene chuckled in response. She had no intention of telling the queen that she planned to tie her son to her bed and use his body as her personal toy for the night.

Lorran reached out and grabbed Keene's hand. "I'm so glad Bren found you and had the sense to recognize his feelings for you."

Resisting the urge to pull away, Keene felt her fingers turn cold. She wasn't comfortable talking about Bren and emotions. They had passion and a growing friendship. If there was more, she wasn't going to examine it too closely. She didn't want to be disappointed. She knew she felt *something* for Bren and it was different from anything else she'd ever experienced but it was frightening as well, strangely powerful.

It was reminiscent of the emotions she'd felt as a child, before she'd gone to the Guild. When her mother had loved her. Not that Keene's feelings for Bren were anything near maternal but it was the confidence she felt in his presence. He would be there for her.

She only hoped he was pleased about her surprise.

"Yes, uhm, thank you. I need to gather a few things for tonight." She felt her cheeks warm as if Lorran could see inside her head. The glow in the queen's eyes let Keene know she approved. Keene smiled and left. She had to find Tiana. Despite the woman's dainty appearance, if anyone knew where to find chains strong enough to tie a dragon to her bed, it would be her.

Keene hurried down the halls to the chambers Tiana and Rainek shared. She tapped on the first door and waited. If Rainek was still around, it would take a few minutes for anyone to answer. Keene leaned against the doorframe and waited. Finally the door opened and a very pregnant, flushed and disarrayed Tiana smiled up at her.

When they'd met, Keene hadn't been able to tell that Tiana was with child. Now there was no doubt she was going to give birth any day.

"Good morning," Tiana greeted.

"Am I interrupting?"

"Nothing major."

"I resent that!" Rainek shouted from somewhere in the chamber. "If you'd give me a little time I could make it major."

Tiana rolled her eyes. "You need to go train," she called over her shoulder. "And I need to chat with my friend." She grabbed Keene's hand and pulled her inside. Rainek stood in the center of the room, a sheet wrapped around his waist and a glower on his face. Keene just smiled. Rainek was a handsome man. Not as attractive as Bren, of course, but still handsome. She admired Rainek's long locks but she loved stroking Bren's short hair and watching the heat in his bewitching green eyes.

Rainek grumbled but trudged into the bathing chamber. Tiana giggled as the door closed. "It's good for him to wait. Anticipation makes it that much sweeter." She smiled and led Keene to the sitting room. She held onto Keene's hand the entire time. Keene suspected Tiana was thrilled to find she could touch Keene and not hurt her. Being a fire witch, Tiana's hands burned most things but the dragon's affinity to fire made Keene immune. "So, what's brought you here so early? I'd guess a fight with Bren but you're not upset enough."

"Uh, no. No fight. I took your advice and played topless."

"And won?"

"Yes. He found it quite difficult to concentrate."

"I don't doubt that he did."

Keene shook her head. "I don't understand it really. I don't have much in the way of endowments." She waved a casual hand toward her chest.

"It doesn't matter. It belongs to you and that's what makes it so attractive."

Keene smiled. It was odd having Tiana to confide in. At the Guild, she'd never had girlfriends or shared secrets.

"I'm going to tell him tonight."

Tiana's eyes widened. "How do you think he'll take it?"

"I don't know."

"You don't have to worry," Tiana laughed. "He loves you. No matter what."

Keene didn't know how to respond. Lorran and Tiana both seemed to think Bren had feelings for her but she wasn't sure and her own emotions were too new for her to risk revealing them.

"Well, I just want to make sure he's constrained when I tell him. Do you know where I can get some chain?"

Eight hours later, Keene stared down at her naked lover, his arms bound above his head, chained to the wall above their bed. She'd been right. Tiana had known where to find chains and cuffs that would hold Bren.

He was stunning—bare and presented before her. Keene felt the warmth start deep inside her sex.

"Baby, I can smell your need," he whispered. The weak candlelight was enough to highlight the desire in his eyes. "Don't make both of us wait."

She looked at his cock, hard and proud, ready for her to mount him.

Mine. Andra's cries were no longer desperate pleas. The dragon had gone from fearing Bren would leave her to demanding his attention when she wanted it. And she wanted him now.

Keene crawled up onto the bed and knelt beside him.

"I have a surprise for you," she said.

His eyes grew tight. "A good surprise?"

"Depends." Before he could ask any more questions, she closed her eyes and let her body change. She felt her hair and breasts grow, her shoulders shrink. When she opened her eyes, she was staring at Bren through Cissa's eyes.

"You can shift."

He didn't sound pleased.

She nodded.

"How long has this been going on?"

She blinked, confused by the anger underlying his words. "I don't understand."

"How long have you been shifting without telling me? This obviously isn't the first time you've done it." He yanked on the chains and Keene was glad she'd thought to bind him.

"I've been practicing for a few months now." Pain settled into her heart.

"Why?"

She had imagined he wouldn't be thrilled but she didn't expect outright anger.

"What do you mean why? Because that's what I am. I'm a shifter," she answered with equal ire.

"Not any more." His voice was low and she could detect traces of Tynan in it.

She sighed. "Bren, I'll always be a shifter." She rolled off the bed. The seductive evening of loving Bren was over. She turned and walked away, stumbling as Cissa's short legs didn't carry her as far as she was used to going with each step.

As she walked away, she recognized the crushing loss. Somewhere deep inside she had hoped he would be pleased, thrilled even, that she'd recovered the ability to shift. But Bren obviously didn't want to be reminded of that part of her life.

Sniffing to hold back the tears she refused to shed, she walked to the garden entrance. The moon was full. There was plenty of light. She could safely fly away.

She took a deep breath, preparing to shift back to her own body before taking refuge in Andra's form. The crack of stone and the clank of chains resounded from the other side of the room. She whipped around in time to see Bren jerk the mooring for the chains from the wall. Bits of rock burst free and scattered across the bed. Once free of the wall, he unclamped the bands around his wrists. For a moment, she saw black filling his eyes but it disappeared as he crawled off the bed and stalked toward her.

This was no pissed off dragon...this was a pissed off human and he was coming for her.

"Bren?" She hated the hesitant sound of her voice or the fact that she took a step backward. She wasn't afraid of him. He just looked a little intimidating—naked and powerful as he took the few steps to stand in front of her.

"You're not leaving."

She opened her mouth to protest. He couldn't stop her from flying. She was part dragon and the animal needed this freedom.

"You're not going back."

The low guttural tone resounded in her chest and she heard the pain beneath his words.

"Go back? Go back where?"

"You're not going back to the Guild. Even if you thought you could shake Tynan loose, did you really think I would let you go?"

Keene felt her mouth fall open. Bren thought she intended to leave him? That's why he was upset. She couldn't find her breath for a moment. How could he even think she would leave him?

"I'm not going anywhere."

"I'll lock the doors if I have to."

He clearly wasn't listening to her. "No, really, Bren, I have no intention of going back to the Guild." She laughed. "Why would I go back there? Here I have a family, I have a purpose." She paused. "I have you."

He put his hands on her shoulders. Keene looked up from the diminutive height of Cissa. Even from so far away she could see his pain. "Then why did you relearn to shift?"

"It's what I am. It just seemed natural to do it." She shrugged. The movement seemed so young and unconfident—nothing like the woman he'd lived with for the past six months. "Besides, I thought you'd find it interesting to have different women to fuck, you know, women with real breasts."

Tynan joined him in his disgruntled growl. He thought he'd shown her, every time they'd made love, that he enjoyed, worshipped, adored her body. But he obviously hadn't been specific enough.

"We need to clear this up once and for all. Change back." Without looking to see if she followed his order, he grabbed her hand and pulled across the floor, stopping when they were in front of the mirror. She stared at him with questions in her eyes.

"I want to show you something and after I do, if you still want to take this form—or any other—I'll gladly fuck you in that body until neither of us can walk."

Keene swallowed and shifted into her true form. The full breasts shrunk to the thin mounds he'd licked and sucked so often. Her nipples immediately tightened and Bren felt his mouth water. He drew himself back. That would be for later. Now, he needed to show her the woman he loved.

When she was complete, she lifted her eyes.

"Good, now come here." He took her elbow and turned her around.

"Bren, this isn't necessary. I accept that you like my body."

"No, I don't think that you do." He stood her in front of the full-length mirror and then stepped behind her.

"Look at yourself."

"I have. Bren, it's fine. I—"

"No, Keene, you've seen yourself through your eyes. Now, I want you to see what I see." He slid his hand down her hip and placed his mouth beside her ear. "Spread your legs a bit, baby, you know how I like to see a hint of that pretty pussy." Keene groaned softly. It was almost impossible to resist him when he spoke like this.

The atmosphere in the room changed. The seduction had returned only she was the one being seduced. She moved her foot a few inches out, opening the space between her legs. He slipped his hand down her stomach and cupped her sex. "That's it. You know how I love looking at you."

She nodded. He'd spent hours stroking her body, watching his hand move across her skin combining the two senses.

"Now look in the mirror and see what I see." He kissed her neck then looked at her in the mirror, capturing her gaze in his. "I don't need a different body. I love yours. I like fucking you with your long legs. I love feeling them wrapped around my waist and holding me inside you like you never want me to leave." His breath teased her skin. "That's what you feel, isn't it?" She nodded, too breathless to speak. "And when you ride my cock. So strong and powerful." He smoothed his hand down her thigh, skimming his fingers in the brief space between her legs. She let her eyes fall from his and watched the path of his fingers across her skin. As he spoke, he rubbed his shaft slowly along the crease of her backside. "And I love your ass. Have I ever told you how much I love your ass?" She shook her head. "I should have done. It's perfect. It fits my hands like it was made for them." His hot palm cupped her backside. "And I love the way it feels against me when I take you from behind. You're so strong. You slam it hard against me, wanting me deeper."

Keene looked up and saw the blush in her cheeks. "Oh, no, baby. Don't be embarrassed. I love it." He held her hips, pulling her back against him. His mouth hot against her neck. "I love being inside you. Don't you like feeling my shaft in you? My body over yours?"

"Yes," she sighed, letting her head fall back against his shoulder.

"No, no, no. We're not done. Besides all the other delicious parts of your body, let me show you your breasts."

She kept her eyes closed. "I've seen them."

"Open your eyes, baby. Let me show you." The sensual command would allow for no hesitation. "You have small breasts."

"Bren—"

"Shh." His hands left twin trails of warmth as he stroked up her skin to cover both breasts. "Small and delicious." He squeezed gently. "And so sensitive." He circled his palms over her nipples, making them tighten even further. He placed his lips on her ear. "I love to feel them in my mouth. They pop right out, like they can't wait for me to suck on them. And you scream so loud when I do. You love to feel my lips on you."

"Yes," she sighed, rolling her hips back against him, moving in the rhythm of his slow circles.

"And you know how I love your cunt." She felt her knees tremble. "How deep you take me and how you hold me. It's the only pussy I want. It was made for me. And me alone."

He seemed to take satisfaction in the fact that he'd been her only lover in this form. The possessiveness of the man was equal to that of the dragon.

"Look at yourself, Keene."

Desire coursed through her body. The warmth from his skin heated her flesh. She stared into the mirror. It was her body, the same one she'd forced herself to accept. But somehow it was different. The peaks of her breasts pressed forward and instead of seeing not enough flesh, she felt Bren's mouth, sucking and nibbling. She looked down. Her legs no longer looked slim—they looked sleek and powerful. The moisture on the inside of her thighs glittered in the pale candlelight.

She felt Bren step away but she didn't move. This was how he saw her—a strong, sensual creature.

This was who she was.

She slowly turned, expecting to find Bren nearby. Instead, he was stretched out on their bed, his arms above his head—no longer bound. He held onto the headboard and Keene knew he wouldn't move from that position until she commanded him. His strength would hold him there longer than any chain.

Confidence that she'd never felt in her form surged through her body. He loved her shape, loved fucking her body. She strolled back to the bedside. His cock was still thick and hard. Keene licked her lips. She would reward him later. But first, she needed to feel him inside her. She crawled up beside him. Bits of rock were scattered around Bren's head. She flicked away a few of the larger chunks and smiled.

"I'm ready for my prize now," she whispered.

"I'm ready to serve you."

The light twinkled in his eyes and Keene knew this was where she belonged. In this body with this man.

Hours later, Keene rolled off Bren and onto her back and smiled. He'd served her well. So well, even Andra was sated. Contentment swelled inside her. This was it. She could be happy with this life.

"I think we should get married."

Keene's eyes popped open and she stared up. Bren had propped himself up on one elbow and was above her.

"What?" The shock from his announcement quickly gave way to fear and pleasure. He wanted to marry her. Did that mean he loved her?

"I think we should marry. It's obvious Tynan won't let you go and I doubt Andra would allow it."

The momentary hope faded away. Bren was bowing to the wishes of their dragons.

"I don't know, Bren—"

He nodded. "That's fine. I'll ask again in a few months. It's a lot and I know you're probably not sure of your feelings right now."

He started to lay back down but Keene stopped him. "Wait. *My feelings?* I'm well aware of my feelings." She took a bracing breath. "It's your feelings I'm not sure about."

"My feelings?"

"Yes. Do you want to marry me because of Tynan or because…of something else."

Bren winced. Tynan urged him to fall on her, bind her to them with passion but Bren held back. He'd grown so used to the physical love between them, he'd forgotten that she might want to hear the words from him.

"I guess I didn't do a good job of this, did I?" He rolled over and knelt beside her. Taking her hand he lifted it to his mouth. "Will you marry me, Keene?" She opened her lips to tell him she didn't need a formal request—she needed his love. She didn't get a chance to speak. "I love you—you, just as you are. I trust you and I want to spend my life with you and Andra."

Her eyes tingled with the threat of tears and for once she didn't try to hide them. "Yes."

He smiled and leaned forward, placing a soft gentle kiss on her lips.

"Welcome to the family, Princess Keene."

She jerked away and stared up at him with wide, panicked eyes.

"Princess?"

"Yes, that's what happens when you marry a prince. You become a princess."

"B-but I don't know anything about being a princess."

He stretched out beside her and pulled her against him, sharing his warmth. "Don't worry, you'll learn."

Slowly she relaxed into his body but he could almost hear the frantic spin of her thoughts. Bren smiled into the darkness and decided now was not the time to point out that one day, she'd be queen.

Epilogue

Keene walked into her chambers and slowly unbuttoned her vest. As the wings sprang apart she sighed. And she'd thought being a mercenary was exhausting. She rolled her shoulders back, trying to loosen the kinks from her neck. It had been a day spent in the library with Lorran researching dragon legends. Some ancient documents had come into the queen's hands and she'd asked for Keene's assistance in deciphering the faded text.

Now, her back, her neck, and her eyes ached. Andra growled making her desires known. The sound could mean only one thing. The dragon wanted to fly—or she wanted Bren. And Bren wasn't available.

Not wanting to lose another pair of leathers to the dragon, Keene unlaced her trousers and pulled them off, dropping them on the back of a chair. The cool rush of air across the skin was a teasing reminder that she would be sleeping alone again tonight.

It had been over a week since Bren had left. The grim purpose of his mission dragged her spirits down even farther. Bren's sister, Kayla, was missing—she had seemingly disappeared from the world. She'd been traveling when her convoy had been attacked. The family was worried but hopeful. Kayla had her dragon to protect her. When reports came of a woman matching Kayla's description in the south, Bren had taken off to investigate. So far, nothing had been discovered. Keene felt the loss herself—having become friends with both her sisters-in-law—but clung to the hope that Kayla was unharmed.

If Andra wasn't still so volatile, Keene would have gone with him. But her dragon couldn't be relied on to stay contained if anyone threatened Bren. Andra's protective instincts were strong but she wasn't good at distinguishing between an honest hazard and playful teasing.

Keene knew she wasn't much better. It was amazing how intertwined their lives had become. Not only their dragons and their desires. When he was gone, and it wasn't often, she missed his body but she also missed him. The hours they spent together talking and working were precious to her. She couldn't imagine her life without him.

Her world had changed completely since marrying Bren. She'd gained a family and, more importantly, she'd discovered who she was. Without the façade of shifting, she'd had to learn to be herself and like that person. She smiled to herself. Bren liked her as well. It seemed that Tynan's instincts about their compatibility had been dead-on.

More had changed in her life. She was a princess, bowed to and served whatever she needed. It was strange situation for a warrior.

The Guild was gone from her existence. She still shifted on occasion but more for practice than anything else. She'd even made love to Bren in her other forms. Confident that Bren loved her body as it was, she occasionally shifted into Cissa's or Vixi's shape to tease Bren. He loved Cissa's wide-eyed innocence and Vixi's ass. He'd loved her long and hard on those nights. She smiled. He loved her long and hard on most nights. The memory crept into her sex and she groaned. Bren wouldn't be home for days. She didn't know how she would survive it.

She missed him—she loved him. And she wanted him back tonight.

She inhaled deeply, preparing another sigh. Bren's masculine scent filled her head. He was back! She raced through the sitting room into the bedchamber.

There he was, tall and gorgeous. She licked her lips, wanting to enjoy the moment of watching him before he noticed her but Tynan obviously recognized her scent as well.

Bren looked over his shoulder, his eyes glowing black and green as she stepped into the room. She ran toward him and leapt the last few feet, knowing he would catch her. And he did. His hands cupped her ass and pulled her forward, separating her legs and slamming her against his hard erection, constrained by his leathers.

"By the Gods, I missed you," he muttered a moment before he captured her mouth beneath his. Keene moaned her greeting, unwilling to release his kiss. She opened to him, accepting his tongue deep within her mouth. The desperate hunger of his touch smoothed the ragged edges of her day. He spun and stalked five feet to the edge of their bed and crawled onto the mattress, never releasing his grip on her backside or on her mouth.

Spread beneath him, she sighed with relief as he began to pump against her pussy.

The increasing pressure distracted her for a moment but concern over Kayla finally prevailed. Keene pulled her mouth away, gasping for breath. "Did you find Kayla?"

The light in his green eyes flickered. "No. We tracked her as far as a slave camp but then she just vanished." Her heart ached with his, knowing his fears, feeling every bit of his pain.

"She's strong, she's tough and she's part dragon," Keene reminded him. "She'll be all right until we can find her."

He nodded but the weight of his concerns dragged him down. Watching Tiana and Lorran, Keene had learned that one of her "wifely" duties was to ease the strain of her husband's burdens.

"We'll find her," she vowed, squeezing him gently. She lowered her voice, letting all her desire flow through her words. "I missed you while you were gone." She stroked her hand up his chest, flicking the ties of his shirt open as she went. "Missed having you inside me. Missed feeling your body on mine."

She stretched up and placed her open mouth against his neck. She laved his pulse point with her tongue, loving the way his heartbeat sped up.

His eyes grew black then fluttered green as Tynan fought for control. Both creatures were in need of comfort.

She dug her heels into his backside and pulled him forward but Bren fought her. Lost in her own seduction, she couldn't believe he'd pulled away.

He separated their bodies by mere inches and reached between them to unlace his leathers. His cock sprung free—long and hard and straining for her. Keene groaned at the sight and Andra growled her pleasure.

Bren must have heard the sound as well. He smiled. "Tynan pushed me hard to return tonight." He placed his cock at her entrance and drove into her in one long thrust.

Thrilled by the full sensation of taking him inside her, she held her breath for one moment. Bren tensed above her, holding himself to the hilt.

"I'll have to thank him," she whispered as Bren began to fuck her. He plunged into her deep leaving no portion of her sex unloved by his shaft. Desperation from days without him sent her body into a climax quickly. Her pussy contracted and she watched Bren's eyes darken as if he felt every flutter. He grit his teeth and continued to pump, going deeper and harder with each thrust. She let her head fall back onto the bed. His control was amazing and he could go for hours, fucking her until she could barely speak. Tonight, she wanted more, wanted to give him the comfort, the release he'd shown her so often.

She opened her eyes and whispered the words she knew he couldn't resist. "Come inside me, my prince."

* * * * *

Miles away, Kayla crouched on one knee in the corner, staring at the twisted body of the most recent man sent to "tame" her. He groaned and rolled over, crawling toward the door.

"Well," Iniz, the slave master, demanded from the hall.

"She just about killed me. There's something not right with that girl. I'm not going near her again. I want my money back."

She felt her lip curl up in disgust. The slave master had taken to selling the rights to try to rape her. So far, none had succeeded. Her dragon's strength had saved her but she didn't know how many more she could fight.

The sound of coins changing hands rattled outside the door. Seconds later, Iniz strode into the filthy room she'd been locked in.

"That's it, you'll not eat for two days."

She shrugged. He'd tried everything to control her and she'd defied him at each attempt.

Instead, she raised her head and stared at him, letting the dragon's anger pour through her eyes.

"Let me go and I can almost promise my family won't rip you into tiny pieces when they come for you."

The edges of his mouth turned white. When she'd first been brought in, he'd mocked her threats. Now, weeks later, she decided he was starting to believe her.

"Masslon!" he bellowed. A young man, slave collar welded around his throat, hurried into the room. "Harvet is coming through tomorrow." Iniz lifted his chin toward Kayla. "She'll be in the group that leaves with him." He smirked when he looked back at her. "Harvet works for the most brutal killer in the land." He smiled and Kayla felt an unwanted shiver run down her back. "You'll wish you'd been nicer to my friends."

Enjoy this excerpt from

Dragon's Kiss

Shadow of the Dragon

© Copyright Tielle St.Clare 2003

Chapter 1

The fire burned across her skin, searing its memory into her flesh. Forever would she feel its touch. Crave it. The heat entered her body as a roaring flame and melted the frozen depths of her heart. Need filled her–turning her fear into desire.

She twisted on the bed, trying to tear free of the dream. She knew it was a dream, knew it was only her mind holding her captive but she had no power. She couldn't break its grip.

Mine.

The voice whispered through her soul and she shook her head.

No!

Her dream-self raced through the forest, running from the creature that wanted to claim her, consume her. He was behind her, ever nearer.

"No, no, please."

Fire broke out across the sky and surrounded her, trapping her. She stopped, faced with the wall of flames. Spinning around, she faced him.

Black eyes stared at her. Inhuman eyes that warned of lust and death. Flames dribbled from his mouth, licking at her legs. She felt the heat but it didn't burn. His long neck craned forward, moving his massive head toward her body. She stumbled backwards and fell to the ground. The rough wool gown flipped up, baring her legs to her thighs. She tried to pull the material down but the creature was there. He nuzzled her hand aside and moved forward, pressing the blunt end of his nose against her sex.

The beast's voice filled her head.

Mine.

"No!"

Lorran's scream shattered the dream. She jerked awake as her own voice reverberated through the cabin. The rapid patter of her heart filled her ears, blocking out all sound. She rolled over, curling onto her side and staring blankly across the room.

She could feel him. He was near, ready to possess her. She shivered despite the warmth of her blankets. The creature hadn't wanted to capture her—he'd wanted to possess her, own her very soul.

Dreams had haunted her for years—horrifying images of flames and death. The screams of the victims. But never like this. Never before had she felt her own vulnerability.

She stared into the pale morning light, unwilling to release the scant comfort of her bed and the childish need to hide under the blankets. The dream was still with her.

The scuffle of heavy feet followed by a loud thump on her front door dragged her from under the bedcovers. She pulled on a robe but hesitated at the door. The villagers hadn't exactly welcomed her. There was no reason anyone would visit her at this hour, or any hour for that matter. Except to demand that she leave. Again.

After the terrifying dream, she wasn't up to more threats.

She waited.

The pounding repeated.

"Mistress! We've need of your help." The deep voice was unfamiliar. "Mistress, are you there?"

It didn't sound like a threat. Still cautious, she cracked open the door and peeked out.

Nothing could have prepared her for the sight. A huge man dressed in full battle leathers with a broad sword belted to his hip crowded her as she opened the door.

"Yes?" she said, backing away as he pressed forward. He entered her house and she saw the reason for his haste—a man, equally as large, draped over his right shoulder. Blood stained the scarred battle leathers covering his legs and the white linen shirt he wore.

"Where can I put him?"

"There," she said, pointing to the bed in the corner. The tiny cabin didn't allow for more than one room. She slept, ate and lived in the single space. Now she'd just offered her bed to a wounded man.

The stranger stalked to the small bed. In a quick but gentle move, he shrugged his burden off his shoulder and caught him, lowering the body onto the mattress. As he stepped away, Lorran saw the truth—the man wasn't just wounded.

A large gouge opened his chest. Blood drenched the torn shirt and dripped down the man's face. She looked at the chest wound.

"That's a dragon bite," she said, speaking the obvious.

"Yes. I couldn't risk taking him to town. I heard you had an interest in dragons."

She nodded. That was probably the nicest thing anyone in town had said about her. Usually they called her a dragon whore.

"Can you help him?"

He asked the question simply. But the answer wasn't simple.

Lorran looked into his eyes. He was young but the grim light of determination told her he knew the wounded man's fate.

"I can nurse him. It will depend on the Gods if he survives."

"And if he survives?" He stared at her with a warrior's eyes—cold and deadly. "Can you help him?"

She knew what he was asking. The warrior waited. She thought about lying, considered giving him the answer he wanted to hear, what anyone would want to hear at this point.

But she couldn't.

"I don't know." She looked down at the torn and crumpled body. The faint smell of sulfur clung to his clothes. Dragonfire. Burn marks stained his leather trousers and the edges of his shirt. The leather chest protector that should have been there was gone. "I can try," she finally said.

"Is there hope? Is there some possibility that it can be stopped?" He placed his hand on the hilt of the broad sword that hung at his waist. "I need to know."

Emotions welled up in Lorran's chest at the subtle threat. She knew what would happen if she said no. The man would die. Better to die than…

"Yes." She turned away. She didn't lie well and feared it might show in her face. She looked at the wounded man. There was something familiar about him. "The sooner I tend to him, the better chance he has." That was a lie as well, but at least it would give her something to do. And it was something to distract the soldier who waited for an answer. She glanced up as she moved to collect water and cloth to clean the wound. The soldier didn't believe her—it was obvious on his face—but maybe, he wanted some hope to cling to as well. In the end, it wouldn't matter. The truth would reveal itself soon enough.

"Do what you can." With that command, he turned and stalked to the door.

"Wait! Where are you going?" She hurried behind him. He couldn't just leave a wounded stranger in her care—particularly not one suffering from a dragon bite. Dragon bites were too uncertain. And the potential damage was too great.

"I have to return," he said, stepping onto the porch. "If rumor gets out that he's been attacked, we'll have a rebellion on our hands."

Lorran watched him walk away. "But—but—I don't know how to get a hold of you. How do you want me to contact you?"

"I'll send a guard from the Castle daily for updates as to his progress."

"The Castle? Who are you?" She looked at the bloodied man in her bed. "Who is he?"

"I'm Riker. That's Kei."

Lorran felt the blood drain from her face.

"Kei the Dragon Slayer," she said unnecessarily.

"Yes." Riker turned and walked away, climbing on the back of his horse before calling out his final instruction. "Tell no one who he is or that he's here. The safety of the Kingdom could depend on it."

His long hair caught the breeze as he kicked the flanks of his horse, spurring the beast along. Lorran watched until he was out of sight and she was left alone to tend to the man who'd killed her husband.

* * * * *

Fire burned through his chest. The flame entered his blood and rode the veins through the depths of his body, burning away the traces of humanity and leaving behind a new creature. The man's body burned. He arched up, pressing down on his shoulders and the heels of his feet, fighting the invasion but it was too late. The beast was there, invading the empty corners of his soul.

"Shh. Relax. Breathe for me. Breathe." The voice poured over his body like cool water, smothering the fire. The tension faded and he dropped back onto the bed. "That's it. Breathe. Long, deep breaths." His eyes were glued shut by pain but he tried to follow her orders. He inhaled and filled his lungs with her scent. It reminded him of sun-warmed hay and a fresh pine wood fire. The sweet smell eased him even further. "That's it. Sleep."

Even with his eyes closed, he could feel her moving away. His hand shot out, snagging her thin wrist. The tiny bone would crack in his hand if he wished it. He tried to ease his grip but couldn't force his hand to relax.

"Stay." The voice didn't sound like his but he knew it was. The memories were returning. He had no idea how long he'd been here or how long he'd been caught in the fire. "Please," he added, some latent etiquette emerging.

"Of course. I'll stay."

She was lying. He knew it. She'd stay until he was asleep and then she'd run. Instinct screamed at him to grab her, hold her. Bind her to him so she couldn't escape.

The human in him grew sick at the thought.

Kei willed his fingers to uncurl from around her wrist. His soul wailed in pain but he rolled away, turning his back to the woman.

He curled his arm beneath his head and concentrated, feeling his body from the inside out. Something was strange—invading his senses, becoming a part of him.

He couldn't open his eyes but he knew Riker was gone. Left alone with the female. He breathed in again and recognized her scent, tasted it on his lips. She was strange, yet familiar. Fog crept over his mind, easing him into sleep—a sleep clouded with dreams.

The woman was there. He couldn't see her face but he knew her taste. Intimately knew her taste. She lay spread before him, offering herself to him. Knowing he was welcome, that she sought his touch, he sank down before her and placed his mouth against her wet, hot sex open to him.

It was perfect. This was what he'd craved all his life. Her flavor, her scent, the feel of her skin against his. He had to have her, hold her.

Panic like he'd never felt in all his years as a warrior dug into his gut, wrapping itself around his genitals like an iron fist. She would leave him. He couldn't let her leave him.

She faded from his hands, disappearing and reappearing a few feet away. He crawled toward her—she backed away. He reached for her. Fear flared in her eyes. She turned, dodging his grip. He clutched at her fading figure. He had to have her, had to keep her. She vanished.

No. Mine! The word raged in his head. She was gone. The heart-crushing panic was on him again and he fought it, sought the strength of a warrior, the stoic face he'd learned as a child. All that remained was silence.

She was gone.

She'd left him.

* * * * *

Lorran chewed on her thumbnail and paced the tiny room. She glanced back every few seconds to the man twisting on her bed. Sweat clung to his body as he struggled. The internal battle would continue. Three days was standard for the trance that accompanied a dragon bite.

He was free of fever. She'd studied enough attacks to know that dragon bites healed quickly and cleanly. But that didn't stop the pain or the torture in the days following the attack. Nothing would ease him.

She'd tried with her husband but her presence had served only to enrage him.

Still, compassion welled up inside her. She couldn't stand to see another human suffer. Giving in to the emotion, she turned her steps across the room and sank down on the edge of the bed.

"Your Majesty, please." He twisted on the sheets fighting and tearing. "Please, Your Majesty." *Dammit*, she said to her herself. Calling him "Your Majesty" was going to get old. Quickly. She took a deep breath. "Kei, everything will be all right." She didn't know what else to say. Even though lying was against her nature. She wanted to comfort him. "It will be fine," she repeated. Her voice seemed to reach him and he stilled. He never opened his eyes but he turned in her direction. "That's it. Everything will be fine. I promise."

She placed her hand on his shoulder. The warm muscle jumped beneath her fingertips. She'd pulled the tattered shirt from his chest while she'd cleaned the wound. She'd left his battle leathers on while she'd bandaged the torn flesh. But bandages were almost worthless on a dragon bite. The wound was already beginning to heal.

Kei sighed as she continued to lightly rub her palm across his shoulder. She watched the tension ease from his body. Sleep was the best thing for him. Lorran sat for a moment. She'd stay with him until he settled.

It had been five years since she'd seen him—and then it had been after a brief and bloody fight. She wouldn't have recognized him if she'd seen him in the street. His face had matured, losing any soft edges of youth and gaining none of the roundness from excess. His long blond hair was spread across her pillow, framing his masculine face.

He looked every inch a King. Even with his wild hair and bare chest, he looked powerful. Having moved to this Kingdom after her husband's death, she was unfamiliar with the royal family. She wasn't a part of that world any longer. If she remembered correctly, he'd been raised as a warrior, never expecting to be crowned King. She knew why he'd been chosen to lead. This was a man born to rule—a warrior leading a Kingdom of warriors.

Women had been rumored to swoon when he looked at them, so handsome was his face. The sharp cut of his cheekbones and a pale scar next to his eye saved him from any kinship to feminine beauty. His face was carved stone, hard even in rest. She couldn't see the color of his eyes but reports said they were crystal-clear green, the color of new grass.

And soon, all this human beauty would be gone.

Emotions flip-flopped through her mind. Anger at finally facing the man who'd killed Brennek, but compassion as well. How strange was fate that his justice had been delivered in such a fashion? She felt no triumph. No human should have to live through the next three weeks of this man's life.

The silence of the cabin grew oppressive as she sat beside him. Her thoughts began to rattle with things she had to accomplish before daylight ended. There was still work to be done. How long would it take for him to fall asleep? She had things to do—notes to make. It wasn't often that anyone got the chance to study a dragon's victim from bite until the conclusion. She needed to write down her observations.

She looked down at him. His eyes were closed but not squeezed shut in pain, his shoulders seemed relaxed, his breathing even. He was finally resting.

She leaned forward, preparing to stand. His hand slipped across the blankets and landed softly on her leg, holding her. The grip was firm but not painful. Lorran froze. He was asleep. It had to be some kind of reflex. His tan skin looked pale against the dark wool of her skirt. White lines criss-crossed the back of his hand telling of his warrior's life. He may be a King now, but he had been raised a soldier.

Lorran reached down to remove his hand but instead he moved, slipping his large palm up her leg, curling it to match the curve of her thigh, delving his fingers into the space between her legs.

Lorran looked around the empty room, as if someone might see her with a man's hand on her thigh. It was an intimate touch but it couldn't be intentional. The man was asleep or, at minimum, in a healing trance. He obviously didn't know what he was doing.

Kei had a certain reputation but Lorran doubted even *he* could attempt a seduction just hours after being bitten by a dragon.

His fingers pushed downward, then up, until they brushed the juncture of her thighs.

"Or maybe he could," she said aloud. The flutter of his fingers against her sex stopped her words. This couldn't be happening. It had been years, *years* since any hand but hers had touched there. Now a stranger, and a King no less, was doing so.

She squirmed, trying to subtly remove him. Instead, Kei's fingers insinuated themselves deeper between her legs until he cupped her, forming his fingers to the line of her sex. A fluttered pleasure zipped through her stomach.

"Please, Your Majesty, Kei…your hand…" She tugged on the heavy weight of his wrist. He growled softly and the lines across his forehead deepened. "Kei, I don't think—"He pressed one long finger along her pussy, teasing her clit with a light touch. "Oh, my." She tensed, sitting up straight on the bed. "I really think—oh dear…" With slow easy strokes, he began massaging her. A spike of need shot through her center. She inhaled sharply. *How can this be happening? The man is asleep!* His fingers continued to move, the rhythm changing to steady pulses. He seemed to know just where to touch her, the perfect intensity.

"This is a bad idea. I shouldn't let him do this," she told the empty room. But her body ignored the logic of her words. She leaned back and arched her hips upward, opening her legs until he had full access. A soft rumble sounded from Kei's throat—a contented, pleased noise, like the purr of a satisfied lion. He rubbed his whole hand up and down, fully massaging her sensitive lips, heightening the tension across her clit. The light wool of her skirt only heightened the sensation. The heat of his touch flowed through the material and warmed her skin.

Her sex was wet and empty. She moaned softly at the sudden sharp desire to be filled.

Lorran pressed the tips of her fingers into the solid wall of his chest. Her hips rolled in gentle movements as she searched for more of the sensations his hand pulled from deep inside her body. She arched against his fingers, pushing him against her clit, focusing his touch and guiding him.

Heat poured from his fingers and flowed through her pussy, driving her on. The pressure grew. Her shallow breath bounced off the cabin walls, echoing back and filling her ears with the sound. Her hips pumped with certainty now, the sweet tightening building until in one sharp moment, it evaporated, released, scattering tendrils of heat through her body. Lorran tensed and held herself still. The wild pleasure captured her, then slowly faded through her body.

After long moments, when her breath returned to normal, she looked down. She'd left tiny nail marks on Kei's chest.

He didn't seem to notice. He slept, his hand still between her legs, but calmed, not moving. The hint of a smile hovered over his lips—as if he knew what he'd done.

"If that's what he can do in his sleep, no wonder women swoon before him," she whispered.

She continued to sit beside him, half-amazed at what she'd let happen and half-stunned that Kei seemed to have slept through it all. Finally, his breathing evened out and she realized he was truly asleep. When she stood, he let her go with no more than a mumbled protest.

Her freedom lasted twenty minutes before he began to twist on the bed and tear at the bedclothes. She returned to his side and placed her fingers lightly against his chest. He immediately quieted and his hand inched toward her thigh.

"Oh, it's going to be an interesting couple of days."

About the author:

Tielle (pronounced "teal") St. Clare has had life-long love of romance novels. She began reading romances in the 7th grade when she discovered Victoria Holt novels and began writing romances at the age of 16 (during Trigonometry, if the truth be told). During her senior year in high school, the class dressed up as what they would be in twenty years—Tielle dressed as a romance writer. When not writing romances, Tielle has worked in public relations and video production for the past 20 years. She moved to Alaska when she was seven years old in 1972 when her father was transferred with the military. Tielle believes romances should be hot and sexy with a great story and fun characters.

Tielle welcomes mail from readers. You can write to her c/o Ellora's Cave Publishing at 1056 Home Avenue, Akron OH 44310-3502.

Why an electronic book?

We live in the Information Age—an exciting time in the history of human civilization in which technology rules supreme and continues to progress in leaps and bounds every minute of every hour of every day. For a multitude of reasons, more and more avid literary fans are opting to purchase e-books instead of paperbacks. The question to those not yet initiated to the world of electronic reading is simply: *why?*

1. *Price.* An electronic title at Ellora's Cave Publishing and Cerridwen Press runs anywhere from 40-75% less than the cover price of the <u>exact same title</u> in paperback format. Why? Cold mathematics. It is less expensive to publish an e-book than it is to publish a paperback, so the savings are passed along to the consumer.

2. *Space.* Running out of room to house your paperback books? That is one worry you will never have with electronic novels. For a low one-time cost, you can purchase a handheld computer designed specifically for e-reading purposes. Many e-readers are larger than the average handheld, giving you plenty of screen room. Better yet, hundreds of titles can be stored within your new library—a single microchip. (Please note that Ellora's Cave and Cerridwen Press does not endorse any specific brands. You can check our website at www.ellorascave.com or

www.cerridwenpress.com for customer
recommendations we make available to new
consumers.)

3. *Mobility.* Because your new library now consists of only a microchip, your entire cache of books can be taken with you wherever you go.

4. *Personal preferences are accounted for.* Are the words you are currently reading too small? Too large? Too...**ANNOYING**? Paperback books cannot be modified according to personal preferences, but e-books can.

5. *Instant gratification.* Is it the middle of the night and all the bookstores are closed? Are you tired of waiting days — sometimes weeks — for online and offline bookstores to ship the novels you bought? Ellora's Cave Publishing sells instantaneous downloads 24 hours a day, 7 days a week, 365 days a year. Our e-book delivery system is 100% automated, meaning your order is filled as soon as you pay for it.

   Those are a few of the top reasons why electronic novels are displacing paperbacks for many an avid reader. As always, Ellora's Cave and Cerridwen Press welcomes your questions and comments. We invite you to email us at service@ellorascave.com, service@cerridwenpress.com or write to us directly at: 1056 Home Ave. Akron OH 44310-3502.